blue

a novel

blue

a novel

Sarah
Van Arsdale

The University of Tennessee Press / Knoxville

Library of Congress Cataloging-in-Publication Data

Van Arsdale, Sarah.
Blue: a novel/Sarah Van Arsdale.— 1st ed.
        p. cm.
"The Peter Taylor Prize for the Novel—T.p. verso."
ISBN 1-57233-238-7 (cl.: alk. paper)
1. Psychotherapist and patient—Fiction.
2. Women—Maine—Fiction.
3. Psychiatrists—Fiction.
4. Jewish men—Fiction.
5. Amnesia—Fiction.
6. Maine—Fiction.
I. Title.

PS3551.R725 B58 2003
813'.54—dc21   2003011958

For Rachel Morton

For technical and writing advice, I would like to thank Alison Bechdel, Rabbi Joshua Chasen, Susan Darke, Dr. Francisco Gonzalez, Matthew Goodman, Dr. Harvey Klein, and Michael Sledge.

Thanks also to the Knoxville Writers' Guild and Congregation Ohavi Zedek, and to Géraldine de Haugoubart and my family, near and extended, for their encouragement and support.

With deep gratitude to my mother, Nancy Williamson Van Arsdale, 1924–2002.

The heart's rue for that which it had scarce possessed,
and yet had lost.

—Leslie Keith

Part 1

All I needed was a little spot, a place where I could drop my satchel and my wounds, a patch of ground to stake me down. The road a black snake under my feet, and the rain smalling down around me, and there the two bridges stitched across the river just like I'd pictured it, just like I'd remembered, and the river so wide you couldn't skip a stone to the other side, so wide you'd need a boat or bridge to cross.

Down by the river, under the bridge, a beast or a troll. Who I could be: she-who-lives-by-the-river. A witch, a river-god, a scaled-up fish, a naiad. Annie Naiad. By the wits of the river, as it is writ. It's not the Jordan or the Nile, but it's so wide that it will do. Here I scratch down from the road, and now the breath of a car shushing past, and I clamber down low into the bushes, and my coat nearly catches on the teeth of the pricker bushes, but they can't nail me with their grins, and then there I am: I'm free.

Down by the river, the riverbank's a spatulate plate littered with stones, stones smooth skulls, smooth as a baby's pate under your hand. Press in, and look out! She's gonna blow!

Bridge number two's a criss-cross of fingers embroidered in steel, no heavy pavement to fall in a block on my head. Here, I'll become real steel under this bridge. A train might come over me, chase me, erase me, erase my me of me's, but I don't care. There's just enough shelter here, just enough cover to keep me from the storm. To keep the body of me warm.

I set up my camp, settle in now to wait. There's not much work to do, just rake out a space and drop my cloth down to the ground, hitch my tent into the stones, right here, under the Bridge of Styx, out here among the baby bones. Out in the night, where I belong. The three best and roundest stones I bring into the tent, and I find them by running my fingertips over their bony ridges. Here, here, and here. The rain starting now fingertips tapping on my head, on the roof of my tent. No one will find me here, and no one is looking, so no one will care.

The cars on the road that mow over the bridge in their watery noise. The cat-squeal of tires, a man yelling, Cocktease! his voice a tar pit, the slam of a car door. Oh, he's mad, that one. I hold onto Kitty, press my cheek to her fur. "The owl and the pussycat went to sea," I begin, I start telling her, but I peer out around the edge of the tent, and up on the embankment the white car jerks away, door swinging open and then slamming shut in one word to mean hollered but I don't know what, a tumbled parcel tossed onto the pavement, and I run my hand fast down Kitty's back, pressing, petting her fingered-down fur. "In a beautiful pea-green boat," I say. It's raining so hard now I can barely see, but the parcel keeps falling, tumbling down the rock in a good pummeling, then lands, comes to a dead stopping drop out among the flattened rocks. I wait, and it waits too, the rain finger-tipping my roof, and then the parcel moves, shrugs, stands; the bones in the valley breathed back to life, bones snapping up, pulled up by a string through the top of the skull. Breathed back to life just like Ezekiel said that it would.

Is she coming this way? Is she coming for me, to breathe the breath of the Savior into my bones? No. She's climbing in a heavy stumble back up to the road, crossing the bridge. Duck back into my tent, quick bunny, Kitty snuggled into the crook of my arm, clicking my tongue on the split of my lip.

I can hear the wolves singing their songs into the night air if I breathe low enough and keep my hands folded like Mary. Sing into the night air here and no one would know, no one would care. Sing a song of sixpence, a pocket full of rye. Four and twenty baby bones baked in a pie. When the pie was opened the bones began to beg; when the pie was opened, the blood was on the page. I close my eyes, and sleep does come, just as it will, just as it does.

⁓

Her first memory isn't of being found, so she won't remember this night rain icing the bridge, the road, her sneakered feet as they dangle over the water. The purr of a pickup truck passing, then passing again, headlights shimmering into the mist. She won't remember what happened to bring her to this bridge: how when the rain began she gave up her plan of hiking town to town, and stood by the highway, hitching a ride. She won't remember the man's rough hand like a rope burning her wrist, how she curled herself into a ball for the fall to the road edge litter, the pain as she thudded to the ground and then down the rocky embankment, her backpack and jacket tossed out after her with a shout to lie lost in the underbrush. She won't remember this night, this rain, or what came before that, or long ago, another night, another rain stinging her upturned face as she waited for someone. She won't remember what it was she wanted, or from where it was she came, or what it might have been that tipped her from her own real life into the smooth sheet of this fugue.

The water is so dark, and yet, she can see how it eddies around the rocks, can see the lights along the bridge reflecting back in white pools. Sitting there in the night, before she comes to, before she notices the wet and the cold, she can almost see beneath the water, to the rocks and stones, the river-washed stuff living under there.

She's been tumbled down the embankment, knocked against the pricker bush and stones; she's felt a heave of nausea and the spinning world as she climbed back up again, and now she sits on the bridge, as if she's patient, as if she's lost and waiting to be found.

Sitting on the bridge, outside some town in North America, at this particular juncture of longitude and latitude, in the autumn rain, free of longing, fear, and trust, with nothing in her body but a pain in her wrist that rings right up to her head, she looks down at the roiling black water, and doesn't remember anything.

~

At first, squinting through the rainy windshield, Rita LaPlatte thinks it's an animal on the edge of the bridge, a deer hit so hard it's been tossed to the side, and if anyone had asked, she wouldn't have been able to explain why she wanted to stop and look. She's seen plenty of deer hit before, knows how wet the stilled black eyes shine, knows how the pitch of blood blooms at the mouth. But no one's asking; as usual, she's alone, and a little drunk, and so at the end of the bridge she turns around at the skirt of gravel, passes again, turns again, then switches her flashers on, pulls the pickup to the side, checking in the rearview mirror for any cars that might be approaching. If she sees one, she plans to wave it on ahead. She's in charge of this, she thinks. She thinks, *this is mine.*

As she approaches, Rita feels a flick of fear: it's not a deer, not an animal at all, so what is it? It's a person, a full-grown woman, sitting on the bridge, as if about to jump, as if she's got nowhere to go, as if she's just been waiting for Rita, or for anyone, to come and pick her up.

The woman isn't huddled against the cold October rain; she's just sitting there as if it's the most comfortable place in the world, wearing nothing but a pair of jeans and a black sweater. White sneakers, clean. Rita notices things like that, what a person wears. No hat, or scarf, her hands bare and red with cold, her black hair damp from the misty rain.

When Rita approaches, gingerly, saying, "Hey, are you okay?" this phrase echoing in her head like something she herself once wanted to hear, the woman doesn't answer, just stares ahead, not looking down into the water anymore, but straight out, at the place where the horizon must be.

"You okay?" Rita asks again, unsure what else to say. She doesn't want to get too close. "Hey. Hey." Ineffectually calling across the rain, the night, the cold, as if what she found wasn't a full-grown woman after all, but an animal injured roadside. An animal who isn't answering, who doesn't understand and can't respond.

But then the woman turns. Her black hair hangs in a limp fringe around her pale, strong face. She isn't pretty, Rita thinks, her features just a little too big, her mouth too mobile and wide. The woman moves her head a little to the right, and Rita sees that she looks dumb, but not dumb like the retarded people from the halfway house who she sees sometimes on Main Street, toddling along with their guardian, heads too big for their bodies, eyes too big for their heads.

It's more like the look of that doe one of her mother's boyfriends took one year, Rita along for the ride, snow melting down into the tops of her boots. The animal had lain in the scuffed up leaves and snow, wounded but alive, looking at Derrick's boots as he approached, snow crunching under each step, the air so cold that Rita could hardly breathe.

For a moment Rita thinks maybe the woman doesn't speak English, maybe she crossed the border from Quebec, and Rita wishes she knew something French to say. Instead, she says again, "Hey," and steps forward, reaches in, touches the woman's shoulder with her hand, ready to jump back, ready to run.

At this, the woman speaks, her voice raspy. "Sure, I'm fine," she says, sounding a little irritated, as if she'd just been minding her own business and Rita had interrupted her thoughts.

"Okay," Rita says then, letting her hand drop. "All right," and she walks back through the rain to her truck, swings into the cab, turns the heater on high, pushes her damp hair from her eyes, smacks a cigarette out of the pack. As a last effort, she rolls down the passenger window, slows, calls out, "Can I give you a ride?" but the woman has turned back to the water, glassy and blank.

—

Maybe it was Rita's voice that began to wake her, as she sits on the bridge unjacketed, emptied out entirely, entirely alone. She looks down at herself: she's got nothing on her, nothing to claim. She reaches into the pocket of her jeans, pulls out a foreign-minted bill, a few coins of American change, a blue cat's eye marble. She holds the bill out in the windy rain, lets it go, watches as it flutters quickly down to the water, watches as the water tosses it up, catches it, tugs it downstream. She's carrying her few things the way a kid would, not in the way of a grown woman with responsibilities and goals, and she stuffs the marble and change back into the front pocket of her jeans.

Or maybe it was Rita's smell that woke her, her smell of cigarettes and newsprint and lipstick, a lingering trace of marijuana still clinging to the sweater she wears underneath her puffy vest.

Or maybe it was something that would have surprised anyone who knew Rita, shelled and shellacked as she is, curling with each year further into her hard self. The palpable feeling of *tenderness*, a feeling the woman can remember wanting, a feeling she remembers, even now, sitting on this bridge in this strange new town, just about to wake.

Or maybe she just got cold, on the bridge in the icy October rain. When Rita finds her, the woman's still in her fugue, lingering on the cusp of consciousness; she still hasn't quite *come back*, and so she won't remember this, meeting Rita on the bridge. She won't remember because she isn't yet there, but is hanging still in the fugue, back in the shadows that threaten the deeper, farther end of the garden. She hasn't come back yet, and so she can't, later, recall exactly how it was that she came to.

Whatever woke her, Rita's voice or Rita's brief touch on her shoulder, a stone inside her rolled over, opening a cave, and then, on a wet bridge some-place with night approaching, the deep wide water below her roiling over the rumbled rockbed, on the outskirts of a mid-size town in the northernmost reaches of New England, she comes at last out of her fugue, wakes, alone, memory still awash but soul restored as after sleep, like waking from a favorite, familiar sweet bad dream.

—

Her first sensation is of cold, and wet, bony damp. Her backside, against the metal of the bridge, feels soaked through, and her unprotected fingers are so cold she can't feel them anymore. She rubs her hands together, palm to scraped palm, looks at her fingers, long, graceful, bruised. *Hers?* she thinks, as she warms her fingers, tries to move them. *They must be real: they hurt.*

Her first thought is one word: *what.* Not the "where am I" or even the "who am I" you'd expect of the person coming to, and not the existential "what am I" that wakes us all, mid-night, jolting us from sleep and straight into mortality. Just: *what.* More of a statement than a question. Behind this thought, this word, float all those other questions, but when the doctors and nurses and psychiatrists will ask her, "What was your first thought?" her answer will be simply, "what."

But now, as she comes to, she knows nothing of what will happen and nothing of what has happened; she hangs suspended on the bridge, timeless, personless, waiting to be found, knowing only the physicality of her reclaimed self: the cold, the damp, her mouth dry and tasting sour, the tightening bell of pain in her wrist that rings right up to her head. When she hears the sirens and sees the pulsing red light coming along the straight stretch of highway, blurry red light in the mist, her shivering begins from deep under her skin, but still she doesn't move, doesn't rise or stretch her limbs.

Instead, she looks up: across from where she sits, another bridge hasps the river, an old railroad bridge, and just before the ambulance stops, she thinks, what if she saw herself over there, a mirror image of herself, sitting just as she is, feet dangling, lost, unnamed, harmed, like her? But no one's there; it's just the black night pocked by the silver rain.

The ambulance attendants are kind, but cautious: the anonymous caller told the dispatcher how she found a woman sitting on the bridge, like an animal, and they think, at first, she may be ready to jump. The older one approaches her, saying his own name, saying that he's there to help, then asking her, "Are you okay?" and she looks at them, still not frightened, just blank. "What's your name?" he says to her, and knowing she has to say something, knowing she must have a name, knowing a name's a special sound made just for you, she casts about, looks down to the deep water and somewhere beyond her conscious memory she remembers a darker water, a deep warm ocean, a patio of blue tiles, remembers looking down at her own bare feet warming on the tiles, and looking out at the indigo sea swelling beneath the clear hot azure sky and says the only word she thinks of: "Blue."

Later, she'll remember only this: the cry of the ambulance as it approached, the blurry hot light washing everything red, then white. The questions pounding, unspoken, in her head: *did I do something wrong? is somebody dead?* and the men from the ambulance, fastening a thick, cushy collar around her sore neck, loading her into the back, using kind words, saying, "We're here to help," and "Does anything hurt?"

Later, there will be just brief glints of this scene, lodged in her memory: the ice like scars down the steel of the bridge as she's led away, the tape winding around her sore wrist like a snake, like a tourniquet, or desire, or something she fears about to transpire. The clean white blanket covering her to her shoulders and chin.

⌒

They handle her carefully, saying: "It's awful cold, don't you want to come in and get warm," and now she responds; she nods, arms folded across her chest. *Yes.* She lies down, at their insistence, on the wooden board, immobilized, even though she's nervous like this, lying down, and she keeps shifting her eyes to look at the attendant riding in the back with her. He tells her to lie still, swabs the cuts on her head and her hands with something that stings. He examines the hand, sees the bruise on the wrist just starting to blue, the blood rushing up under the skin. He doesn't try to diagnose, just carefully splints.

She lets him wrap her wrist in tape, compliant, looking up at him the whole time, not wincing, not crying out, not saying a thing.

He's a good kid, and he smiles a genuine smile at her, says, "We'll do everything we can to help you," and just as he's been trained, he doesn't say, *You'll be okay.* But the news that they'll help her, that someone has come for her, is so reassuring, so much *just what she wanted to hear,* that she puts her head down on the stiff bed, watching the ceiling of the ambulance, white, sterile, bright, as the three of them sweep down Route 3, their siren a ribbon of lightning splitting the night.

In the emergency room, it's one white-coated woman or man after another, wheeling her under an X-ray machine, asking her questions, removing the collar from around her neck, saying, "It looks as if your spine is fine," taking off her wet clothes and holding out a gown, and she plunges her arms in the arm holes, trying not to panic, but *what are they doing, what do they want,* and they cover her with a warmed blanket, and then she's left alone, staring into the white light overhead. She's so cold she thinks she'll never be warm, but now, in the bright, lit-up emergency room, she wishes she were back by the river, back on the bridge. At least it was known.

In the hospital, her impressions are scattered, disconnected: a man who gently lifts her right wrist, presses it with his fingertip, looking down at his watch; a woman with three tiny braids at the back of her head, who sits by her side, asking "Do you know today's date? Do you know who the president is?" The answers swim away before she can catch them in her fist, and all she can think is this woman looks like a giant bird, *a raven,* she thinks, and then says. It's all a jumbled mess, her arm laid out on a thick metal plate, someone saying "Hold still, just like that," and a noise like a giant shutter clicking open, then shut. A needle stick pricking her vein, the cold stethoscope on her chest, until they all leave her again and it's all just a mess, a big *disconnect,* like *connect-the-dots* she thinks, and sees a drawing of something, a rabbit maybe, without lines, with only dots for each ear-point, each paw, three along the back, three for the round cottontail. This image is so absorbing to her that in her mind she starts connecting the dots, drawing the outline of the rabbit, but she's interrupted, the curtain around her bed scuttling open, and a nurse—"Has this one been in before?—saying, "They've got a room all ready for you, Blue," and wheeling her in her bed toward the elevators, into the room, saying "Here, swallow these," saying, "there, now you'll have a nice long sleep."

⌣

She won't tell anyone, Rita LaPlatte thinks as she pulls into her parking spot in the paved lot that runs the length of Main Street, behind the row of buildings that hold shops below, offices and apartments up above. The walkway to her building's slick with the rain now turning to sleet, and Rita's careful picking her way up the steps, holds on to the rail, even though, ungloved, her hand winces at the cold.

Inside, she climbs the wide marble stairs, passes the lawyer's offices on the second floor, then goes up again to the top. Once in her apartment, she stands at the window, looks down at the river tumbling below.

If she wanted to tell anyone, she would call Bart, and she checks her watch: just after midnight, she knows he's at the radio station covering the boards. Maybe she'll just see what he says.

"KID Radio," he answers.

"Hey, it's me."

"Oh, hi. You home already? What excitement did I miss?"

She can picture him there at the station, his green WKID T-shirt stretching a little too tightly over his gut, and she pictures again the woman on the bridge, but something inside her says, *no.* The familiar *don't tell.*

"Let's see. Pretty much I just talked with Stelly after I lost my place at the pool table. No good male meat."

"Yeah, tell me about it."

"Oh, Bart, come on, you get better chances than I do."

"Huh."

Rita twists the phone cord around her finger, still looking down at the river. What was the woman looking at down there? What could she see?

"So, that's all you have to report? Listen, it's still early, why don't you come down to the station and keep me company? You can bring me some doughnuts."

"No, I'm going to bed. I'm beat."

"Okay, if that's the way you want to be. What's eating you tonight, anyway? You're in a pissy mood."

"I don't know," Rita says, and this much, at least, is true: she doesn't know. All she knows, as she hangs up the phone, is that there was something about that woman on the bridge. That it's the kind of thing that doesn't happen every day, finding someone like that. That this must mean something, must mean that something, finally, is going to change.

Rita changes into her pajamas, and even though she's still a little bit high, she makes sure everything's in its place, the velour blanket neatly folded and laid out on the armchair, the water in the bowl of floating candles replenished, dishes washed and clothing put away. She then turns out the lights, but just before she gets into bed she stands again at the window, looks down at the river, looking down at it as if she's never seen it before. For now, and for as long as she can make it last, the secret's hers, and she won't tell anyone.

What was she watching down there, and for how long?

⁓

She wakes to a nurse saying right near her head: "Blue, Blue," and to the woman lying in the bed, to *her,* it sounds as if the nurse is telling her the color of this drug-sleep seawater she's treading. Or what *indigo* is. She's woken more by the sound than by the meaning it represents, but then, as the sound peels away to leave the meaning behind, she thinks she can smell the color, the cold alcohol wipes and white, starched sheets. She wakes thinking blue is the color of something you might want to keep.

She tosses her head, opens her eyes, and here's the room, the nurse pressing her fingers first to Blue's swollen left wrist, then to her right, looking at her watch, and leaving, quick and swift and efficient, *brisk,* Blue thinks. Leaving the room.

Blue sits up in bed, pushes the pillow up under her head. Her head pounds, *boom boom boom like a drum.* The room's white, and pale green, just the bed she's in, tightly made, a tall tray, and a little laminated cabinet to one side. Inside the cabinet, where she can't see them, her clothes lie silently, laundered of her scent and folded into neat squares by the hospital staff who work deep in the basement. No wallet, no driver's license or wedding ring. No clue. Just the handful of change, the marble, all of it now bagged and set inside the drawer by the sweater and the jeans.

Out the small window, she can see a pine branch move a little in the wind, and it's at this she feels a panic rise up: *where am I* comes now, and she searches the room for something familiar, but nothing is there.

Blue, the nurse said. *Blue. Is that my name?* She tries to remember anything at all, but quickly finds there's nothing there: no name, no place, no childhood phone number or an address that she knows. There's only this room, this white blanket, this pine tree filling the window.

When the nurse comes back in, she affects her cheerful attitude, saying, "Well, I'm glad to see you're up," and here, something inside Blue clicks shut: *the old lockdown, the don't-tell-anyone. Pretend, pretend.*

"Yeah," she says, uncertainly. "I'm up."

"Well, then, I'll just get the doctor," the nurse says, and from the room, Blue hears the speakers in the hall switch on, sounding the page for the doctor on call.

A woman, slight and small, comes in, her hair a pale copper tangle down her shoulders. *Like*—Blue starts to think, but there the thought stalls, as "Do you know where you are?" the woman says, her voice a bright piping noise in Blue's aching head.

"Sure," Blue says. "I'm in a hospital room," her tone making it clear this is obvious; it's the tone of an adolescent, and for that moment, Blue's closer to her thirteen-year-old self than to any other self at all, and even this young new doctor, younger than Blue is, small, seems like a grown-up with all the control.

"Good," the doctor says. "And do you know why you're here?"

"The accident," Blue says, her mind jumping the quick connections: *hospital, doctor, accident,* but even though she's making this up, scrambling for whatever seems right, the right answer, as she says the word "accident," her head pounds harder, and she wants to cry. But won't. *Don't cry, don't.*

The doctor asks about the accident, and Blue names the pictures that come into her head, fractured images, the words tumbling out as if by themselves, as if out of control: a car, a rain-slicked black road, a skidding slur into a ditch.

The doctor says, "We found you sitting on a bridge outside of town. You're in Maine, in New England. Do you know where that is?" Blue nods, and the doctor makes a note. "We're here to help you," the doctor says, leaning forward a little, and Blue thinks, *maybe she does care about me.* When the interview's over, Blue lies back, the stiff starched pillow scratchy behind her head, watches the doctor leave the room without looking back.

Nurses come and go throughout the day, bringing in a meal, a cup of medicine, switching on the bedside lamp at dusk. But Blue's still only just emerging from her fugue, staring out the window at the shivering pine, watching the rain streak up the glass. She thinks of the words she's heard since she came in, since she came to: *past, remember, day.* And there are other words inside her, too: *avenue, sienna, shore.* If she wrote them on a paper pad, would they turn out to be random, thoughtless words? or would they prove to be clues?

—

Night, Blue's given her dose by the same nurse who was in the night before, a young, moon-faced girl, who watches Blue swallow the pills. But as she turns to go, Blue panics: "Don't leave," she says.

"Excuse me?" This nurse is new, and not too-well-versed yet in the kinds of oddity she'll see.

"Don't leave me, please," Blue repeats. "Really. You're the only here I know. I recognize you," she whispers, and the young woman, fresh from nursing school, is flattered and scared at the same time.

"You recognize me?" she asks. Maybe she'll be the one to bring this mysterious woman back.

But as quickly as Blue catches, attaches, clings, and won't let go, she releases her hold. Maybe the sleeping pill is starting to work. By the time the nurse has focused on what's happening, Blue's turned back to the dark window, her blue eyes closed as if in sleep.

—

Early morning, coffee in his moss green mug with the handle long-since broken off, Bob Reichman stands at the nurses' station, fingertips scratching his beard, reading over the intake note, preparing to enter the room, a luxury of time he didn't have in residency in New York, where the patients flocked through the psych ward like birds, a constant distressed wing-beat in the background. Here, he reads over the note on this new patient, the one found on the bridge, over the spot where sometimes migrating psychotics will pause for a few days of shelter, spring and fall, on their way to roost before the winter snows. This new patient he's landed is the one everyone is saying has amnesia, even though he's loath to make such a quick and easy, such a made-for-TV diagnosis.

PATIENT NAME: DOE, JANE, AKA "BLUE"
PATIENT NUMBER: 31-100214

Patient is a white woman of approximately thirty–thirty-five
years, who variously states her age as fourteen, twenty-two,
and thirty-four. She is not oriented to time or to place,
appearing to make guesses when asked, saying sometimes
she is in a hospital in England during World War II, at
other times asserting she is in a prison.

The patient came into care via ambulance, following a report
by an anonymous caller, who reported seeing her sitting on
the Route 3 bridge on the east-bound side. The caller reported
that she was unresponsive to questions, and that she did not
appear to notice the cold and rain. She was wearing only jeans
and a sweater. Ambulance attendants reported that when they
arrived she was somewhat responsive, possibly in shock.

In hospital, blood tests returned normal. Urine sample clean.
Pt. treated for shock.

Physically, the patient's most remarkable injury appears to be
severe bruising to the left forehead and left wrist and forearm.
Superficial scrapes on palms, face, and arms. A hairline left
navicular fracture on X-ray. CT scan negative. Pt. appears
to be left-handed. She has a long-healed scar along her left
anterior thigh.

PHYSICAL EXAM: Pupils round and reactive to light. Ears clear.
Lungs clear. Heart regular rate and rhythm, no bruits, rubs or
gallops. Abdomen not tender, soft.

The most striking symptom in this patient is her apparent
absence of memory. She reports being unable to recollect how
she happened to arrive at the bridge on October 2, or any
events leading up to that time. She cannot state her profession,
marital status, or familial or religious affiliations. She says she
can recall no memories of childhood or adulthood.

She does not appear overly distressed. She appears frightened upon meeting a new person, but her memory for recent events (i.e., since she "came to" on the bridge) appears to be intact, in that she recognizes the health professionals who work with her, and her own recollection of the story of how she was brought in remains consistent.

TREATMENT: Abrasions cleaned. Wrist wrapped and taped; no cast necessary at this time. Monitor for further pain. Tylenol 3 for pain. Ambien to sleep.

Standing there at the nurses' station, Reichman thinks, okay, it does sound like amnesia then, and he knows that in most cases, nearly all, the memory comes flooding back soon, within days if not hours. A family member will appear, or a random association will jostle loose in the patient's brain, and the veil of forgetting will lift, sometimes to reveal a condition far more threatening than amnesia, a tumor pressed against the pons, or a borderline personality disorder or psychotic break. Or uniquely worse, perhaps, than any of these, an unremembered trauma that kicked the patient out of the present and into the fugue.

He raps with his knuckles on the patient's door, enters the room, and as he does, Blue pushes up a little in the bed. Another change. Another doctor coming in. *Why won't they just leave me alone,* Blue thinks, but doesn't say, because as much as she's annoyed and so tired that all she really wants to do is sleep, they're all she's got, these strangers coming through.

"Hello, Blue," the tall man says. He isn't wearing a white jacket like the other doctors do, with their names embroidered in ice blue stitching above the pocket. And so he has no pocket from which to take a little light disguised as a pen, tilt her chin with his hand, watch her eyes glide back and forth, back and forth. And he doesn't have a stethoscope slung around his neck, so he won't be leaning down to her chest, pressing the cold circle to her bare skin.

No. This one is wearing a green checkered shirt and a thick tie the color of egg yolks, and khaki pants, and he doesn't look like the others. Blue has no way of saying what it is he does look like, but he reminds her of the kid in the ambulance on the shrieking ride here. *On the ride home,* she thinks.

"Hello," she says back. Then, she can't help it: "Do you know the man in the ambulance?" she blurts out, knowing that when she's blurted out things like this before, to the nurses and the other doctors, they've just looked at her and blinked their eyes, and haven't answered, as if they don't know what to say. Is this is why they keep her here so long?

But this man says, "What man? Which one?" and leans against the doorjamb. She tells him, describes the man, how he looked so young, how he wore a tiny gold earring in one ear, how his hair was the color of, the color of, the color of, but she can't think of anything. "He rode in the back with me when I first came here," she says.

"Oh, no, I don't think I do know him," the tall man says. He wrinkles up his forehead. "Wait a minute, maybe that's the Mercer boy, Jackie Mercer. Yes, I'm sure of it. I think I do know him, or know his folks anyway."

Folks. People who care for him. People he loves. Blue nods, happy that at least he's understood her and has answered her seriously.

"May I have a seat?" he asks, and she nods again, and he then pulls the straight-backed chair around and sits down, crosses one leg over the other, folds his hands in his lap.

"Blue, I'm Doctor Reichman," the man says. "I know I don't look like the other doctors you've seen, and that's because I'm a different kind of doctor. I'm a psychiatrist, and you and I will be working together to figure out what's going on here," he says. He doesn't say, "to figure out what's wrong."

Blue looks at him. *Now what?* She nods.

Reichman goes over the uses of psychiatry, the methods, the tests he'll run. The promises he can't make. He doesn't use the word *amnesia* yet.

~

At Crystal 'N Sands on Main Street, Rita fingers through the big bowl of polished stones, amber and tourmaline and cat's eye and jade; she likes the way the stones feel against her skin, smooth and as lightweight as if they were empty. But she isn't here to mess around with the stones; she's on a mission, and soon she moves to the shelves of candles, carefully chooses one, the one for bringing back people who have been lost to you.

She takes it to the counter hesitantly, knowing that the proprietor, Crow, always nosy, will ask her about it, but Rita's got an excuse that will prevent her having to tell Crow the truth; she's trying to get her mother back, she'll say. She's trying to contact the dead.

Of course, this isn't true. She wouldn't want her mother back even if she could work some magic like that, which she can't, because her mother, she knows, won't respond to anything, can't be reached even by the spirit world, has floated out beyond the reach of magic and of souls. Her mother, dead, is just as unreachable as she was alive.

Sure enough, in the curling tendril of incense at the cash register, Crow sweeps her sheaf of dark hair back around her head, inspects the candle as if she's never seen it before, carefully reading the cardboard tag complete with recommended incantation tied around its stem, then says, "Trying to find someone who's lost?" and Rita nods, but feels her clever story, her *ploy* (her word of the day from her learn-a-word-a-day calendar) drain out of her, and she leaves it at that, even though she can tell Crow is miffed at her lack of response, twitches her lip in disappointment, and curtly says, "Five ninety-five."

Back down Main Street in the October dusk, and at the Emerson Block, the name of the building etched in stone over the stationer's shop, Rita pushes open the heavy glass door, mounts the stairs, eager and yet at the same time, reluctant. Why should this incantation work where all others have failed?

On the third floor, the sheet of opaque pebbled glass in her apartment door seems illuminated as if from within; it looks almost bright. Rita shimmies the lock open, twisting the key to the right as she pulls hard on the door; after ten years in this place, she's accustomed to this quirk, but still thinks she's got to get the landlord to fix it. Inside, the room's lit by the streetlamp that shines on the dark rippling river water all night. Rita shrugs out of her jean jacket, then goes to the Formica table by the window, where she unwraps the candle.

Across the room, there's a small bookshelf, the topmost surface covered with a dark blue cloth, decorated with two photos, one a photo of an angel that Rita bought at Crystal 'N Sands, then framed. Beside it, a postcard she picked up at the Book Nook, a photo of a wolf, in silhouette, on the curving back of a mountain ridge. Here, at her altar, Rita carefully lights the candle, reads the incantation from the cardboard square out loud, calling out to invoke the return of a person who's lost, or missing, or strayed. "May all this be only for good," the incantation ends, as they all do.

The directions tell her to picture the person as clearly as she can, and then three times to say the person's name, but this is difficult, since, Rita's sure, she hasn't seen the person in question in more than thirty years, and has never had a name to match with the blurry face as she imagines it. So she pictures her own face, angular, too thin, with the heavy brows that she has to pluck, the mop of hair she tries to keep trimmed.

She pictures the woman she's believed for years could exist; she pictures the woman she wants to believe could be her own twin.

There's nothing new in any of this; Rita LaPlatte's been looking for her missing twin since she was six and for hours would sit on the dirty springtime front stoop of that year's apartment house, waiting, peering through the scrawny forsythia branches to scrutinize every kid who approached from further up the block.

Initially, when Rita was small, her mother was patient, saying, "Sweetie, you don't have a twin," but later, as Rita grew, her mother was more often just plain mad all the time, exploding like fireworks on the fourth of July, gripping Rita's small shoulders: *"You do not have a twin. You don't!"* until Rita was too scared even to cry, and just nodded, turned, and walked to her room, where she sat on the bed and cuddled her stuffed rabbit close to her chest, the ache of longing pounding in her small head.

"You don't have a twin," the lie—Rita knew, it had to be true!—ringing, echoing, like the sound of a door slamming shut.

Now, Rita imagines her twin as she's always imagined her: looking like Rita, but prettier, smiling in recognition. As Rita's grown up, and older, so has the image of her missing twin, and now, if a person watching could see through to the imaginary world, she'd see Rita's twin appearing beside her, there in the room that's perched like a bird's nest over the river that tumbles and coils under the streetlight, shiny and blueblack as the thickest black oil.

Blue wakes on her fifth morning, alone, from a half-dream, a druggy dream, something of a cat, an ocean wave, a cool, dark room. As quickly as it comes, it's gone, slipped away with the other stuff of night, and here's the nurse, waking her. Here's her breakfast on a tray, two white and yellow eggs, look-ing up at her like eyes, or pools. She eats, eats everything on her plate, *good girl,* and then the nurse's aide takes the tray away, and Dr. Reichman comes in again. This time, Blue recognizes him.

"Hello, Blue," he says, coming into the room. This time he's got his notebook out, and he pulls up a chair to sit by her bed.

"Hello," she says.

"I'm back again to ask you some more questions, to see if together we can figure out what's going on here."

"Okay. Ask away. But I don't feel many answers here," she says, tap-ping her head with one forefinger.

"That's fine. Now, first of all, do you know where you are?"

"I'm in a hospital."

"Have you ever been here before?"

Blue doesn't know the answer, and so she says again what she's said so many times since she's come to: "I don't know."

"Okay. Now, do you know me?"

"Yes. You were here the other day. And also you and I knew each other a couple of years ago, when we were working together in a frame shop. A farm, I mean a farm."

"I see." Dr. Reichman is busy writing, and Blue thinks, *I must be on the right track, for him to be writing so much in that notebook,* but then she's suddenly tired, and says so, and he goes.

⌒

Friday afternoon, dusk, that yellow strip of light that lingers late on these autumn afternoons still clinging just above the red and orange leaves at hori-zon's edge, Bob Reichman parks his car in the lot of the YMCA, sighs, and then, before he can convince himself that heading straight home would be a better idea, he gathers his gym bag and heads into the low brick building.

Reichman's always a little nervous about running into patients here, even though he rarely does. Instead, it's the men he knows from work, or from his infrequent visits to the synagogue, whom he dodges in the locker room, telling himself it isn't that he's anti-social, it's just that he spends all day talking, it's just that he wants a little time alone. "How's it going," one man, a lawyer for the hospital, says, and Reichman says, "Fine, you?" smiles, and turns; that's it, that's all he has to do.

In order to offset the first slap of cold water, he thinks of something hot as he makes his headlong dive into the pool, thinks of the sauna that waits for him afterward, thinks of a hot afternoon in July. But by his second lap down the lane, he's warmed up, and thinking as he does whenever he swims on a Friday afternoon that it's Friday, erev Shabbes, and he should be in shul, he should be home making a chicken dinner, inviting someone over to light the candles, say the blessings, and sing the prayers with him.

And as usual, on this Friday, he smiles at how regular is his self-castigation, how predictable his thoughts, how deeply embroidered the pattern that his parents so carefully stitched in him. When was the last time he went to services at the jerry-rigged havarah in Intervale? When was the last time he had a Shabbes dinner, not counting his trips to Boston to see his dad? Even before Amy moved out, *before Amy left,* he forces himself to say in his head, Friday night wasn't special, was just the end-of-the-week, just the time to curl into the nest, make love, and sleep.

Soon, the water produces its anesthetic effects, and Reichman doesn't think anymore of where else he could be, doesn't think of the past, of what he could be doing, or what some say he *should* be doing right now. It's just *breathe, breathe, breathe,* and finally, in the cold water of the long, shallow pool, for a few minutes, Reichman forgets.

～

While Blue lies in her hospital bed, face turned to the big window in her room, in the blank reach of *nothing past,* just a pale wash of light where the memory should be, the *Intervale Gazette* picks up her story, running front-page articles about the mystery woman, with her photo and the oversized caption, "DO YOU KNOW ME?" One story makes an appeal for donations of women's winter clothing, size 9, and the good people of Intervale rush forward, but it's hard to say whether this charity comes more from simple kindness to a stranger in their midst or from a desire to brush near the mystery, to be able to think, *she's wearing my girl's sweater,* or *she'll be lacing up my old Bean boots.*

After three days of observation on the internal medicine floor, Blue is moved upstairs, to the quiet part of the psychiatric ward, the part of the hospital where the respectable drunks and women suffering depression are kept until they can pull themselves together and resume their lives, where the occasional teenager who snaps gets sent before being shipped to the big hospital downstate.

It's here, upstairs in her new room, that she dredges up from sleep the remnants of a dream, trailing behind her a shredded ribbon of images that unravel before she can remember them. She wakes in a blue nightshirt, something donated from one of what she's come to think of as *the people,* wakes feeling that *oh no* of the unfamiliar, remembering the medicine floor where she first stayed, longing for the slant of light that came in just so, for the bleep of monitors and the smell of the narcissus someone had deposited at the nurses' station, the scent like something cool and something hot at the same time. She wakes longing for this, wakes missing it; it's all she knows: her only home.

A nurse comes in, a new nurse, and Blue feels the pull toward what she's rapidly beginning to think of as *the old days,* the Tuesday through Friday she lived on the medicine floor. She longs for the nurses there, even the brusque ones who treated her as a malingerer. If asked, she wouldn't be able to name this feeling as *longing, nostalgia, rue*—to her, it's a deep visceral feeling in her gut, an ache, sore and tender like the purple blotchy bruise that started blooming on her wrist when she first came to.

But this nurse is friendly, and not dressed in the remote white uniform of the nurses on the medicine floor. She's wearing pale brown slacks and a light green sweater with a nametag: Alison Crue, R.N.

"Good morning," she says, coming in the room. No clipboard this time, and again, Blue misses it, even asks, "Where's the clipboard?"

"Oh, we don't use those up here as much as they do downstairs," Alison Crue says, briskly walking to the windows and opening the curtains. "I think you'll find a lot of things are different up here." She stands at the window for a moment, looking out, then turns.

"Well, don't you look smashing in that blue nightshirt," she says, and Blue, sitting up now, still feeling dreamy, still struggling to bring back the stones and the rain and the crooked hallway from her sleep, doesn't know what to say.

"I do?" she says, then realizes she has no idea what she looks like. She pulls her hand self-consciously through her short hair. *Short hair,* she thinks, *I am a person with short hair.*

She doesn't know it, but the blue of the shirt, a deep indigo, is the same color as her eyes, startlingly bright and intensely blue. Her hair is dark, coal black, and her eyebrows are black too, and thick, and Alison Crue is right, she's striking, and in her own odd way, beautiful.

"Would you like to see?" Alison Crue says, and brings from the bathroom a hand mirror with a plastic back, on which has been stenciled a flower. A daisy.

Blue looks into the mirror. Now, she feels nothing, and staring into the mirror, she's staring into the flat pool of non-feeling. A steady hum. It's like looking at any one of these strangers she's found herself among—she could just as easily look like Alison Crue, with her long razor-straight blond hair. *Is this me? Is this how I've looked all this time?*

In the flashing second as she hands the mirror back, Blue hears a tiny warbling noise inside of her—*just like sleeping beauty*—but the voice is gone before it even becomes a voice in her head.

"I don't want to look," she says to Alison, then adds, "sorry," knowing that she should look but unsure, really, why. Instead, she turns to the window.

"Well, then, it's time to get up. No staying in bed all day up here." Alison walks from the room, and Blue swings her feet out from under the sheet and thin pale blanket, lets her legs dangle, and then looks up to the window.

Outside, she can see a granite rock face mountain, far off, beyond the roads and houses, skirted with red and yellow trees. Closer in, just below the window, a tall white pine—the same one she saw from the other floor, a different angle, in her first hospital days—shivers in the wake of a crow landing on its topmost branches, and there's something in the shivering, that pulsating rivering motion, that stirs Blue. But then it's gone, and she stands, dresses, goes into the bathroom. Another mirror here, this one bigger, hanging over the sink, and Blue looks into its glassy reach, stares at the face of this stranger, the black hair, blue eyes, her skin too pale, cheeks drawn in, deep crevasse forming in the divot between her eyes, the perfect curve of her lip.

Who are you, she thinks to herself, but even now, she doesn't cry.

⌒

Down by the riverbank, Annie Naiad keeps herself tented under a parcel of cardboard, cardboard she carries folded under her backpack on her endless hegira. She likes building the fire each night, likes rolling a big metal drum that she finds by the side of the road down to the water's edge under cover of dark, likes stuffing the scraps that she finds, the newspapers and pieces of wood, into its perfectly round metal mouth. The best part is when she strikes the match on the flint, the best is the sound of flame touching tinder. Settled now, she keeps herself warm with the fires she builds on the riverbank's beach, just around the corner where the water slips past the railroad bridge, where the flame won't be seen by the drivers in the cars passing on Route 3.

This is a good spot she's got, and Annie Naiad settles in to her job of watching the river pull past her encampment. She's been here before; she's set up like this under this old railroad bridge, a good spot to stop as she makes her annual rounds: Boston, Portland, and deep in summer's heat one time she went all the way up to the border of Canada, hoping to see, or at least to hear, the wolves she knows must pace through the forest up there, that far to the north.

Now, this patch of ground under the bridge is quickly becoming her home; after one night it's familiar, it's as if she's lived here forever, as if she belongs. Last time she was here, there was a rabbit, and now, one morning, she wakes in the frosty cold that creeps around the edges of her cardboard tent and lifts up the flap, smoothing the cardboard with her fingertips, watches without moving, and at last there's a rustle in the underbrush, a movement that could be the breeze from the river, but no; here he is, and she wants to shout, wants to tell him she's back, too, but she knows better than to do this, and keeps very still, watches the rabbit sit upright, stare out ahead, and then hop away. She can barely contain her pleasure at this, and giggles to herself inside her tent, one hand covering her mouth.

Annie Naiad talks to herself there, under the bridge, under the stars. Or rather, she talks to something inside herself, some part of herself that doesn't live in her body, but lives in the world outside. She's muttering, and if anyone were listening, if anyone wanted to bear the stench that rises from her clothes and skin, the clinch of dried sweat, urine, the food that sometimes spoils in her knapsack, if anyone dared lean in without her seeing and could hear what she said, he'd hear her sputtering what appears at first to be nonsense. He'd be frustrated by her difficulty with articulation. But if these words could be transcribed, if someone could swim into her head and write them down, it would be clear what she said, if not what she meant.

Down by the riverbank the sleeping is good, my red-lined sleeping bag the shroud of Turin wrapped all around me. I'm cozy and dozy, a pocketful of posies, nothing to worry me, no dreams or stupors or lights shining on and off and on with my pulse.

In a hospital ward it's all so bright there's no sleeping anywhere, even if you curl up tight against the light that shines into your hammock. One blanket per customer, please, the ladies say, so there you are; you're stuck, dumb duck stuck to the ice with its rubber feet frozen down.

Down by the riverbank, here at home, that's where I do my sleeping best. The cars on the bridge a whisper, a lullaby, and no trains on the rickety track at night to wake me from my rucksack dream. The man with the rope, the choke in the throat, nothing I can't spit out in one stroke.

———

When Rita first sees the story in the *Intervale Gazette,* what catches her eye isn't the word *reward* but is the simple phrase captioned under the photo: DO YOU KNOW ME? The photo's pretty clear, considering it's been reproduced on newsprint, and Rita's one of the first to see it, in the newspaper's pressroom, where she ties up the bundled papers to be sent out on the trucks. She recognizes it immediately: the woman on the bridge, the woman she found. She pulls the papers off the conveyor belt one at a time, stacking them by tens, over and over seeing the face and the phrase until it becomes numbing, until she can't think of anything else. *Do you know me?*

At 11:30, Rita sits with the others as usual in the break room, selects her hot chocolate mix from the machine, and drinks from her Styrofoam cup.

"Get a load of this," Roger says, then bites into his doughnut. "'Woman Remembers Nothing,'" he reads from the headline. "One of those amnesiacs. Did you see that movie on TV, where the guy never got his memory back?"

Rita looks at the photo, at the article, mesmerized still by the phrase she's been reading all morning: DO YOU KNOW ME? Except for that rainy night on the dark bridge, the weird way the woman looked at Rita without seeing her, stared at her as if from a deep blank reach of space, Rita doesn't recognize the woman, even though she tries to think: has she ever seen her buying groceries at the IGA, throwing darts at Bodeo's, or out at the road-house on a Saturday night? No. This she would have remembered, of that she's sure. But still there's this lingering feeling: she wants to know, wants to lift herself to float out beyond Roger and Ross and the others, to float up to where this mysterious woman with the funny name belongs.

She doesn't mention any of this to the guys, doesn't tell them about the night, the rain, how she touched the woman's shoulder, how spooky it was when the woman looked back. *As if she'd seen me before, as if she knew who I was.* They wouldn't understand. She just lets them go on.

She keeps the secret of the mysterious woman no one knows inside herself as she goes about her job, tying up the bundles, delivering the bundles to the stores around town. She holds the secret inside herself, and thinks of it that way, even though she knows she doesn't really have much of a secret to keep, just wishes she did.

At home, Rita finds her scissors in the kitchen drawer, takes them out, and carefully, precisely cuts around the edges of the photo, then clips the photo to the magnetic Kitchen Klip she keeps on the fridge, stands back to look at the picture that the picture, the fridge, and the kitchen make. It's a little crooked, and Rita adjusts it, adjusts it again. She couldn't say why it has to be just right. She's left the caption on: DO YOU KNOW ME? and from the newsprint, the woman stares out at her, asking.

If anyone asked, Rita would say she wants the reward, wants to be the first one to lay the puzzle pieces together, to say, *oh, this is her, I know who she is*, and cash in on her five hundred bucks. Rita convinces herself of this to the extent that at night, she lies in her bed, thinking of what she'd do with the money. Is five hundred enough for her to take a trip somewhere? Where could you go on five hundred? Could she get someplace warm, the Bahamas, like she's seen advertised in the paper on Sunday, the happy couple pushing each other into the gin-clear waves in their dress clothes, holding their shoes up over their heads?

Probably not. A trip like that would cost more like a thousand, plus, what would she do when she got there? She wouldn't exactly fit in, with her old summer sandals and her pale, pasty skin.

Five hundred dollars. She could get a new kitchen set, new table and chairs that match. Spruce up the apartment.

But if she had five hundred dollars just like that, what she really should do is spend it on her pickup, fix the exhaust so Bart will stop teasing her about riding roughshod all over town. She really needs to do something about her truck, she thinks, turning onto her back, giving up now on sleep.

~

Blue wakes in the night. The hallway hospital lights leak in under her door, and on that cusp of sleep to waking she's a very little girl in a bedroom, the light of her parents' grown-up life, the sounds of conversation, of laughter, of forks and knives on plates. Blue knows what she's supposed to do: close her eyes, try to float inside the memory, allow it to expand, so she does, lying in her bed, but then she sinks back down into sleep, and by morning she's forgotten even that brief glimpse of memory.

~

Ready for her first appointment down the hall in Dr. Reichman's office, not here in her hospital room, Blue walks through the door as if leaving her only home, turning at several points along the hall to look back. There's Alison Crue, R.N., standing at the nurses' station, and the next time Blue turns, she's crossing the hall with a tray of medicines.

Left, then right. Follow the colored strips taped to the floor. The yellow strip veers off here, the blue turns left, the white goes straight ahead. *Red, red, follow the red. Like a single brush-width of carmine, like a bloodline.* For now, it's all she can do to follow the red line taped to the speckled brown linoleum tiles, look up for the occasional signs: "PSYCHIATRY" with a little white arrow pointing the way. She passes the library cart stacked high, hears the voice of the man who delivers the books boomerang out from a patient's white room.

In her first longer sessions with Dr. Reichman, he's cautious with her, still not entirely sure if she's truly amnesic or somehow faking it, maybe borderline? but she doesn't possess the manipulative charm of a borderline, seems too depressed, uninterested in reeling him in. A pathological liar? Perhaps. We'll see. He learned a long time ago that diagnosis isn't a wooden drawer into which he can slip a patient; it's simply a way of naming a behavior, and they're not all mutually exclusive. Being human, patients don't always fit the list of possible diagnoses, but they spill out, unravel, make a mess.

Blue's wary too, and even as she follows her feet following the red line down the hall, she just wants to go back to her room. She likes Alison Crue, R.N., and Betsy, who comes at night, gives her the nighttime pills. These people feel more familiar than the doctor, who seems so far away, on the other side of his big questions. The nurses don't make Blue remember, don't ask her anything, except how is she feeling today.

Today, today, today, Blue sings in her head as she opens the door to Dr. Reichman's office. *Today, today, today,* and she sits in the overstuffed chair opposite him.

"Good afternoon," Reichman says.

"Good afternoon," Blue parrots.

"How are you feeling today?" he asks, and Blue's relieved: *Today, today.*

"Okay," she says. "Fine, really."

"Are you sleeping all right?"

"Sure, I mean, they give me these pills that knock me right out, so if I couldn't sleep I'd say there's something wrong with me," she says, laughing, then thinks she's laughing too loudly, and quiets right down.

"Well, we could try cutting back on them if you'd like. See if you can sleep without them, and if not, we'll increase the dose again."

"Oh." Reichman thinks she looks disappointed at this. Is it the disappointment that sometimes comes with the first tentative steps of trust? If he proves himself, she has to start trusting him, and if she starts trusting him, she must start to unshutter her guard. If he's reading this right, in a way it's a good sign; it means she's most likely able to develop trust.

Or is he misreading her altogether, and she's disappointed at the thought of losing her sleeping pill? Or is she disappointed at something else entirely?

"How would you feel about that?" Dr. Reichman asks, and Blue starts feeling the pain in her head, soaring across her temples and into her brain, but she knows this isn't what he means, he isn't talking about feeling like that, like this shrieking pain in her head or the bruisy ache in her arm where the bandage is wrapped.

"What do you mean?" she says. "How I feel?"

"Well, I mean, what emotion would you feel if you didn't have your sleeping pill at night? Happy, sad, disappointed. . . ." Reichman doesn't like suggesting feelings to patients, fearing he'll influence them, but he fears that with Blue, they'll never get anywhere if he leaves it entirely up to her.

Balance. Measure. *Step forward, step back,* Reichman thinks.

Feeling, Blue thinks.

"I guess that would be okay," she says, and Reichman thinks, okay, she wants to stay in her head, can't move into the realm of feeling yet, but then she says, "Do you think it will help me get a memory back?" and Reichman sees that there are tears welling in her eyes. Welling, but not spilling over, as she swallows down hard.

"I think it may help you to have some dreams," Reichman says, leaning forward a little in his chair, then becoming aware he's leaning forward, and leaning back again. Don't scare her with your interest, he thinks, and sees in a quick blush of memory one of his first dates with Amy, four years ago, how he leaned in to kiss her, came on too strong because he liked her too much. And nearly lost her then.

"And allowing yourself to engage in dreams at night can only be beneficial," he finishes.

"Okay then," Blue says, swiping the back of her hand across her eyes. "Can I go now? I feel kind of tired."

Reichman glances to the round-faced clock on the desk. As usual, he's surprised how long such a superficially simple exchange can take, but he's encouraged by this: there is something deeper at work, he believes, when these small negotiations take such time.

"Sure, Blue, go ahead. I'll make the changes on the medication, and I'll see you Wednesday."

Blue leaves the room, closing the door behind her. *Follow the red, follow the red,* and she walks back to the ward, recognizing each turn in the hall, each open door, noticing that the library cart is gone, there's a new bouquet on the nurses' desk. How can anything be wrong with her memory? She could name any number of details of life here on the ward. But now she's tired, as if by claiming fatigue she's conjured it, and in her room, she lies on her bed, face to the wall, and sleeps.

On Blue's bad night, her worst night, she wakes and panics, wakes with a soundless cry coming from her throat, trailing the nightmare behind her: a bat clutched with its terrible tiny feet to the window screen, waiting to take flight, and around her a noise of celebration, and a man in the house, in the next room, waiting for her. "Next!" he'll call and she'll go the way of the others.

Blue wakes with the cry coming from her throat, vibrating into her chest but silent, and then she's sitting up in bed, sweat matting her hair to her scalp. She looks around the room, the panic now rising in her, says, to no one, "Where am I?" and begins to cry, sobs shaking her shoulders but her eyes staying dry.

By the time the night nurse comes in, Blue's huddled back beneath the covers, rocking. "Where am I, where am I," she repeats, and the nurse, Betsy Long, R.N., can't resist breaking protocol, and sits on the edge of the bed, lifts Blue into her arms, and Blue cries, *like a baby,* Betsy thinks, Blue's arms slung all raggedy and loose around Betsy's shoulders.

"Come on, come on," Betsy says at last, as Blue's sobs quiet. "It's okay." She rubs Blue's back, and has that fleeting fear that someone will see this pieta, that someone will see and think, *queer.*

Betsy holds this mysterious woman close, pulls her to her breast, more like a friend, or a mother, than a nurse or a lover, afraid someone will see, but more afraid not to respond, sure that this response, the warm human blood of touch, is what this patient needs.

No one comes in the room, and Blue cries herself out, and Betsy finally pats her back into the covers, and returns to the nurses' station to write the nightmare, the long tearless sobbing, into Blue's widening chart.

While Blue wakes in the starchy rough hospital sheets, the light from the hallway and the sting of alcohol and ammonia seeping under her door, across town and out on Pequot Road off Route 3, Bob Reichman can't sleep, and finally, once again, he gives up trying. If only he had more time to swim laps at the Y, maybe he'd be able to sleep, but as it is, he's lucky if he gets to the pool on a few weekday evenings, Saturday afternoons. And so he's tugged from his dreams after midnight, not fully awake but not asleep, as if his ancient cerebellum's sleeping but the new cerebrum's suddenly on the lookout. On alert.

He lies with his eyes open, looking out the French doors that lead from the bedroom to the deck, doors Amy had suggested they put in. "We can wake up in the summer and open the doors, and it'll be like we're outside," she'd said, and for one summer that's how it was. Now, when he wakes, the doors are shut against the coming cold, two long black squares of night. His mind skitters away from Amy, gallops to his patients, but then he thinks of events long past, in a patchwork of importance: the pitch of embarrassment at his inadvertent insult to one of the nurses at the hospital picnic in August; a still shot from their trip to Greece, Amy laughing, pulling the suitcase on its leash through a crowd; and then the car careening toward him when he was seventeen. Briefly, he sees a friend's tiny, urban backyard out in San Francisco, how it was split in a sharp line, sun from shade. He thinks now of all the wrong things he's said and done; he thinks of the mistakes he's made. On this night, as is usual of late, he winds up by thinking of his father, alone in the house in Brookline, bumbling room to room, forgetting to switch off the heat before bed. Leaving the gas flame flickering on the stovetop until the kitchen fills with the sharp scent of aluminum gone hot. But what's the choice: this, or a retirement home somewhere, his father shrinking further away from him among strangers, in some nicely appointed, sterile old folks' home.

Reichman knows there's nothing he can do right now; if he's going to move his father from that house somewhere else, someplace with supervision, he certainly isn't going to do it at two A.M. It's best to get up, give in, switch on a light in another room.

In the kitchen, he rummages through the fridge, cuts a slice from the deli meatloaf, heats some milk in a pan. *If you hadn't married a* shiksa, *you'd know how to keep a kosher home,* he hears his father say in his head, but still, he eats his snack, light on overhead, leafing through the pages of last Sunday's *New York Times.* News of the outside world. He knows that any sleep-inducing properties of warm milk result from the placebo effect, but it works for him, and after reading the paper, he's grateful enough for his own life, a life free from war and famine and, for the most part, from despair. And so he shuts the light, returns to bed, and in some manner, returns to sleep.

By the riverbank's light, in the light only of the moon and the diffused glow from the town's sheltering streetlights that rim the bridge and the section of Route 3 that leads into town, Annie Naiad sleeps through the night, her face as relaxed and tender as the face of a child, cheeks curving under the strings of her hair, sleeping bag twisted around her like a cocoon, arms swaddled too, head tucked in, Kitty sleeping at her feet. If anyone saw her sleeping there, she'd appear to be dead, she lies so still and needs so little air. She dreams, lying there, of the wolves that she knows are out there in the night, even though she can't hear them, even though they never come close. She dreams of a tunnel, a chute, and she's riding down the curving slopes, like on a bobsled, only this isn't like that, this isn't like anything, this is a dream.

She's grown accustomed in her wandering to the animal sounds of the night, and she doesn't rouse with the mice that tremble their tails past her cardboard box; she remains dreamward as the river otter slips up onto the bank on its wriggling legs, fur black and wet. She continues to sleep as Castor and Pollux pass and shift overhead, and sleeps until dawn, when the light shimmering into her cardboard safe house and the song of the birds that remain all year long break open the seal of the night to make a new day.

Rita LaPlatte's bedroom is neat, sheets and blankets tucked in at the mattress' edge, the fake brass headboard like a curling circus ring. Everything in its place, and a place for everything; that's what Rita says. At night, the light from the streetlamps that glimmers off the river shines in, but still, Rita sleeps, most nights. Some. When she can't sleep, she gets up, lights a candle, rolls a joint, and smokes it out on her balcony, watching the river water three stories below in its persistent tumble and fall.

Asleep, Rita doesn't remember a thing. Here, in her own bedroom, she's in charge of everything, and she keeps her dresser bare and neat, her clothes folded in their stern drawers, or hanging straight and ironed behind the closet doors. Just as she did when she was a kid: "the kid's got the neatest room in the house," her mother would say, and laugh. "Me, I'm more, how would you say, more happy-go-lucky than that," and she'd lean in toward whatever man was listening.

Now, grown, Rita's got just one of everything, and she likes it that way: one pair of heels she hardly ever wears, one pair of sneaks, one pair of boots. Her down vest, her blue leather jacket, in a feminine bomber style. A single bedside lamp, a single pair of sheets. On the nights she goes out to the roadhouse or stays out late at Bodeo's, she drinks, and drinks, and those are the nights that she can't sleep, but instead wakes tangled in the sheets, even in wintertime overheated. On the nights that she stays in, she doesn't drink so much, and looks at her scrapbooks, or watches TV, makes sure the apartment's clean and only then goes into the bathroom and with a Q-Tip swabs the mascara off from her eyelashes, erases the black lines that rim her eyes, wipes the blusher from her cheeks. Only then does she go to bed, sing the song her grandmother taught her the first of the two times she saw her, the song she's sung to herself each sober night since she was a kid—*there'll be bluebirds over the white cliffs of Dover*—and then she sleeps, the only noises in the room the sound of the river tangling over the waterfall and her breathing chest as it moves beneath the sheet.

While the people of Intervale struggle with sleep or dive right in, the night river tumbles past Rita's street, passes the row houses lined up like Monopoly buildings on River Road, then plunges under the bridges, out past the town, out to the reservoir. Here, maple and oak leaves, once swollen into soft pads of red and orange, have dried and fallen, and now lie in dried windblown bunches along the forest floor, and tumble around the edges of the wild meadows. The black trees scratch outlines against the trembling lavender October sky, the dark water motionless as a dropped penny. In the woods, the deer sleep easily in their nesty beds of fallen leaves or meadow grasses trampled into whorls, their predator, the wolf, having not been seen in so many generations that the deer have nearly erased the memory of the howl. The horned owl watches for mice skittering across the State Forest road, and a few miles north, up past the far end of the reservoir, the Rousecut River bisects Maine from Quebec, and on the far side, in the wild forest lands, stitching farm to farm, the wolf pack trots and clusters, waiting for the freeze.

⁓

Reichman starts slowly, trying to tease memory out of Blue's bottlenecked past. He starts by asking her to shut her eyes, tries deep breathing, relaxation, moves into hypnosis. "Just tell me what comes to mind," he says, but Blue can only cough up current images: Alison Crue waking her in the morning, the hospital room view. Even with hypnosis, the furthest back she can reach is the night she was found on the bridge, and from that night she's retained only the sketchiest sensory details: the damp cold, the siren firing red against the misty rain.

After their first sessions together, it becomes clear to Reichman that it isn't going to happen this way, and he changes course. He can't unblock her memories, and so instead of trying to get Blue to remember, he starts each hour by simply asking how she feels.

A few days after he cut her sleeping pills, she looks out his window at the grey sky. From where she sits, she can see the granite mountain that she sees from her hospital window, but it's different from this angle: bigger, more real.

"How have you been feeling since we cut down on the sleeping pills?" he asks.

"Okay, I guess. But I had a bad dream," Blue says. She pulls her shoulders in, squeezes her eyes closed. "I remembered a bat, a little bat on a window screen," she says.

"How did you feel when you remembered it?"

The room's silence grows huge around them. Outside, a thin veil of snow begins, high above Intervale, and Dr. Reichman waits for Blue to answer.

"I guess I didn't remember it," she says, at last, feeling her fear slide down as if sliding down behind a thick screen. "It wasn't a memory; it was a dream."

—

Under the bridge, Annie Naiad scrambles through the underbrush, muttering, looking for sticks for the fire she'll feed to the big mouth of the can that night. She's not too bad at planning ahead; she can predict what she'll want hours away, and knows she'll be wanting the color and heat of the fire as the chill dark night descends.

She mutters under her breath, sometimes laughing, sometimes so angry she's seething, spit spraying from the chink of her lip, pushing her tangle of matted black hair from her face. To see her like this, a passerby would think she's an old woman, unless he could see under the crust and despair that's aged her too soon. There's a quickness to her motions as she reaches for the sticks and the trash she'll turn into heat, a power that's only possessed by the young.

Annie mutters her way into the underbrush, away from the railroad bridge, up toward Route 3, and the cars passing over the bridge don't bother her: she's in her fantasy, and is gathering sticks by the banks of the Mediterranean Sea, sticks she'll weave into a basket, or light as a beach fire for the Hebrews to see as they make their way across the desert years.

And here, buried in the scraggled, leafless bushes, something red: a flash of red cloth, and Annie approaches, cautious, then tugs it free: a parka, with a heavy lining, a hood, big pockets that zip open and shut. Annie pulls it on over her sweater, straightens her spine and looks down at herself, just like a woman in a department store would. She primps a little, turning left, then right, as if she's being watched by a mirror or a friend.

It's a little bit small, and if she'd take off her tattered sweater it would fit, she could zip it up, but she doesn't; she can't let go of that sweater, and so she picks up the sticks she's bundled up, turns to go, but then, there it is, off to the side, up higher, up by the road: *a knapsack, a daypack, I'd say by the size, by the lies it could hide in its insides.* She collapses it under her arm as best she can, looks back up to the bridge. *Did anyone see?* and crouches rabbit-low to the ground as she scurries back down the embankment, back to her camp, back to her home.

Only in her cardboard tent does Annie open up the sack. Someone sent it to her, she's sure of that. Inside: two good shirts, a green and a blue, some underpants, two pairs of thick scratchy wool socks. At the bottom of the inner pocket, squirreled away like a secret surprise, a wallet, and at this, Annie goes gleeful, giggles like a girl, giggles like she must have when she was a girl, before. She opens the cuff, and there's a driver's license, a sheaf of bank machine receipts, and money inside. She counts out the bills: *twenty, forty, eighty. That's just fine.* And secured in a leather envelope, some papers, a passport. She looks at the passport picture: could that be someone like her, someone she knows? *Could it be me, the me of me's before which God and man will flee?* In another pouch of the knapsack, a few sheets of paper, thin and blue as a baby's skin, the red edge looking ragged but new, the red edges looking like the stains of blood that would come from a deep paper cut. It's a letter, and slipped into the crease, a photo of two women looking into the camera; in the background, the blue sky and bluer sea. They're laughing, just like the people in the picture Annie keeps, torn from a magazine, of a man and two women having a picnic on a beach, and just as she thought one of the women in the magazine photo looked so much like her, looked like her but with her harelip fixed, so too she thinks one of the women on the beach is her, and she thinks this photo, combined with the one in the magazine, must be of her and her friends, the friends she's been looking for, the reason for her traveling.

Annie reads the letter as if it's her own, as if it was written to her, and this is easy to believe, because it starts out, simply, "You"— then says, "I was looking for you in the track of all those dark years and didn't know it was you I was looking for"—Someone's looking for me, Annie thinks, and that small hard knot of hope clogs up like a plug in the back of her throat, and she folds up each page of the letter, to save it for later.

In her cardboard tent, her home, Annie's got a stash of her most special things, the odd collection of bits she's gathered or kept, her documents, the photo of her friends on the beach. She takes out the letter, the new photograph, the wallet's contents, the leather envelope, and tucks them into the Maxwell House tin with her other treasures. The knapsack she shrugs onto her back; she can carry more firewood home from the fields like this, she thinks, and she does, humming now under her breath. Something good's going to happen, now that they've sent her the pack and the jacket and the letter, now that someone's looking for her. Something good is coming: she can feel it in the twitch of her lucky lip.

~

Blue leaves the hospital her first day out alone with trepidation, self-consciously pulling on the old fisherman's sweater and corduroy zipper-front jacket that were brought in with the donations early on. Blue thinks, *Early in my career as an amnesiac,* then smiles. She's excited, and scared, and now she can name these feelings, wrapping a scarf around her neck, unsure how it will feel to be out alone, out on her own.

As she lopes down the hall, the nurses gather like birds around the nursing station, saying, "Have a good time, Blue," and "Don't do anything I wouldn't do," and Blue waves back to them, turns back as she's walking, calling out, "Don't worry," smiling, loping, feeling *normal.* As she passes through the lobby, then approaches the glass doors, she thinks, see, I'm just like everybody else. I could be anyone, but then she catches herself up short as she sees her reflection in the doors, and panics: *I can't leave!* The hospital has become all she knows, but she pushes the door open, hard, and names the feeling like Dr. Reichman's taught her to: *defiant.*

Outside, she's heading down Hospital Hill, the air clean and clear and bright with oxygen and cold. The hospital smell scrubbed away by the air.

Down the hill, past the big sturdy houses with their wide lawns, a few of the lawns blanketed with brown leaves, some lawns neatly, recently, raked and mown, ready for the snow. Blue looks left and right without embarrassment or shame, peering closely as if memorizing this brick edifice or that wide porch.

In her head, she starts to hum a little tune, originating from that plane of nowhere in which everything, to Blue, originates: the space without the web of stars to catch her memory. It's a little tuneless hum that seems to match the day in its variety of wind and sun and cloudy cold. Down the big hill, humming, as if she could be anyone. As if she is someone.

As the wide boulevard narrows to a city street, Blue thinks back to the map in her jacket pocket, the one the social worker gave her, and she can see in her head the details laid out before her; she can remember the names of the streets and how they intersect: Main, Charlebois, Maple, Elm.

At the corner of her street, as she thinks of it, Elm, and Main, there's a traffic light swinging from the wires up above, and Blue waits, stopped, for her turn to cross. At the other side, as if anchoring one corner of the intersection, pinning it down so the hardy wind won't loft it off into the blowy sky, there stands a store, with a plastic white sign: QwikMart.

When the light changes, Blue crosses to the other side, pushes in the market door, and once inside it's the smells that hit her: something thick and heavy, something stale, not at all like the hospital smell, which now means *home,* not *sickness* or *fear.*

She looks around, and wouldn't say she remembers anything, here, but nor does she have to be told: she knows the aisles will be stratified with shelves and that the shelves will hold loaves of soft cut bread in brown plastic sleeves, glass jars of mayonnaise. There will be refrigerator cases of beer and milk, and a row of colored candy. It's here Blue goes, realizing too late she doesn't really want anything in the store, no pickles or wine or soda or Cheerios— she just wanted to come inside. Behind the counter, a small woman sits, waiting, not reading or anything, just staring out the window at the corner of Elm and Main, watching the light change, while Blue chooses a flat tape of gum and a handful of fireballs.

She's got a five-dollar bill in her pocket, given her by the social worker for this trip. The woman takes her money without a word, gives her the change. She's surprised by nothing, not even a woman, past thirty, breezing in on a weekday morning buying candy.

Outside, Blue pops a fireball from its tiny cellophane envelope home into her hand, then into her mouth, and as she walks it burns brighter and brighter, like something powerful and new.

⌣

It's not lost on Bob Reichman that his new patient doesn't seem to care that she's erased her past. *La belle indifference,* it's called, he knows: the patient isn't upset that the broad net of his mind no longer catches the pretty krill and toothy fish of his memory's deep sea. This term is familiar to him not in work with amnesiacs, but with those floating out the other end of memory's telescope, the Alzheimer's patients. All around them, their families dither and worry and cry "He doesn't know me," and the patient himself sits happily piecing together a jigsaw puzzle, pleased when the curved ridges fit.

Early on in Alzheimer's, the patient will forget, then laugh and shrug; in recent visits to Boston Reichman has seen this with his own father, his father mistaking Reichman for his brother-in-law, or suddenly unsure of his location or the time of day. Once, he stood up just after lunch, announcing that he was leaving for the synagogue, to help make a minyan for the evening prayers. When Reichman said, "No, Dad, that's not until later, not until six," his father shrugged, and laughed a little laugh, saying, "Oh yeah, yeah, that's right," as if he'd only made a small mistake in calculation. As if he hadn't confused the times of day he's ticked off all his life, chanting a different set of prayers for afternoon or evening-bleeding-into-night.

Now, this patient, *Blue.* Like Reichman's dad, she doesn't care, but nor does she have anyone around her caring in her stead. No one's panicking when it's clear she doesn't remember a face or recognize a name. There's no one there to get upset when she says, "Do I know you?"

Reichman's been trying to jar something loose in Blue, and the frustration he feels is the same he felt twenty-five years ago when he started in this field and he first encountered patients whose resistance was so thick their hearts were mired, and sometimes he wished he could slap them. One short hard smack across the face, and then they'd start to cry.

It's been years since he's imagined this fantasy; now, Blue brings this out in him too, but he doesn't want to slap her face, make her cry; he knows that she isn't suffering from the usual resistance. If anything, in these first weeks she talks too easily, the normal defenses one carries for protection in the world melted like sugar walls by her amnesia. By her condition. He thinks her memories are like a bowlful of marbles, jumbled and stuck in her brain, and he wants to shake her by the shoulders, give a solid palm to the back of her skull to unstop that bottleneck.

It seems as if she really did just appear, Reichman thinks, leaning back in his chair, turning to his window, pursing his lips as he scratches his fingers into his beard. He's met with her nearly four weeks now, three sessions a week, and in each session he's had a new test to try, or a new exercise, and he finds in his diagnostics that she's educated, and she's retained some of her memory from the distant past: she can name states and their capitals, she can figure mathematical equations, she has a grasp of history.

But nothing else is there. She has no personal memory, can recall the lessons taught in school but not the teacher's names or her home address. She has no notably distinctive accent that could point him to a city or a region. She's got the knowledge of a well-educated woman, but no personality to go with it. No, that's still not quite right. She's got a personality, tentative, frightened, nascent.

Reichman has two questions: who is she, and what happened to propel her into her fugue? What trauma jarred her into this blank reach of *I don't know*? And what could jar her back?

Reichman lets his thoughts of Blue float away, takes in what he sees from his office window. The leaves have turned to yellow, gold, and now to brown, and all this week have been falling steadily from the trees along the ridge; in the next rainstorm, they'll all be down, and then winter can begin.

By five P.M. the light's a rope of dusty yellow-pink banked along horizon's edge, beneath the dunderheads that now are crowding in. This is still the summer side of daylight savings time, but next weekend Reichman and all of Intervale will turn their clocks back, as if forced to stop backpedaling into the past, reminded again they can't keep summer in their midst. But

Reichman, he'll be happy to tick the hour back; he'd rather move on to escape the summer's deep hedge and the long circular mow of the lawn's wide apron around his house, mowing it out as if the lawn could be a moat to keep the forest and all its creatures out there, where they belong.

In the spring, just after Amy moved out, he sold the power mower and got an old-fashioned hand mower. All summer he pushed it in wide circles, watching the concentric rings widen as he walked, beetles and crickets spraying up in his mower's wake as he walked away from their life together. Now, in preparation for turning the clocks back, or just out of absent-minded need to turn away from the worry that chafes like a sharp tack in his shoe, Reichman lifts his round-faced clock from the table, winds the butterfly key at the back to keep it ticking. Autumn and he can expect his melancholic patients to start getting blue, even as they ride the steep climb toward mental health, if not toward happiness. It's true for him, too.

Even though he tells himself he wants to move on, as he shuttles his papers now into neat folders, slipping the folders into their file drawers, as he switches off the lamp he keeps on the desk, Reichman thinks maybe he'd rather stay in this measurement of time, in June, July, August. He wants, perhaps perversely, to stay in this first season of grief.

Reichman heads out his office and down the hall. He's a psychiatrist, for Christ's sake, he chastises himself as he waves to the secretary, calling out, "Have a good weekend." He knows all about this, about the cold hold that the past exerts, about recovery from loss, and says to himself that he can't go back. If he took the advice he thinks his patients should take, "Move on ahead," he'd say. Let's leave that season in the past, push through autumn, then into winter's deep collapse.

~

On her delivery rounds the late October freezing rain is pelting down, and Rita's got her windshield wipers slapping high, but she can hardly see the road. Friday, and Rita's got five more stops to make, and then she's free. She'll call Bart from her last drop and tell him to meet her at Bodeo's.

When she crosses the bridge and heads back into town, she's thinking only of her evening to come, of what might be said, what might be done, but the rain is drumming down, and she remembers, as if she'd forgotten, the rainy night nearly a month ago when she stopped and brought the mystery woman back to life. She remembers that this is the spot, this is where "the woman was found" as the news story said. Smug, Rita leans back in the seat of her truck, nods to herself, slows, looks down to the roiling river below. She's never noticed before what a long drop it is, what a steep fall it would be from the bridge to the water. *Maybe I saved her from jumping,* she thinks. *Maybe I saved her damned life.*

Rita doesn't see as she glances below, trying to keep her eyes on the road, Annie huddled in her cardboard tent, snug under the railroad bridge, amidst the brush and brambles, running her fingers over the ingredients in her packet of things, whispering to the people in the picnic, pressing her face into Kitty's soft fur.

Shivering in the brightly lit QwikMart, "Hey, meet me right after work," Rita says into the pay phone, with no preliminaries.

"What, like at five?" Bart says, in his usual whine. He's going to complain, but Rita's used to this: he always resists.

"You're not working tonight. It's Halloween. Wouldn't it be nice just to relax for a change?" she says into the phone, aware that she's sounding a little desperate, and suddenly aware that the clerk behind the counter probably assumes she's talking to a boyfriend. *Strident,* one of her new words: is that what she is, what she's become?

"Who knows, maybe one of us will get lucky," she says a little too loudly, and laughs.

"At least you have half a chance of that," Bart says. "Me, the next time I get laid will be when I'm laid into my grave."

"Oh, come on," Rita shifts her weight. "Listen, I'm at a pay phone. Just show up, all right? See you there." And she hangs up the phone before Bart can say no. She wants to stick out her tongue at the guy behind the counter, or at least to glare, but then she sees he's such a young kid he's not even listening, he's just nervously pulling at the edge of his QwikMart uniform, pulling at a thread that's come loose, and instead she passes him the delivery sheet, officiously clicks her pen, and with her index finger, the nail painted, chipped, points him toward the right line to sign.

Swinging into the pickup, Rita wonders if anyone at Bodeo's will wear a costume tonight, and then the memory of that one Halloween plays like a movie through her head, the familiar memory, the one that runs of its own accord whenever it's triggered as if there had been only one Halloween, the bright days under the leafy golden canopy, cacophony of jays and black-birds in the wings of the trees, everything washing yellow and orange and red, the colors so big and bright that Rita thinks, at ten, she could eat them. Sometimes walking underneath the trees on her way home from school, the afternoon sun saturating the leaves, she thinks she'd like to put them in her mouth, on her tongue, just lay a big leaf there, so she could taste it. How would it feel?

But Rita doesn't do this, doesn't really think of it, even. It's silly, something a little kid would do, and she knows better than to tell anyone, even herself, that this is what she wants. Instead she settles for scuffling her feet through the leaves, in her new shoes, even though she knows her mother would scream at her for ruining her shoes. "Those shoes have to last a whole year, so you'd better not wreck them, 'cause I'm not buying you another pair," her mother said when they walked out of the department store, Rita clutching the box in its crisp white paper bag, the name of the store spelled out in white letters.

Still, walking home from school, she allows herself to scuffle through the leaves. *This can't hurt, can it?* Besides, as soon as it snows she'll be wearing her boots to walk to school and back, and she'll save the shoes for when she's in school, and everything will be okay, she tells herself, even as she notices a pebble has worked its way into her right shoe, and when she bends to untie the lace, she sees that two of the white stitches have started to come loose, right where the brown part of the shoe meets the white, *right where they show*, and she brushes at them with her fingertips, then walks the rest of the way home with care, thinking of how she'll keep the shoes tucked by her mattress. Maybe this is just what's meant by *breaking them in*. The rest of her walk is quieter, without the accompanying scutt of leaves and twigs beneath her feet.

Halloween, and Rita thinks she'd like to be something different, really different. No witch or hobo, no cartoon character from a TV show. She'd like to make something, make a costume from a box. Couldn't she be something like a mailbox or a pack of cigarettes? She imagines her costume in her head as she walks, cleanly painted red, white and blue, perfect, her fantasy distracting her sufficiently from the problem of her shoe.

Home, she goes straight up the long flight of stairs to the second floor, opens the apartment door into the kitchen. The boxes she and her mother moved last week are still piled up around the room, some of them opened, others still closed. The apartment is empty, she knows, she can feel it, and besides, usually when she gets in from school there's no one home. She puts down her satchel in which she carries her books, looks in the fridge for something to eat, but then thinks she isn't hungry, and instead starts to unpack a box, and that's where her mother finds her when she comes in, putting away the forks and spoons, layering the plates in the cupboard.

"Well, aren't you industrious," her mother says, and Rita can hear that slight wheeze of sarcasm in her mother's voice, that high, long note. "Your lazy mother couldn't manage to unpack anything," she says, sitting heavily at the kitchen table.

"That's okay," Rita says, "it's almost done."

"That's okay," her mother repeats, mimicking Rita's nervous squeak. "You've got so much energy, why don't you pour me a drink?" and Rita goes quickly to the counter, then gets a glass from its new spot on the shelf, pleased and proud that she's found just the right place for the glasses, the perfect place, in the center cupboard, bottom shelf. The handiest spot.

She takes ice from the tray in the freezer, pours half orange juice, half vodka, holds it out to her mother. But her mother is busy taking off her high-heeled shoes, rubbing her feet. Rita stands, waiting, looking out the window. From here, she can see over the neighbors' yards, the fat red and yellow maple leaves, and then, beyond that, the mountain that drops down to the river covered in the shimmering leaves of golden beech. The leaves are waving so softly in the last light that the whole mountain looks like a big animal, ready to run.

"What are you standing there for? Just put it down on the table, for God's sake," her mother says, and then, as Rita turns away, she adds in a softer voice, "Thanks."

"Mom, I think I know what I should be for Halloween," Rita says, turning back to the boxes, and then, before her mother can cut her off: "I want to be a pack of cigarettes."

"Ha," her mother laughs, in that way that means that Rita's made her laugh, that Rita's said something funny.

"Ha. That's a good one. Marlboro? Or maybe Virginia Slims?"

Rita isn't sure how to answer, so she laughs. "Or Camels," she says, unsure if this is part of the joke. Unsure what the joke is.

"Well, that's a great idea, and I think you'd make a great pack of cigarettes, but I sure don't have time to make a costume like that. Christ, I wouldn't even know how to begin. Halloween's tonight, isn't it? Why don't we just get you something at Woolworth's? Why do you have to be so damned different all the time?" and she lights a cigarette, turns to look out the kitchen window, fluffs her hair with her fingers.

Because they're high up in this apartment, on the second floor, from the kitchen window they can see the horizon of Intervale, and now, October dusk, the sky is going purple-blue like a second-day bruise, like a wrist burn, like the round, soft-looking grapes Rita wishes her mother would buy at the IGA.

Rita goes back to counting the things in the cupboard over again to make sure everything arrived from the last apartment to this one, all the plates and cups nestled tidy and safe in their cabinets, her mother's gaze caught on the horizon line, like a bird snagged by a wire, the sky going dark.

"I know! I've got it!" Rita's mother says suddenly, waking Rita from her worried reverie about her new shoes, how to fix or hide the pulling stitches.

"What?" Rita asks, thinking for a minute her mother has come up with a solution about the shoes, then remembering it's her mother she's trying to hide the shoes from; her mother won't be her pal in this.

"For Halloween. You can be a grown-up. Oh, sweetie, it'll be perfect."

"A grown-up?" Rita pictures herself dressed like one of the teachers at school, Miss Bliss, or Mrs. Trout, with her big black shoes that squeak across the library floor.

"Yeah. Look, don't worry about anything."

Six o'clock and Rita's sitting still in the straight-backed chair, the wooden chair with the fraying mesh seat, while her mother makes up her face. Rita likes the feeling of her mother's hands on her own face, how her mother puts her fingertips delicately on Rita's chin, tilting her chin up into the light, so her mother can better see what she's doing. Rita's dizzy with this feeling, that her mother is paying such close attention to every pore in her face, to the line of her mouth and the slope of her cheek. Rita doesn't even mind when her mother tweezes out the hairs of her eyebrows, one by one, warning her by saying, "Okay, here's a pinch," and then the sharp tick as she plucks out the hair.

When she's done with the makeup, Rita's mother stands back, says, "Wow, you look great. You look about eighteen!" but she won't hand Rita the mirror yet. "No, wait until it's all done, so you can get the full effect," she says.

Then to Rita's hair. With a comb and brush, her mother teases and combs, pulling so hard that Rita wants to say, "Stop," but doesn't. Instead, she doesn't make a sound, just sits still, squeezes her eyes shut as if by squeezing hard enough she can squeeze out the pain.

Downstairs, the front door of the building slams open and shut, and then there are the steps coming up, a quick rap on the door and here's Derrick coming in, filling the room now with his smell of gasoline and oil, saying, "Jeez, Colleen, what're you doing?"

"It's Halloween," her mother says. "Look," and she stands to the side to show off her daughter, eyes darkened by blue shadow, brows tweezed to two thin lines, the puckered bow of her lips red and glossed. She's wearing a mini-skirt of her mother's pinned tight and short, and a tube top, and fishnet pantyhose rolled up at the waist, and by now, her hair's been teased into a big messy swirl resting on the top of her head.

"Jeez, you two could just about be twins. What's she going as, a sex kitten?" Derrick laughs, and her mother laughs too, pretending to slap his butt with the back of the hairbrush, and Derrick grabs her wrist and Rita doesn't know, is he going to hit her back? Is he really mad, or just pretending? Her mom shouldn't have hit him with the brush, even if that only was pretend, because you never can tell with him.

But Derrick doesn't hit her mother, instead roughing her wrist in his hand, twisting just the tiniest bit, pulling her against him and kissing her hard. Her mother gasps, says, "Derrick, the kid," and he says, "What do you think got me so hot?" and Rita shuts her eyes again, presses her hands under her thighs, until the pattern of the rattan seat cover and the pattern of the fishnet tights ridge into her skin, making the skin of her hands look not like fishnet, but like the skin of a fish, a big huge fish, slippery, salted, able to swim down the Rousecut River and out to the sea.

As she pulls back onto Route 3, Rita isn't looking back, she's just looking ahead, into the night and what it might bring.

~

When Blue first arrives at her session, this important session, her last as an inpatient, she sits in the waiting room, right leg jigging up and down, worried, nervous. She can't concentrate on the waiting room magazines with their bright pictures. Once she's ushered into Dr. Reichman's office, she scans the room before she even looks him in the eye. Where's the glass ball with snow inside that sits like a clear marble on Dr. Reichman's desk, holding down by its watery weight a sheaf of papers, on the sunny days the light glinting off its skin? *Where is it?* She looks to the desk, while Reichman sits, waiting to see if she'll begin. There it is, half-hidden behind a stack of books, and her breath loosens, she breathes, *it's okay,* she tells herself, and starts to talk.

Blue's amnesia still has the effect of making her less inhibited than most people, and later in the session, when she gets that restlessness that creeps up her legs, that feels like it's pulling right into her bones, she leans forward in her chair, picks up the ball from Reichman's desk in her hand, and tilts it slowly on its axis, watching the snow drift up and back.

Inside, there's a little house, a chalet, and three tiny pine trees, with an even tinier bluebird perched on the roof of the house. At the bottom, there's a miniature plaque with the word "AUSTRIA," spelled out in curly old-fashioned green letters on a red background.

When she picks up the ball, she isn't concerned with the papers lying under it; maybe in her other life, *before,* she would have loved the chance to rifle through these neat leaves drifting across the glass desk top: Dr. Reichman's reminder notes to himself, names and numbers of Boston nursing homes, a letter from a colleague about a shared patient, requests for transfers, for prescription pills. Maybe the woman who became Blue would have tried to sneak a look for her own name ribboning out in black ink or in the crinkled blue that soaks through carbons to the final yellow sheet, but now, she isn't curious. She tells herself she wants more than anything to know who she really is, but she wants this the way she wants chocolate, or a sunny day: now, and without complication. Her curiosity lies glazed under the skin of her disinterest like the stuff of river life now lying under the frozen skin of ice that forms around the pooling eddies, between the rocks and ledges over which she dangled her legs when she first came to.

After her session, Blue returns to her hospital room, collects her jacket and scarf, then leaves the building for her last daily walk through Intervale, stands at the top of Hospital Hill, looking down across the town, through a light swirling mist of flurrying snow. She thinks Intervale is like the glass ball on Dr. Reichman's desk, and she can imagine it all tucked inside a globe: the hospital at the top of the world, the streets and avenues and rail-road tracks laid out below, the river cutting its dark liquid path through the neighborhoods, under the bridges, and out beyond the glass ball's range. Blue thinks, standing there and looking down, that whatever lies beyond this little world, she doesn't want to know.

⌐

Reichman notices that Blue attaches quickly but apparently randomly to people and to objects, and although this isn't unusual in cases of amnesia, he writes a few lines on this in her chart after each session, the weakening early winter sun giving him just enough light by which to write, until he sighs, resigned, and switches on the lamp.

By her last session as an inpatient, he notes that she's gotten attached to this paperweight globe, and sometimes, at certain crucial junctures, she'll pick it up, tilt it in her hand, stare in.

"How do you feel about moving into your own place?" Reichman asks.

Blue tilts the glass ball, watches the snow slide over the tiny pines. "Okay, I guess." Then she looks up. "Lonely," she says, her eyes filling in that immediate way that Reichman's come to expect. He knows it's just that her defenses are down, knows she's without her presumed usual inhibitions, knows her tears don't mean what they'd mean in another patient. Not necessarily.

"What is the loneliness about?" he asks, and then Blue's words erupt, volcanic. At last.

"What do you think it's about? It's about not knowing anyone, even myself. I don't know one person in the whole world, and not one person knows me. How do you *think* that would feel?" she says, her voice not rising louder as one would expect, but going quieter, stretching out like piano wire.

"Pretty bad," Reichman says, preparing himself for more of her anger, reminding himself as he does at these times that the anger isn't really directed at him, even though, with her especially, it feels that way.

"Pretty bad." She mimics him, like a thirteen-year-old would, and he can almost see her as a thirteen-year-old, hair falling over her eyes, wary and angry and never surprised. "Well, it's more than pretty bad, it's terrible. You have no idea what it's like to not even know who you are, and you're pretty damned presumptuous to sit there pretending that you do."

Her face is reddened, and she looks more alive right then than Reichman's ever seen her; she looks genuine, as if, at last, she isn't calculating every word she says, watching every motion of her hand. The emotion is so real that he thinks, this anger is very old. Original. Pure.

He leans forward, elbows on knees. "You're right, Blue. I can't imagine how lonely you feel right now."

With this kindness, this *tenderness,* the air is stilled out of Blue's angry sails, and all that's left is her sadness welling up inside her, and she covers her face with her hands, alone, watching how black the curtain is when she shuts her eyes against the crying. She'd cry now, she's sure of it—Dr. Reichman's sure too—if she could, but the tears are choked off so firmly that all she has is the motion of the crying, the quaking shoulders and shivering hands.

After she leaves, he has two more patients, the more usual neurotics, a nervous young man who laughs inappropriately and dodges Reichman's every attempt to get in, and a woman who's started dating yet another man who, Reichman can see, will treat her just as badly as the others have.

When he's through, he leaves his office, heads down to the gym. Once in the clear, cold water in the lane, he's free to count his laps as his body passes over the tiled floor of the pool. It's here he thinks best, and here he thinks first about Blue, feels the snap of her anger. *You don't know how it feels,* he hears in his head. And then he thinks again about his father, worrying as he swims *what to do, what to do, what to do.* On his last visit to Boston, Reichman came into the dim living room just as his father was curtaining his tallis on for the evening service, and he had to say "No Dad, that's just for the morning." Reichman feels like a little boy at these times, pulling on his father's sleeve, pulling his dad back to the present, and then he feels guilty as his father pronounces the lengthy Hebrew prayers just right, as if these were embedded in him in a place beyond his memory. As if there's nothing wrong. Is there? How will he raise the prospect to his father of moving, of selling off his furniture and going into a home? How could he even think such a thing?

In the pool, Reichman has a moment, just as he's about to curl into a flip turn at the wall, in which he knows what he has to do, and concentrating on his breath and his turn, he repeats Hebrew words as if they're a mantra: *Eliyahu,*

Eliyahu, hoping he'll find the strength to do what's right, to do what he knows he must. He chants *essa einai* in his head, and catches himself, reminds himself that he doesn't believe, that his only strength, if he can muster it, will come from the place it always originates. It will have to come from himself.

~

Her last morning in the hospital, Blue wakes with a feeling: *sadness,* so real that she curls her fingers into the palm of her hand, expecting to feel the sadness there like a big blue marble, weighty and solid, but instead, nothing's there, just the tangle of sheet and her own dry skin. Nothing's there.

By the time Alison Crue, R.N., comes in Blue's up and dressed, packing the donated clothing into the cardboard boxes that the social worker brought up from medical records in the basement. She carefully holds up each piece of clothing, folds it precisely, then lays it into the box as if laying an abandoned infant at last down into a crib. When Alison sees her, packing her few things, these few things that aren't, really, hers, she can think of only one word: *tenderness.* It's the tenderness with which Blue's packing these things, a dingy pair of sweatpants, a T-shirt with a garish cartoon splashed across the front, stone-washed jeans that went out of fashion years ago, that makes Alison's breath catch in her throat.

But she's a professional, and instead of breathing out a long sigh, she says, "All set?" and Blue looks up. "I guess." It would seem to anyone looking in that the woman packing was eager to leave, up at dawn, ready to go. But Alison can see in Blue's eyes the fear, although even Blue herself doesn't quite know that the only reason she's packing now is that she's afraid to stop: if she stops, she may not be able to leave.

At the doorway, papers signed ("Blue Doe," is the signature she uses now), boxes packed, Blue sits on a molded green plastic chair just inside the double main doors. Next to her, the nurse's aide, a young girl just out of high school, cracks her gum, taps her foot. Blue's got one of her two boxes firmly set between her feet, the other on her lap, her arms wrapped around it. She's hanging on tight; it's all that she's got.

What's out there for her? What if she can't live on her own? What if she never remembers? What if she does?

But then, the lockdown comes to save her in the nick of time, the *don't cry,* the *go on.* Here's the taxi pulling up in the small swirling snow, the driver stepping from the car, hiking his belt up over his gut, the hospital doors sliding open for him. He hefts both boxes easily in his meaty arms. Then, the musty back seat of the cab, the *goodbye,* and the plunge down the hill, into Intervale, into the world.

— ⁓

"A tisket, a tasket, I'll weave a little basket. A tisket, a tasket, into the depth I'll drop it," Annie sings in her high cricket voice under her breath as she slides another water-softened stem into the fabric she's creating from the milkweed and the grasses drying by the riverbank. When it's complete, she scrabbles through her coffee can of precious things, picks out a few of her favorites, *something old, something new, something bloody, something blue,* all wrapped in the blue bandanna, tied with a knot. *I'll keep you safe, my little things, my darlings. Now aren't you a pretty dish to set before the king?*

At the water's edge, Annie pushes the little basket into the water, and the current takes it downstream, playing it along the crest and fall of the water as it goes, until, even to Annie, who knows what it is, it looks like just another clump of grasses tumbling in the river's wake. *There you go, just you, little Moses, all alone, waving your fat baby hands at your mother standing so handy at the riverbank, safe and dry. Goodbye, goodbye,* and then she turns, and picks up the timbrels of her Maxwell House can and a silver fork that washed up, and dances the dance of Miriam by the shore of the Reed Sea, there, under the Bridge of Styx, in the near-dark, her shadow dancing along in the orangey-glow of the streetlights of Intervale.

Part 2

*D*own by the riverbank, on the other side of town from the hospital and park and the big solid houses that wait like patient dogs for their owners to come home at day's end, Blue's apartment feels empty, as if the wind could blow through and everything would disappear. Someone donated an old kitchen table, white enamel with thin red lines painted all around the edge, and someone else got rid of an overstuffed chair, forest green with tufts of white snowing out the arms, and with the emergency fund money from the hospital, she bought a bed. "I hope it's enough to get you started," the social worker said, and Blue nodded, because the social worker had made sure she'd have what she needed: two plates, a bowl, a scattering of flatware, an aluminum pot and cast-iron pan.

Her building's an old row house, a warren of apartments built for the mill girls a hundred years ago, and the whole block's in disrepair, as if cursed by the mill girls and their constant gnawing lack, the central stair covered in worn carpet that once was red and now looks black, the dim hallway smelling rabbity, strongly of cigarettes and must, smelling of *need* and *never enough.*

After she's unpacked her few things and laid her clothes into the cock-eyed built-in drawers in the bedroom, Blue makes a foray out to the market, walking past the other row houses, then left onto River Terrace, right onto Williams Street. At the little market she's unsure what she would have bought *before,* what she would have wanted, but knowing which of the hospital offerings she liked to eat, she puts together a basketful of groceries, eggs, milk, bread, frozen fish sticks in a pack, a box of cereal, a cardboard can of oatmeal, and walks home in the sunny cold, a brown paper bag in each arm.

At her building—*home?*—she turns the metal knob on the glassed front door, climbs the stairs to the second floor. Her own apartment, once she keys open the wooden door, is just three rooms: first the kitchen, then the living room, last the bedroom, facing out over the river. "A railroad flat," the social worker said.

It's an empty place, the kind of place where a person either wouldn't stay more than a month or two, a place temporary as a tent, or it's a place where a person could get trapped, always meaning to move on, but never finding reason. Always thinking, good as any, better than some. Not so good, but good enough.

Now, Blue doesn't care except that it's hers, her first place: this is where she'll begin. Month to month; plus, the landlord, whom she's never met, waived the security deposit. He's a friend of Dr. Reichman's, "a very understanding man," Dr. Reichman said, and between this and the old junker car someone donated and the job at the Intervale Diner ("Do you think you could wait tables?" the social worker asked), Blue's set, for now, for the moment, for this long moment yawning into her new life.

When the social worker suggested she get a phone put in, Blue shook her head, no. "I don't need one," she said, thinking, *who would call?* Now, after putting her groceries away, boxes lined up neatly on the shelf, Blue goes to the bedroom, stands by the window that looks down on the river, and knows that even without a phone, she's waiting. Still waiting. Waiting for a call *back then* that never came in, waiting in the silence for the jarring, purring ring.

Standing at the window, the water down there roiling in great wild wells, eddying around the big boulders, she twists the cord of the shade around her finger, tighter and tighter until she can't feel it. *Numb.* Maybe it isn't that she's afraid no one from her new life will call; she doesn't want a phone because without a phone, she won't be waiting for someone from before to call her now; she can begin excising her hope that someone will want to track her down and take her home.

Home. She knows that there's a place called home, knows what home means: someone's waiting by the phone. An apartment or a house, familiar furnishings, the great-aunt's candlesticks and granddaddy's photo in a frame.

The particulars whisper their history throughout the house: the battered brown globe on its stand, the favorite floral pillows on the bed. The accumulation of things, forks and spoons lying flat in their tray, books half-read and impossible to discard, the drawer full of bank statements adding and subtracting a history, the rolls of half-used tape and slips of scrap with a phone number in a forgotten hand, both face and name gone now, tugged away in the surf of where you met and why you cared.

Blue stands at the window, unwraps the cord from around her numb finger, then picks up the marble she keeps on the sill, palms it, rubs it between the palms of her hands, looking out at the river in its tumble and roll.

She is, herself, like Dr. Reichman's glass ball with snow inside, she thinks, looking out the window at the river freezing over. It's like she lives in her own miniature internal world, occasionally shaken up and made snowy inside by Dr. Reichman, this stranger who has the power to change the weather, if not the climate where she lives. But it's her glass-ball world, hers alone, and until she remembers something, until she remembers who she is, she'll stay there, trapped beneath the drifting snow.

Friday afternoon, and Reichman pulls in the driveway of his childhood home, notes that the trash barrel is neatly tucked by the garage, the leaves raked up from the small front yard, and thinks, at least that's in order, at least his dad's able to corral a neighborhood teen to take care of the necessary tasks.

Reichman carries his overnight bag up to the door, without knocking steps inside, out of habit touching his fingertips to the mezuzah on the doorframe and then, briefly, to his lips. The house smells the same, the decades of his mother's heavy European cooking having saturated the walls and furnishings with the smell of dumplings and chicken soup, challah and sweet strudel, so that the smells linger even now, years after her death.

"Dad? It's me, Bob," he calls out, shutting the door behind him against the cold and the approaching dark, despite the familiar claustrophobia that wells up in him at doing this. Click of the latch and shush of the wood fitting into the frame.

"In the kitchen," his father calls back, and Reichman sets down his bag, walks down the hall, past the array of photos of himself and his sister, their past arranged by his mother years ago along the wall, and now dusted every other week by the cleaning woman who comes in.

His father's sitting at the kitchen table, not reading, just sitting, a coffee mug in front of him on the pink placemat, the white Formica wiped so clean that Reichman can see each fleck of gold sprinkled in it.

"How was the drive?" his father asks, and "Fine, fine," Reichman says. "I missed the traffic—that's the good thing about getting here for Shabbes," and immediately he regrets this, immediately knows he's said the wrong thing.

"And keeping Shabbes isn't the good thing about getting here for Shabbes?" his father says, then goes on: "I got us a chicken, pre-baked, at Rosenthal's deli. We just have to heat it up."

"Great," Reichman says, only then realizing that he's shown up empty-handed, again, again he's brought nothing. He wouldn't think of visiting anyone else without a bottle of wine, or some delicacy from Maine, maple sugar candies shaped like women and men, or a box of hard squares of dark fudge. But what can he bring to his father, who insists he needs nothing, who insists on keeping kosher?

The only thing that he has brought is an idea, an idea that's kept his mind busy all the way down from Intervale, an idea that makes him feel excited and sick at the same time. He'll await the right moment, he says to himself, and then sees that his father has gone back to looking out the kitchen window, up beyond the curtains to the sky, as if Bob isn't there, as if he's alone.

Upstairs, Reichman washes up, stows his bag in his childhood room which is still furnished, like a shrine to his adolescence, with his old single four-poster bed, the little dresser and the bookshelves crammed with childhood books: the *Just So Stories, Huckleberry Finn, The Jewish People,* Books One and Two. In this house, he feels huge, as if his five-foot-nine frame, considered normal outside, here makes him a giant in a dollhouse.

Dusk is approaching; he only has a moment to sit before heading downstairs to make *kiddush* with his dad. Up here, Reichman sighs out a single long breath. It will take forever to pack up this house, even if he hires someone to help. What will he do with it all, with the blankets and photo albums, the tools in the basement workshop, the few treasures pushed into his parents' child-hands when they left Europe?

"Bob? Bobby," his father calls up the stairs. "It's almost Shabbes," and at the familiar words, Reichman's on his feet, heading downstairs.

But as his father's lighting the candles, pouring the wine, he stumbles on the words of the prayer, saying not the blessing for the fruit of the vine, but the blessing for fruit of the earth, and not seeming to notice, not seeming to care. Only one word in the prayer is different, and Reichman knows that if he corrected his father, his father would shrug, say, "Oh, did I?" But this is a prayer the man has spoken or heard each week for over eighty years. A prayer he once said perfectly, singing it out in his baritone, extending the words, making the children giggle and laugh when he raised his glass and they shouted, *"L'Chaim!"*

The chicken looks better than Reichman expected, and as soon as it's on the table, the table set with the good Shabbes silver and plates, Reichman feels so hungry he thinks he could eat the whole bird. His father's also stirred up some instant mashed potatoes, and there's a challah from the bakery, and boiled frozen peas. Far more food than the two of them can eat.

Reichman looks down at his plate; it looks like a pale palette imitating his mother's Shabbes best. When she was alive, she'd spend the whole day cleaning the house, preparing the meal, slowly roasting a chicken, and baking the plum and sour-cherry tarts. Sometimes, in winter, when he was very small and his big sister Roz was at school, he'd be given the job of mashing up the potatoes with margarine and salt. He'd get to lick the spoon. In summer, he'd have the task of shelling the peas, or later, when he grew too old for this, when his father told his mother this would make him a sissy, he was taught how to make *kiddush,* how to carve the chicken, using up all the meat, leaving nothing to waste, leaving nothing on the bone.

"Dad, I've been thinking," Reichman says now, after eating in silence, after satisfying the edge of his hunger. "This house is so much work for just one person; it's huge. I've been thinking it's too much work for you."

"No, Bobby, it's fine. How's that chicken? Not bad for from the deli, huh?" His father takes a sip from his wine glass, and Reichman sees he's left a thin lip mark along the edge, and he feels a little sick.

"But, Dad, I worry about you being here all alone. What if something happened?" Even though he's able to keep his voice steady, to keep the trembling out, Reichman feels scared: what if something did happen? What if something went wrong?

"Don't worry about me, Bobby. We all get forgetful as we get older. It's part of life."

"But also part of life is accepting that things change."

"You think this is something I don't know?" his father looks up at last from his plate, with the look in his eyes that Reichman knows so well, the shadowy reflection of *what he saw* back in Europe, when he was a boy.

There's nothing Reichman can say to this; there never has been, and he sighs again, again wishes his sister had stayed closer to home, hadn't moved all the way to the coast of England, as far as she could get.

Just when he's thinking he'll never convince his father to leave this house, his father surprises him, puts his fork on his plate, says, "Look, Bobby, I know what's happening to me. I know my memory isn't so good anymore. I know I shouldn't keep living here alone. But I don't want to go into a home."

Reichman tries, says, "Maybe you wouldn't have to. Maybe we can think of something else," but his father has dropped it, shakes his head. "Let's not speak of it on Shabbes," he says, and the two men finish their meal in silence, the chicken drying on the plate, the peas and potatoes going cold, the candles slowing burning down.

~

MYSTERY WOMAN RELEASED FROM HOSPITAL, the headlines read as Rita bundles and packs the papers, under the fluorescent lights of the *Gazette*'s pressroom, the machinery thudding around her like a river, or a waterfall.

She'll be living among the people of Intervale, the story says, and Rita thinks: wolf-woman living among us. She'll be working at the Intervale Diner out by the interstate. Some big landlord has offered a deal on one of his apartments, one of the row houses down on River Road, igniting a flurry of protest from the social workers who work to find apartments cheap enough for their clients to afford, yet still in good repair.

There's news here, at last, weeks after the story of the woman's arrival in Intervale has been edged off the page by the other stuff of life, the mayor's latest scandal, the kids who died in a car wreck out on the interstate. At break, the others will talk again about Blue, and again Rita will remain silent, then take her paper home at day's end, clip the story, scissor out the new photo, paste them into the scrapbook she's keeping, then head down to Bodeo's, where she won't tell anyone. If anyone asked why she's doing this, what would she say? She has no legitimate reason, no excuse, for why she even cares.

The picture of Blue that runs with the story is much clearer than the first, having been shot by the *Gazette*'s premier photographer under somewhat better conditions; now that Blue's been released, she's more talkative, more willing, and although in the photo she looks wary, she doesn't look terrified, not like she did in the first bleak photo, the one taken just after she arrived, just after she was found. *After I found her,* Rita thinks.

At break, Rita stares at the photo, and thinks she sees a likeness. Look at the eyes, the dark hair, the pointed chin, the features a little to rugged to be called pretty. She rests her own chin in her hand, pretending to read, but really she's just staring at the photo. *Could it be?*

But she won't ask, won't say, "Don't you think she looks like me?" She wants to keep the possibility a secret, wants to wonder alone, and besides, so fragile is her small balloon of hope that she doesn't want it popped by Ross or Mert saying "What, are you nuts?" When the others come in for break, they look at the photo and don't look back at Rita, just blow on their coffee to cool it down, tear open their cellophane bags of Danish and doughnuts.

They don't mention any likeness, and Rita doesn't ask, just bites into her jelly doughnut. Maybe she *is* nuts. This woman in the photo must be younger than Rita is. Or older. Maybe there is no resemblance there, and anyway, who can tell from a grainy photo reprinted again and again in newspaper dots?

All Rita knows is this, her own unglamorous history: born and raised in Intervale, where she and her mother moved apartment to apartment, trying to stay ahead of the landlord demanding his rent and her mother's boyfriend of the moment and his full or empty threats.

But there was that one night Rita remembers, early on, she was very young, her mother, drunk, crying into the phone, crying something about another baby, something about a twin.

Nearly all her life, Rita's imagined a different scenario: what if the woman she called "mother" wasn't her real mother after all? What if she was abandoned thirty years ago in the forest of the night, left by her real mother, left in the forest swaddled up in a blanket and towel, blood still streaking the soft wool, the smell of the blood drawing the wolf? And what of this: what if there'd been two? Two of her, and the wolf nosing the babies, allowing them to suckle at her teats until the rescuers arrived.

Since then, she's imagined a twin, in her loneliest moments, imagined that person who would be so like her they'd both feel a shock when one was struck by lightening and the other one not. She's imagined the made-for-TV reunion. Her twin, the one that was left behind, raised after all by the wolf, surviving the northern clime, surviving to adulthood as a wild wolf-man— no, wolf-woman, she corrects herself. She's imagined how this twin, this sister, would come loping in to save her, would find her, take her on a sled piled high with soft pine branches and furred animal pelts, take her deep up into the mountains, up to her mountain home.

Rita hasn't considered this other possibility: what if she was born, just as she's been told, to her own mother, but a twin was born too, a lucky twin adopted into a real family, all these years living the high life in Boston or New York, going to a private school, living the life Rita sees people living in clothing catalogues and magazines. Couldn't this twin also come to find her, come to save her and take her away?

Rita and Ross load the bundled papers into the trucks, and she swings into the seat, checks the rearview, pulls out of the lot. She shifts into second, then third, and drives out Route 3, out over the bridge.

⌒

That night, Rita eats her supper, a big plate of macaroni and cheese, sitting at her kitchen table, overlooking the river down below. By this time in the winter the water's nearly hidden underneath a sheaf of white ice, and she can just make out a few swirls of black water hesitating there before the water tumbles into the rumpled waterfall, free.

Eating her supper, looking out the window to the river lit by the street-lamp, Rita makes up stories, stories about her missing twin, or other stories about the situation of her birth: the she-wolf nuzzling her cheek, whispering wolf-words, secrets, to her newborn ear, marking her, making her different, making her real.

In addition to the wolf postcard on her altar, in her living room she's got a big poster of a wolf, a close up of its head and shoulders; she even got a frame for it at The Frame Up down at the mall. This wolf is tidied up for the camera, nearly smiling, not looking dangerous or anything, tinted a little blue, with a blue border going all around the edge. Rita cut off the bottom where it said "MONTANA" in big white script; she didn't want to be distracted.

After she eats, and washes her plate and fork and glass, Rita wipes off her makeup, brushes her teeth. From under her bed, she pulls out the wolf scrapbook she keeps there, neatly trimmed newspaper clippings with stories of wolves: the occasional appearance of a wolf who drifts down from its pack in Canada, kills a farmer's sheep or cow, and ends up shot. The photo of the wolf hanging like someone's old coat from a post. Or this: the pack of wolves seen trotting along Route 3 when Rita was a little girl. Sometimes, at night, home from hanging out with Bart or shooting pool, Rita in her beery haze pulls the scrapbook out, sits up in bed, lights a cigarette and reads it through again. She's nearly got it memorized, but she keeps reading anyway, running her finger over the photos she's collected, slowly turning every page.

But tonight, she isn't drunk, or feeling bad, or *maudlin;* she's looking for some evidence, thinking of the mystery woman, thinking of her twin.

The best picture is the scariest one, and this is where she lingers, tonight, thinking of the mystery woman, thinking of her twin: the picture from the article she tore out at the doctor's office two winters ago when she had the pneumonia. She'd been sitting there waiting and waiting, her lungs feeling like they'd burst from the pressure and the pain, and she reached for the *People* magazine, thinking, *let's see what Cher wore,* but there on the cover of another magazine was a picture of a wolf, and she'd opened it up: a pack, coming in for the kill, their terrible wide jaws and their white teeth sinking into the flesh. The photographer must have had a lot of patience, because the pictures showed the whole thing, the deer first turning, wild-eyed and frightened, then in the next shot collapsing into the snow, and finally just the deer's carcass, gutted, spoiled, the eyes like the glass eyes of a toy bear, the snow all around trampled and tinted red with deer blood.

"Rita LaPlatte," the nurse had called right then, and Rita realized she'd forgotten all about the pain in her lungs, forgotten where she was and what she was doing, forgotten everything not in the world of wolves and deer and hunt and kill.

She'd torn the picture out when the nurse turned down the hall, then quickly jammed the pages into her purse, collecting herself, pushing the hair from her eyes, wheezing a little as she tried to catch up, hand on her chest as she tried hard to breathe.

Under the stars, the fire splutters and slips up my hickory stick, ignites the next fire down the beach, and all the way down the beach I can go, lighting the fires as I walk, lighting the fires as I need, because I bleed the need for heat and flame. The pillar of smoke following the Hebrews as they crossed the Reed Sea, here I go, my me of me's, not for my own sake alone, not but for the grace of God go I.

The fires now all lit, all ignited from the wick of the stick I dipped into the holy flame of the fire, nestled in its big pit down by the teeth of the bridge. Look at the flames, flickering in the dry night. Look up at the stars, Kitty, look up and see how the stars are just a reflection of the fire and the flame. "See how many stars there are?" the lady said that night, the night she took us from a bed, on our way to the next stop somewhere down the line, ready to wander through more desert dark just like Moses and the wandering Jews.

And then I'm so much with crying I have to bite down hard on my fist, like this. See? Tell me, Kitty, tell me. What was her name? Where did she go?

Where did she go, that lady with the smell like a flower? The shout and the cry, the way the parents said "eat your soup or die," the man of the family, his hand always tickling someplace it didn't belong. Here, I nestle down with Kitty into the rocky graveyard of the baby bones, thinking maybe she just stepped out, maybe she'll soon come back. Far from my tent, far from my Max of precious things, far from my self, far from everything, waiting and watching while the firelights sparkle, while the gasoline can does explode, explode into stars sparking down on me, to breathe God's life back into me, sweet breath of God breathing back into my baby bones.

The flames are easily seen from the Route 3 bridge that passes over the river, and by the time the fire's going, several calls have come in to Intervale Rescue, and down the rocky beach they come, with their hoses and their spray. It's easy to get the fire under control; it's just brush, beach grass and thicket of hedge, with just one fire spot that's fed by gasoline.

But as the fire's doused and the firefighters are preparing to leave, one turns, sees something balled up to the side, here, up the slope from the burnt grasses, and he feels a frightened kick in his chest: it's a person, lying curled on the ground, swaddled in a puffy red parka that's now blackened with fire and smoke, the hood pulled over the head, oblivious to the heat and smoke. Dead?

He calls to his partner, and together they approach, but as they near, the body, the person, comes back to life: it's muttering something under its breath, and the firefighter says, "Hey, are you okay?" knowing the answer, even before he touches the shoulder, before he tries to roll her back and over.

He snaps back from her snarl and spraying spit, and sees then, as the hood of her parka slips back, it's a woman, her hair matted as filthy black fur, her lip curled up in an unrepaired cleft.

When the ambulance attendants snap on their rubber gloves, they're not just following protocol, they're nervous, and don't want to touch this patient. This animal.

The ambulance siren calls through the clear night, Annie trundled into the back willing to lie there, absorbing the bright light, under a white blanket *clean as a scream heard through the night.* In the hospital ER, the doctor gets her a bed, assesses and dresses the burns on her arm, hand, and face, then leaves the room, writes out the order for Haldol to put her to sleep. The M.D. who comes in tomorrow can deal with this one, he thinks. He's got enough other things to do.

In her hospital room, Annie Naiad's breath comes steady and deep; *where's Kitty?* but the sedative is making her woozy and weak until she can't fight anymore, and drifts into sleep, her only dreams shadows of themselves, a fire exploding, a woman's hand brushing her little girl's cheek.

—

Was it such a good idea to release Blue so soon? Bob Reichman's not too sure. He knows that if he'd kept his strange new patient under lock and key, she'd probably never regain her memory; he's read the studies, but this kind of complete, retrograde amnesia's so rare there wasn't much research to be done. Still, keeping the patient sequestered in the wards keeps her in the pathological social setting, where she can only absorb pathology from the others, and so it's best to get her out as quick as he can, set her free, let her start anew. Besides, it's still unclear just who will foot the bill for a patient with no insurance, no Social Security number, and no name.

Late Friday afternoon, the sky already bleeding into black from blue, at his desk Reichman leans forward in his chair, tips the glass ball side to side, watching the snow drift up and back. There's nothing, really, wrong with Blue, besides her understandable situational depression. She's free of psychotic features, of personality disorders; it's nothing a good antidepressant and a schedule of seeing him twice a week won't palliate, even if it can't be cured.

Reichman lets the dark descend outside without turning on his desk lamp. He enjoys seeing the streetlights' glimmer start to glow a little brighter against the dark, enjoys watching the squares of light switch on in the houses across Elm Street. Keeping Blue would only prevent her from encountering all the sundries that might, eventually, trigger her memory and bring her home. The small surprises that make a life, that can recall a history. But Blue's case is different; usually an amnesiac's memory "comes back" in the forty-eight hours following trauma, and the psychiatrist sees the real, original person, the who-he-was return like light shimmering out in a scotoma from a candle's thin, lit wick.

These are the questions that rumble through Reichman's head on a Friday night, even after he locks his office, drives down the hill from the hospital to Intervale's Unitarian Society, where once a month services are held by the *havarah* members, the Jews who refuse the Orthodox synagogue but want something to stitch them to the holidays and ritual. Why is it Blue exerts such a pull on his imagination? Is it only because she's the ideal clean sheet of glass onto which he can project anything?

At the door of the hall, he presses a *kippah* onto his head, even though as he makes this motion, every time he wonders why, then tells himself it's out of respect. Habit.

Now she's been released, he's certain Blue will start showing more signs of depression as she comes face-to-face with the truth: this is it, there's nothing more that he or anyone can do. She's got to start a new life, and she may not be able to. Standing for the silent prayers, Reichman feels his helplessness like a tangible thing, like a pressure in the back of his neck, and he allows himself to sway from side to side, comforted by this motion, knowing it isn't that any spirit is moving in him, no divine presence lulling him to sway; he knows it's just the rocking that comforts the distressed.

"God of our ancestors, God of Abraham, God of Isaac, God of Jacob," he chants with the others, "God of Sarah, God of Rebecca, God of Rachel and Leah . . ." and thinks of his father, wonders if tonight he made it out to the old synagogue in Brookline. Here, in Intervale, the few Jews have pieced a service together, haggling out differences between the Reform and Conservative and Reconstructionist movements; a few, like Reichman, the disaffected grown children of Orthodox Jews who can't quite shake their obligation. Some chant the prayers in Hebrew, some whisper in English, and Reichman isn't even sure why he comes here, except that on a Friday night it gives him something to do. He can tell himself he made an effort to connect, tell himself he's getting out.

When Kaddish is chanted by the mourners, he remembers again that slice of pain, that first Sunday after Amy left him, waking alone, and later, how he swam his laps hard, as if with each stroke he could bring himself further from the pain. He doesn't want to remember; he wants to forget, and he murmurs the prayer, glad he's got familiar territory here, glad his memory's good for hanging onto these comforting, familiar words.

He's well-trained enough in the Hebrew prayers that they feel like a physical memory, like an instinct, like knowing how to wake in the morning or how to sleep at night. Even though here they chant the prayer announcing the new moon at night, still it binds Reichman back to something ancient, back to the time when the sky was just a clear sheet of black overhead.

As he chants, Reichman imagines the new moon waxing, imagines all the moons waxing and waning backward, the seasons shifting back and back through time, summer folding back to spring, then back to the autumn two years ago, when he and Amy first bought the house on Pequot Road: how he rounded the back of the house, and there she was, kneeling into the flowerbed, her hands covered in dirt, the sleeves of her black T-shirt rolled up past her shoulders. How she turned from her work, looking at Reichman as he approached, wiping her hands on her jeans, standing. How, while they talked, she rubbed the papery tulip bulbs in her hands, as if rubbing the delicate skin of a favorite, injured animal.

Reichman sways to the prayers. Why can't he forget this one scene, why does this scene, out of all those he could recall, seem burned into his brain? He's embellished it, he knows, colored it in like a tinted black and white photo, washed in a passel of jays screeching in the pignut hickory tree, a dog barking far off, the river wind coming up, ruffling Amy's hair around her face. Was there a sign he should have been heeding, something foretelling that too soon, she'd be leaving?

He knows he shouldn't question this, shouldn't run his hand over the blade of *if only, what if*—and he knows he shouldn't try to forget; he's a psychiatrist, for Christ's sake, he knows what to do. Knows it's just a matter of time, of waiting for the memories to extinguish, then quit, a matter of getting out, lunch with his colleagues or long swims at the gym. A matter of coming, half-good Jew that he'd like to pretend that he is, to these scanty services.

After the final prayers, there's the *kiddush,* which Reichman always dreads. What does he have to say to these people? What is their common bond, after all? He sips his sweet wine from the little paper cup, standing at the edge of the group, nodding to the people he recognizes, feeling yet again that awful pull to socialize and then the pull to pull away from the bright chatter of this odd collection of displaced, dispersed Jews. Reichman leaves the hall, walks to his car, not looking up, not seeing the silky night sky above him littered with stars.

~

Her first day on the job at the diner, Blue's nervous: *why couldn't they find me a job where I don't have to talk so much?* Instead, here she's on display: *step right up! see the amnesiac!* She's the freak in the sideshow, and if she remembered, she'd be able to say this is familiar, this feeling of difference, of *what's wrong with me,* and if she could remember a feeling she swam in like swimming in the waters of a deep, bluegreen pool, it would be this: *loneliness.*

But she doesn't remember, and she suspects she doesn't feel any different from anyone in this town. Is she different? Or is everyone wandering away from their former selves and into their new lives alone?

She's introduced to the chief waitress, Eleanor, tall, stately even in her uniform. And Tiffany, with a pillow of stiff curly hair puffing out around her head, her uniform too tight, clacking her chewing gum even as she says, "Hi." They both look at Blue warily, each of them wondering if she'll become their friend or if she'll just end up taking their tips away.

The first day on the job Blue keeps screwing up, can't get the numbers for the tables straight, brings plates of eggs to the ones who wanted pancakes, but she perseveres, and by day's end, by after-lunch, she's got it down, and feels satisfied, as if she knew she would.

And then, there's the short drive across town to River Road, past the IGA supermarket, past the turn for the bridge *where I was born,* she thinks.

The lights around the town are winking on, and Blue can see the last strip of yellow umber light, low along the horizon's edge, and if she could remember, she'd think it's like a river of color in a dark-hued painting hanging over a lover's too-soft bed.

Home. Across the broken-down yard littered with trash, up the long flight of steps, into her place. Now she's got a job, a place to live, now she's been released, Blue isn't quite sure what to do.

What do people do? Blue wonders then, watching the last ribbon of light elide from the horizon, watching the river bleed from dark blue into black.

What does she want? Who can she be? She sits on the bed, looking out at the river now gone black, invisible. She can't help it; she's waiting for the phone she doesn't have to ring.

Sitting cross-legged in front of her altar, Rita lights a candle, not the new one for returning lost people and things but an older one, one she's had a long time, the one for remembering.

The lights are all out; the only light comes from the streetlamp and the candle's soft glow, and Rita closes her eyes but then lets the lids drift open a tiny bit, so through the scrim of her mascaraed lashes she can just see the candlelight, the things clustered on her altar.

"Remember, remember," she says to herself, and sees the moss and feathers and fur, the hide-smell of the skins. The crunching leaves, mother's warm breath and grizzled fur. The sky above so blue. Warmth, warm breath. Cold sky. The snow lacing down around them, around the two human babies nestled close to the wolf's warm chest.

This must have happened; this must be real, Rita thinks, but then, instead of being enveloped by the memory of the wolf, she's intruded upon by a familiar old memory, one that's visited again and again. She's leaning against the doorjamb of her mother's room in one of their big, drafty apartments, watching as her mother leans in to the mirror that hangs over the dresser, closes one eye and pulls on the lid, hard, then pulls her lips back against her teeth, slips the lipstick across them, making her face look, for a moment, disfigured, as if it isn't flesh, as if it's made out of clay.

Rita hangs, watching, at nine wanting to learn some facial decorating tips but not wanting her mother to know she wants to know. Not wanting to ask, not wanting to do anything that will illustrate that she's in league with her mother, or that she wants to be.

Instead, she chides her mother, and this isn't hard, this is easy to do: "You've got way too much eyeliner," she says, shaking her head. It's true: her mother's eyes, when she goes out on weekends, are heavily lined, like a raccoon's eyes, Rita thinks, and thinks then of the night she woke, late, hours after her mother had gone out, and heard a noise outside: it was her mother rustling through the trash bin in her mini-dress and heels, downstairs by the apartment house door.

"You always think that," her mother says now, but she goes easy then on the green shadow. "Men like a lot of makeup, that's one thing you'd better start learning now, Miss."

You should know what men like, Rita thinks, but doesn't say. Instead, she hangs in the doorway, and realizes she doesn't want her mother to go out at all, wants her mother to just stay home, here, with her, to watch a show on TV. The same feeling the adult Rita had while her mother was dying last year: *don't go, stay.* Rita would make them a dinner of frozen green beans and fish sticks; she'd bake a couple of potatoes, and later, she'd make for them both ice cream sundaes, with walnuts on top.

But because she knows this fantasy is no good, won't happen, she disposes of it before it really takes hold. Her mother's humming *"Someday he'll come along, the man I love/And he'll be big and strong, the man I love,"* and she'll be going out tonight and the next night too, because she's in that flirty in-betweeny time when one boyfriend has left and the new one hasn't appeared just yet. If Rita wants to watch TV and curl so close to her mother on the sofa that her mother says, "Rita, please, you're all over me like a bad suit," she'll have to wait until the next man comes, takes them over, and then vanishes again.

"Mom," Rita says, just to hear her mother say, "Yeah?"

She wants to say, "I love you," but this wouldn't make sense, so instead she says the next best thing: "That dress looks great on you," and her mother turns, looks at Rita. "Well, thanks, sweetie, that's very nice of you. Let's just hope somebody else notices that, too."

Rita smiles with her lips pressed closed, nods, and swallows. Her mother's done, clicks her compact and her lipstick shut, snaps them into her purse, then scans the room. As usual, her room's a mess, even though Rita makes regular attempts to tidy it up for her: clothes scattered everywhere, a glass with dark liquid, probably scotch, moldering by the bed, and odd things where you wouldn't expect them: a single hair curler that's rolled, forgotten, to the side of the dresser, a nearly empty cereal box standing on the kitchen chair her mother brought in last week so she could change the light bulb in the ceiling fixture. *Etcetera,* Rita thinks.

"Okay, I guess I'm ready," Rita's mother says, and Rita nods from her slouch by the door. Her mother clicks down the hall, saying, "Keep the door locked, sweetie, I'll be home late," Rita bobbing along in her wake, and Rita thinks forward, forward, into the evening to avoid this part, so she doesn't have to think of this part, so she doesn't have to be here, in the dark hole that swallows the house as soon as her mother goes.

First thing, she switches the TV on, turns it up loud, just to hear it speak. In the kitchen, she turns on the stove, reads again the instructions on the package of IGA fish sticks, even though she knows how to make them, knows this by heart: *350 degrees for 35 minutes or until golden brown.* Rita prefers them crispy. She tumbles the hard sticks across the aluminum pan, counting out five, two on each side and one in the middle, thinking for a moment this configuration looks perfect, looks just like a picture.

Later, after her dinner, after she's washed all the dishes and put them away, after she's watched a TV show or two, Rita returns to her spot, leans against the doorjamb of her mother's room again. She imagines her mother there, standing again at the dresser, peering into the mirror. Then she pictures her mother asleep in her bed, and shuts the door on this image, closes her eyes so it will stay in her head. So she can pretend.

Then Rita goes to her own bed, gets her blanket and pillow, carries them into the living room. That's where she falls asleep, with the TV voices on, as if they're talking to her, as if they are real.

Sitting at her altar, remembering this takes only a second of time, and Rita wonders why it is this memory stays stuck in her head, detailed and perfect? Why can't she conjure something more interesting, something more wild, something with the wolf she's sure she was born to? Why can she remember so well her mother, the series of apartments they lived in falling like dominoes down in a line, but can't for the life of her remember her twin?

~

In the psych ward of the Intervale Hospital, the doctor searches Annie for some kind of ID, but finds nothing on her except a little stuffed toy cat, so worn and matted and sooty he slips it into a plastic bag, and a page torn out from a magazine, so badly crumpled there's no telling why she would keep it. On one side, a stock clothing ad, on the other the first page of an article: LOSE THOSE TEN POUNDS BY JULY!

After three days on the ward, Annie at last answers when he asks her name: "Annie," she says, "Annie Blaze." Under her breath, so soft and high and sloppily articulated that he can't hear, she adds: *When I lived at the riverbank it was Annie Naiad, and I lived in the river, by the wits of the river, but now the river's gone, the Reed Sea parted by the flames in the fires I set.* The doctor, a native of Maine, writes it down *Blaise,* like the name of the dairy down the road when he was a kid, and doesn't think this is odd, and sends the information to the social workers, who'll take weeks to get to that strata of the paper piles, who'll begin the long search state by state for anyone by that name who's been reported lost or stolen or strayed.

During her first days on the ward, the nurses insist the aides try to wash her, give her a bath, cut back her matted hair, but even the burliest guys on the staff have trouble holding her for long in the tub, and so she ends up rinsed, but not scrubbed, sent back to her room, where she huddles into the corner of her bed, muttering still under her breath.

I told them I'd been down by that stream a long time, but I knew they didn't believe me, no way.

Where were you living before here, the doctor says. Says she's the doctor but she's got these three tiny braids back of her head and no makeup, no white coat. She's not looking like a doctor but she's got that doctor way, looking at me sideways, like she's always thinking of me.

Where before this, she says, and I say in the tent, in my tent. Where was the tent, she says, like she don't believe me but like she's pretending to believe me. She's all the time making notes on that pad of hers, but she don't wear the loopy metal ears, so I don't know if she can call herself doctor.

Where did you get the tent, she says. I know she don't believe me on account of why should she? She thinks there's no way I could get a tent.

By the stream, I tell her. I tell her by the stream when I turn my head towards the wall, so maybe she won't quite hear me. I kind of don't want her to know, but that other one does want her to know. I turn towards the wall, and it is blank, and beige, hospital beige, and I say, by the river.

She makes a note and nods. I want her to believe me about the tent and the stream. I want her to understand how I did it. I nod and nod and nod, and the doctor doesn't like that, and she stands up and says I guess you've had enough for now. I've had enough, I remember the father hollering and then the glass bowl thrown against the wall and the sparkling glass shards in their spray like announcing the Savior coming to stay.

In the pool, Reichman counts his laps: *twelve, twelve, twelve,* repeating the number in his head until his right hand taps the tiled wall and he curls his body fetus-like, then springs back: *thirteen, thirteen, thirteen.*

Blue's memory isn't coming back. Certainly not in the near future, certainly not anytime soon. Reichman realizes this with the feeling, *disappointment,* he's most accustomed to, and pushes off from the wall even harder on the next turn.

Some patients recover, or heal, or change the way he wants them to, and he can see the progress slowly going forward, the long unraveling of family myth and dream landscape and present-day crises all falling apart and then together, in the end making neat parallels, or at least making sense. This may happen with the new patient who came in just this week, calling herself Annie Blaise, although she's got no ID, and no records in all of Maine can be found for her, and he knows it might take quite some time before the police get an answer about her fingerprints. She's clearly psychotic, and by all appearances has been for quite some time. Chances are this isn't her first stay in a hospital ward, and Reichman's sure other psychiatrists have tried with her. Still, there's always that chance, that hope, that his remedy will do the trick, even though, swimming in the cold water now, he deeply doubts it.

Reichman stops at the lane's end to catch his breath. It wasn't long ago that he could swim seventy-two laps, two miles, straight through. What's happened to him? Has he really gotten this old?

He pushes off again, this time with his head out of water, arms propped on a kickboard. Maybe this Annie Blaise will prove a success; maybe he'll get through, and she'll be released, a whole person reassembled from her fractured parts.

But Blue. He'd thought at first this case would prove simple, a knock on the head that jarred something shut, like a cabinet door of memory that just won't open after the earthquake's hit. With a little time, a few well-chosen drugs and a little talk, the door would pop open, revealing a husband, a house in a town somewhere, maybe some kids, a set of parents, a friend, someone who would take this woman back to her origin.

Now, he sees this isn't in the cards. Was it something he said, something he did? Some wrong move that he made? He's had patients before like Annie Blaise who are nearly impossible to repair, they've been so damaged so early on. And he's had his share of patients who resist. But with Blue, he's got a new feeling, a bad feeling: *who's in there?* Almost as if there's no one there to reach, and he hasn't a clue how to go about finding her.

At lane's end he pauses, drops the kickboard onto the tile, snaps his goggles on again, and pushes harder off the wall, plunges into the water. Faster, faster. It's the only way he'll be able to sleep.

It isn't that the drive itself is familiar; on the way to Portland, Blue checks her progress against the directions, glancing down at the neat handwriting of the social worker. But the driving itself is what feels familiar, and out on the highway in the bright winter day, Blue knows she's done this before.

The highway spits her into downtown Portland. As she walks to the big office building to get her papers stamped, notarized, and signed, she thinks, *I'm here to claim a number and a name. Blue Doe,* she's settled on; nothing else makes sense to her, and when the social worker argued with her, saying didn't she want something easier to understand, something more common, say, Elizabeth or Jane, didn't she want to choose a last name of a famous woman, say, Dickinson or Woolf, Blue just shook her head. *No. Blue Doe.*

At the government building, she signs the papers, passes the hospital documents across the countertop, waits for the supervisor to approve this unusual case. The long wait, winter sun eking in through the wire-covered windows, steam leaking from the clanky old radiator in a long warm hiss. Like something, some other place she's been, she feels rising up in her like a balloon. Then the photo, a flash and a click, her face paralyzed into a smile because she really did want to laugh when the woman said, "Look at the birdie," and held up a photo of a yellow cartoon bird.

Then here are the papers, signed and stamped with an impressive raised seal, looking regal and feeling real.

Her new cards in her wallet, tucked in the big pocket of her down vest, she looks like many young women in Portland on this Tuesday, her hair tufting out from under a white wool cap, her heavy cable sweater and black down vest, jeans, boots. No one would notice her, no one would stop and say where did she come from? Who is this stranger in our midst?

Blue tries to let herself get a little lost, but her sense of direction is good, as she and Dr. Reichman have noted and discussed: was she an out-doorswoman, an explorer, a taxi driver, or just one of those people everyone turns to when they want to say, which way?

No telling, but now, in Portland, she follows the streets around, up into the neighborhoods of big houses with their wide front porches. A walk-way, where she can look out over the cold grey Atlantic, rising and swelling. Then down the hill, where the houses grow smaller, more rickety, cars parked up on the snow-covered lawns to avoid the jaws of the plough, everything disheveled, a baby stroller left outside and tumbled over by the wind, big plastic garbage bins spinning down the center of the street. There, in among that web of crooked streets, on a corner lot, she sees a dog, a pup, his brown and white splotched fur tufted up by the wind, ears flopping past his chin. He's tied to a metal stake plunged into the center of a cement slab embedded in the scrap of yard, sitting upright, as if at attention, as if wait-ing for someone to come home.

Blue stops walking. The rope running from the pup's collar to the stake, she sees, is so short that the pup can neither lie down nor move away onto the snow; piles of his excrement lie scattered on the concrete slab around him. The pup doesn't move as she approaches, doesn't bark in warn-ing or wiggle in anticipation, but when she reaches out her hand to let him get her scent, the pup pulls its head away, looking at her sidelong, emitting a grumbling growl of protest and alarm.

Without pausing to think, in one motion Blue pulls off her gloves, reaches to the stake, unclips the chain, and then continues walking away, not afraid of the pup, not sure if the pup will follow. At first, it doesn't: initially, the pup doesn't move, but stays put in its soiled sentry spot as if it's still tied up. Had it been an older dog, it probably would have stayed. And then, in a sudden bound and leap, up it springs, expecting the backward snap of the master's muscled command or of the rope's choke to the neck, but not feeling it, and being still a pup and not fully inculcated in the ways of man, it scrambles toward Blue, runs to keep up, leaps to her side, all energy and fur, canine heart pumping nearly loud enough for her to hear.

At her car, the pup won't get in on his own, and Blue has to lift him up, sit him on the front seat. They drive together like that all the way back to Intervale, the pup looking out at the scenery, then curling up on the seat, sighing, falling asleep, his nose resting on her lap. In the descending dark that levels the highway and the landscape around it, as she turns on her headlights against the night, Blue now becomes something more than what she has been, in addition to becoming a thief. She can feel it, as she drives, looking over at the pup, singing along with the easily learned songs that come on the radio, her hand resting on the pup's flank. She's becoming a person who lives in relation to other animals, who agrees to throw her lot in with that of her captive. She's becoming attached.

Now, she belongs to someone; now, she's got to make a home.

~

Rita's fingers stain grey with the black and white ink from the newspapers she ties up tight, then stacks until Ross comes in to truck them to the loading dock. Every day she scans the front page for another story, but it appears the story she wants has slipped into the litter of all that's unimportant, and the mystery woman, Blue, has disappeared from the news.

Rita's known Blue better and longer than anyone here, she tells herself, smiling a little when she thinks of this. She still hasn't told anyone, not even Bart, that she's the one who found her on that rainy night, sitting not like a real woman but like a statue of a woman on the Route 3 bridge. She hasn't told anyone that she's been watching out, watching the paper daily for a new story and watching the streets of Intervale as she makes her daily rounds in her truck. She knows better than to try to switch her route with Mert's, knowing Mert will never give up the diner delivery, never give up the complimentary coffee and pie he's served there every Friday, but she's driven by the diner, and one late afternoon, she could swear she saw that face she's sure looks like her own pressed against the big plate glass window that looks out on the parking lot and road.

She hasn't told anyone that she's certain, she's sure, that Blue is her twin.

Rita tells herself she's stealthy as an animal in this, in her pursuit. She's got to be cautious; she doesn't want to scare Blue off, doesn't want to risk the possibility that seeing her, Blue would startle, then bolt. Or worse: refuse to recognize her. She's got amnesia, after all. Hefting another bundle of papers, papers she doesn't care about because they have no news of Blue, Rita thinks, how could she recognize me? Or, maybe this is all it will take to jolt her memory back: seeing me, seeing her twin. And then what? Once Blue starts remembering, won't she simply leave again, go off in search of her adopted kin, the good people who raised her better than the mother who raised me?

She could just start following Blue, couldn't she? Couldn't she get some kind of disguise, she thinks, and imagines herself dressed in a costume, face painted or masked to look like someone else.

As Rita pulls out of the parking lot, the bundled papers rise up and fall back with a thump in the back of the van, and Rita doesn't think of the disguise on that Halloween long ago; that's how quick it is, that's how thoroughly it's woven into who she is. Instead, she switches on the radio, hoping, she's not sure why, to find a song that's sad.

She's got to find a way to meet Blue, she's got to find a way through. She's got to be careful, and not blow it the way she's blown everything else. But maybe, now, things will be different, now that her twin has come home to roost; maybe, now, she can do something right.

———

Late afternoon and Reichman heads out Summer Street, stops at the intersection, waits for the green. No late patients on Wednesday, Reichman knows he should have gone for a swim or at least to run some errands, but instead, he just wants to get home, and pictures his house, with all of his things, waiting for him.

From here, heading out of town, he can look upriver, north, and see the early-winter light making a pink sheen on the water down below, and he can see the path the river cuts through the boulders and the bank, all the way up to the north end of town, where the river curves, then disappears.

As he crosses, he looks to the side, tries to see down. On the river's far side, there's a pull-off for the fishermen who spring and fall park their pickups with their tows and unload boats and gear into the water from the rocky beach. Now, of course, it's empty, covered with a thin sheaf of ice and frozen snow, but Reichman pulls in, parks, and leaves the car.

He walks back over the bridge, on the inbound side, the side where Blue was found. Halfway over he stops, looks down: below, the water swirls around the rocks, the fastest parts of the river not quite frozen yet, the ice forming concentric rings in the stiller pools.

He looks around, as if looking for clues, as if he'll see Blue's hand-prints still embossed on the rail of the bridge, but there's nothing, and he rubs his own gloved fingertips across the frosty metal. From here, he can easily see the railroad bridge, and imagines he can even make out the place where Annie Blaise encamped; he thinks he can see a corner of the old card-board box she called her home poking out from the rocks and snow, the low shrubbery still blackened from the fire. There's no way she would have survived down there past November's end, that much is sure, but still Reichman's bothered by how hard he pushes a patient like this, how much they all insist that she improve. That she conform. That she join them.

Up here, it's cold; the wind picks up as it slices down the river gorge, and Reichman shivers, claps his gloved hands together, his warm breath puff-ing out and disappearing in the cold air. Back in the car, Reichman switches the heater onto "high." Here, Route 3 straightens out, and he settles in for the long, straight ride. Turns on the radio, hears a snippet of news, then switches it off, preferring instead to listen to the quiet fading winter light.

At home, Reichman gets the boxed menorah down from the attic where cardboard cartons stand stacked in two neat rows, labeled, against what event? His sudden death, when his sister will fly in from England and flutter around, ineffectual and bothersome, until a couple of his colleagues take control? He presses his palm against the floorboards in the spot where some winter's water collects, and finds the wood is dry.

Downstairs, he sets the menorah in the window, as custom dictates from the days when Jews lived in villages and the passersby could see the flickering lights from the street when looking in. He says the prayers, lights the candles, even though he knows that out here on Pequot Road only the night animals will see the burning little lights.

As he usually does at this time of year, Reichman wonders why Jews should feel any more responsible to their collective memory than anyone else. Why does he remember to light the Shabbes candles, or to spiral into self-reflection in the days approaching Yom Kippur?

Next week, after Hanukkah, after Shabbes, his father's moving in. Then, he'll have to keep track, have to watch himself. He's told his father he won't keep his home strictly kosher, but he knows that starting next week he'll be giving up his favorite foods, chicken and cheese enchiladas and shrimp scampi.

Why does he bother with these menorah lights? No one is watching, nobody cares. Maybe he should have gone to the Hanukkah party the Havarah invited him to instead. He mumbles the prayer, thanks the God he knows doesn't exist for saving his ancestors, and feels silly, just silly—why does he even think that his life is threaded to the lives of these ancient Jews? Before the Jews were Jews, they were just another band of nomads, in a world where warring factions fought and made peace and fought again, the factions pulling apart, separating, then coalescing again in a new configuration. Who could say, even back then, who was and who was not a Jew? When you figure in all the intermarrying, pogrom rapes, secret love affairs, the sheer heft of confusion in the centuries that followed, it seems crazy to hang on with such tenacity as he sees in his fellow Jews to this idea of biological destiny, of "choseness" residing in the genes.

Still, he thinks these thoughts not on a night in the dark dead pit of winter, alone, but on a dark night in the light—look how the brightness rises every night to the stellar shimmering of the full-blown menorah! And he feels again that thrill he felt as a child, chin resting in his palms, his father's voice singing, as the eighth and brightest candle was lit and the earth spun away from darkness and back toward the light.

He thinks, then, oddly, of Blue. The axis of the earth, the spinning planet turning slowly, achingly, back toward the light. This young woman, lost, alone, without a past, without a home. Without a past to climb back into, to long for, to rail against, what is she? Or who?

The forest animals don't see Reichman's menorah flickering behind the window glass, don't wonder at the days all shortened up on their leash of night, don't long for summer, don't long for light. They move against the night, watching for eye-shine, the rabbits and the squirrels, the great wild wolves moving down from Canada, toward the bright pale glow of Intervale.

⌒

It can't be that the snow has woken her. She sees the impossibility of this as soon as she wakes, but countering it there is the window, curtains pulled back, and outside, in the mill lights that illuminate the river dusk to dawn, the snow falling light and restless, a white scrim drifting, drifting, solid and loose at once. *Snow,* she thinks, sitting up in bed, and up from her amnesia's waters there rises an island of memory, a small memory like a marble between her fingers, and she thinks, *snow day,* and there's an overheated bedroom, steam essing from a radiator, a hallway with a pretty patterned carpet tongued down its length, there's looking down a long steep building to a white courtyard, the sound of a radio scratching into clarity, the smell of coffee percolating and onions frying, and outside, there's *snow.*

Is that a memory, Blue wonders, knowing it must be. What else could explain a thought like that? Not so much a thought as a picture. Seeing his rare chance: *she's awake!* the pup scrambles up on the bed, and Blue rubs his soft ears, excited at her memory, but scared. "I think I remembered something," she says to the pup, and he lifts his face so she'll scratch him under the chin.

"Come on, let's get up," she says, and together they leave the bedroom, cross to the kitchen, and Blue opens the kitchen door to the rickety wooden steps, the cold air hitting her full in the chest, through her cotton pajamas. *Oh.* The pup slips down the steps, desperate to reach the yard, and while he's out Blue dresses, looks at the clock: four. She's got an hour before she has to leave for the restaurant, so she gets the pup back in, suits up in mittens and scarf and hat, dutifully layering everything as she's been taught, and then she leaves, slipping to keep up. In the dark, the pup runs back to her, leaps up, as if to verify that she's coming along, then runs ahead. Out on the road, he snaps at the snow, wiggles, wags, prances ahead. Blue tilts her head back so her face is kissed by the snow, by the cold air, but this movement isn't natural to her, it isn't done with the grace of someone loving the snow, tilting her face happily up to the wet weather; Blue tilts her head back stiff-necked, winces a little, stands still for a moment, waits.

They walk along River Road, which soon dead-ends, then narrows to a path, the mud now frozen into ripply ridges that make it hard to pass. If someone saw Blue, walking the path along the river, bending to snap free the lead from the pup's collar, he wouldn't think, what's wrong with her? Instead, he'd more likely take no notice: just another white woman in New England, not too tall, not too short, her features a little too craggy, too angular to qualify as pretty. If he looked more closely, he might see something terrible and sad in her eyes when she looks up from the pup. She might give a little nod, frightened, shy, and pass him on the path.

It's so quiet Blue thinks she can hear everything: the whir of the electric lights, the occasional car passing over the bridge, the hum of very early morning life in Intervale. It's so cold that the river is nearly frozen, great chunks of filigreed ice filling in the black spaces, but under the ice she can see the water moving. *Snakes in the water, snakes in the deep water,* she hears in her head, but she keeps walking. Now it's two memories so far, and it isn't even five A.M.

Dr. Reichman told her to think about what triggers the memories: "What's the feeling behind them? What are you feeling at the time?" he'd said, saying they might grip her at any time, ignited by the most commonplace sensation, a taste, a smell, a sound. *Like snow,* she thinks. He said she should immediately sit down and write whatever she is feeling, write whatever memories come to her.

"Write it like a story; if you're unsure what comes next, just make it up," he said.

Blue knows she should do this, and she's got in her pocket the tiny notebook and pen she bought just for this purpose, but she doesn't want to, and feels her reluctance like a piece of wire winding in her chest. She doesn't want to sit around writing; she wants to walk down to the place where the river collects in a slippery pool; she wants to see if the pool, where the water doesn't run so fast, has frozen over. She wonders how she knows it will freeze here first—*I must have learned that someplace*—but she continues walking in the snow. The ground is covered, all the rocks and tree trunks becoming white bumps, the path getting trickier to follow, everything softening with snow. *Make for me a snow angel,* she hears in her head, a woman's voice, a voice she knew, and her heart kicks in excitement, but she can't place the voice, just the immense sadness in it, the loss, and the wrong syllables stressed.

Snow angel, she thinks. This memory—if that's what it is—feels different to her, feels newer, she thinks. With her gloved hand, she brushes the snow off a big boulder, and dutifully sits. The pup has sprinted ahead, is busy sniffing around in the snowy leaves and the laurel that rakes up around the trunks of the trees. Blue closes her eyes, breathes in deeply, just the way the doctor taught her, letting the cold air in, feeling her skin stretch tight against the pressure of her ribs. She focuses on that voice, conjures it again: *make for me a snow angel,* a woman's voice says, and the word to describe it that drifts up to Blue is: *tender.*

Blue takes out the little notebook, writes what she's captured so far on this day: the *snow day,* the radiator, the voice. She thinks, this is the way she wants someone to talk to her, the way the nurses sometimes did, in the hospital, a note like that tenderness in their tone. But there's something else in this voice, too: there's *goodbye.* Someone tender who is leaving, or who is far away. There's the other thing about the voice, too: the slanted stresses on the syllables, and the funny softening of the "g" in "angel." What could this be? Blue wonders, but knows she can't figure it out: Don't try to figure it out, Dr. Reichman said, just explore it.

She tries to explore it, sitting on the rock in the cold near-dark, but she feels again the wire tightening in her chest. She mouths the words to herself, the snow falling on her shoulders and hatted head, watching the sky streak paler, white and grey and rose, and then she says the words aloud, as if in this way they'll come to life: "Make for me a snow angel." But after a little while, the words lose all their meaning, and she's left with nothing but a little collection of sounds in her mouth. Sitting on the boulder, hearing the voice well up inside her, Blue feels sad, sadder than she's ever felt, a swelling loss like a bubble that will only grow, and never burst. "Oh," she cries out, and the pup waggles over toward her, rests his whole long snout across her knees, looks up, looking sad too.

Blue rubs his head, squeezes his ears between her gloved fingers. She's crying now, and whispering to the pup: "who am I? what did I lose?"

The pup tries to scramble onto her lap with his big clawy paws, and she pushes him off, pulls off her mittens, wipes her hand across her eyes, blinks, takes off her hat, holds it between her fingers, runs one finger across the knitted lumps, counting them in their concentric rings. Since she left the hospital, her hair has grown, so now it falls to a straight line just above her shoulders, and when she replaces the hat, she can feel with her fingertips how the ends of her hair peek out in a smooth black fringe. She calls the pup again and the two walk back, walk home.

In the apartment she fixes herself a quick breakfast, changes into her nylon waitress uniform, not thinking anymore of the woman's voice, not thinking of how she got here, just getting herself to her job, as if she's just another woman working to pay the rent and heat. As if she knows where she's going, as if she knows who she is.

⌒

On a mid-December Thursday, at her stop furthest out of town, the QwikMart out on Pequot Road, Rita jokes with old Perry, as she drops the bundle of papers by the register, but she doesn't make up a pretense for why she's lingering here, doesn't pretend she needs milk or beer. Perry knows it's the tickets she's after, and on this Thursday there's a new game out, just announced in today's *Gazette,* and Rita's got a feeling *this time,* a feeling that she'll win. After all, isn't she on a roll?

Down here, at the turn for River Road, everything's a little wilder than it is right in town. Here, Rita can feel the wild icy river tumbling in its great frozen gulfs, just a few steps away from her. In summer, Perry can hear the river from his perch atop his stool, but now, he turns the radio on, listening to WKID, "KID Radio," the announcer says just as Rita puts down the bundle and takes off her gloves.

"Hey Perry," she says. "What's going on?"

"Same old same old," he says back. "Hey, but the wife won a trip to Atlantic City."

"Really? Wow." Rita is impressed. She did win fifty dollars once, on a lottery ticket, but the only time she ever won anything else was at the hardware store when she reached into a bowl of keys and happened to pluck the one that fit the lock on the display, winning a free set of keys made. She only needed her one set of keys, but she got another made anyway, just so she could get her prize.

"Yup, I guess we'll be going down there in a couple months, just for a weekend, just as soon's we can both get the time off," Perry says, scratching behind his ear like a dog.

"What can I get for you, Rita? Here to try out the new game?"

"Yeah, I've got a feeling about this one. I guess I'll take five," Rita says, as if this is a different number than her usual, but it isn't; she always buys five tickets, and is careful to keep them articulated like the spine of a delicate animal she cares about.

Perry hands her the tickets and she hands back a bill, and Perry says, "Exactamundo," and rings up the sale. He knows better than to expect Rita will scratch off the tiny circles of gunmetal grey there in the store; even if she wins, she never brings the ticket back that day, but stows it in the van, tucked safely up behind the visor, waiting for the time when she feels her luck is right to claim her free ticket.

"Thanks, Perry. I want to hear all about your trip when you get back," Rita says, opening the door. She makes a point of being polite in this way, of taking her time, forcing herself to wait; *don't hurry,* she tells herself, tells herself: *breathe.*

But by the time she's gotten back to her truck and pulled herself into the driver's seat, the cushion of the seat familiar with the impression of her body, her heart is racing. It's here: her chance, her possibility.

From the niche in the dashboard she plucks out a dime, the special dime she keeps there and always uses for this trick because with this dime she won that fifty dollars, once.

Rita looks at the new cards, with their pictures of wildlife. Each one is different: a moose, a wolf, a big blue-grey bird, a raccoon, and a snake. Instead of going in order down the row, keeping everything precise, Rita saves the wolf for last, thinking, this has got to be it. Of course she'll hit the jackpot with this, her totem.

The first card yields nothing, nor does the second, but this only increases Rita's excitement: they never have two winners in a row, so her chances are better at hitting it big on the wolf. On the third, she holds her breath, and there, slowly revealed under the metallic disc, are the words she didn't want to see: FREE TICKET.

The wolf will be a bust, she knows, and tucks the whole row, now messy with her scrapings, the edges bent, behind the visor, starts the van, and heads back to the loading dock, switching on the radio, but not singing along with the old, familiar song.

~

They keep asking me about my fires, why did I make them, what were they for, and if I could have said anything I would have told them how the first one was just for keeping warm, keeping my little me out of the storm; what could be warmer than fire? I picked up sticks and tented them up into a pitch over papers I'd taken from the big barrels out behind the stores on the road to Damascus that goes over the bridge. Lit my match like a flit, and zip, there was the fire.

Then the others I had to light, because if you have one you have to have two and if you have two then three's a need, and on like that, and each time I turned around there was another spot calling me for a fire, until they were blazing all up and down the beach, the fire a moving riptide, waving together, until they were just one fire, one big conflagration of memory's elation.

When they started to crackle and creep toward the bushes, into the bulrushes, I tried to persuade the flames to edge back toward the water, but hell no they wouldn't go, like everyone else they couldn't understand me, and before I knew it, it was out of control, fire outracing me, and even my tent was pitching into the flames, so I ran inside and grabbed at my special Max of special things, what I hadn't sent for safekeeping down the river with Moses in the reedwove basket, tucked my Max of my remaining things in the pack the woman tossed to the bushes that night of the man with the teased cock in the bloated car and the sirens pitching out. I saved it, ran back out, tucked the pack under the rail bridge with its metal legs and away I went into the dark landscape, telling the rabbit keep this safe for me, *and then the sirens started to scream, and my arm licked by flame, singed with the name.*

They came with their water and doused the flames, even though I tried to tell them don't, don't water this fire, fire of my heart's desire. I lay wrapped in the new red parka, curled against the sirens and the flames, hoping they wouldn't find me there, leave me alone, just let me be, filthy pig in a blanket, the pig that is me.

Now they won't stop asking me, and I shiver away and turn to the wall. Where were they, then? Why should they care? Here, they've got me right where they want me, they've got me under lock and key, and out there some where's all my things, my special packet of things, the letter I found and the shell from the park, the rabbit I touched and my locked locket heart.

~

In Dr. Reichman's second-floor waiting room, Blue can stand at the window and look down to the street, watch the people coming and going from the pharmacy, and she can watch the big black hands on the old clock face inch toward four o'clock. In these moments of waiting, before his office door opens and he says, "Blue? Come on in," it seems as if all her thoughts and feelings are crystallized, a ball of feeling in her hand that she can turn and examine from any angle, but none of her examining brings her any closer to learning who it is she is. Who it is she's been.

"Blue? Come on in," Reichman says, and she turns, follows him through the door, sits on the end of the stiff white sofa.

She isn't sure, this time, how to begin, and feels a sudden panic: *maybe it wasn't a memory. Maybe I'm making all of it up.* But even as she's thinking this, she says, "I remembered something," and then backpedals, quick. "I mean, I don't know if it was a memory or not. Maybe it was just an illusion or some kind of trick."

"Well, let's try to figure it out," Dr. Reichman says.

Blue tells him then about waking up to the snow, tells him about the vision of the long carpeted hallway, the window that looked down to the courtyard below, *ailanthus tree* outside the window, the man's voice on the radio saying, "snow day," and when she comes to this, her voice quivers and cracks.

Reichman's thinking he can't possibly track down this fragment to a place specific enough to help him find Blue's identity, but instead of going down that path he says, "What's the feeling?" and Blue waits a long moment, then says, "Sadness, I guess. And fear. I think I was afraid."

"What do you think you were afraid of?" he asks, and she starts trembling again, looks out the window, looks back at him. "I don't know. Something." She rubs her forehead with her fingertips. "Maybe being alone?"

Reichman tries having Blue close her eyes, tries to get her to go back into the memory, but there's something in there that won't let her in, won't let her past the vision of the room. Still, it's good, a good start, a good sign, the memory, the feeling, and it doesn't matter to Reichman how small this beginning may seem: it's the first hook into Blue's memory, into her past.

"Do you think this will help?" Blue asks, and he hears again that quiver in her voice. "I mean, it's so vague. It could be anywhere. And how do I even know that it's real?"

"Real?" Reichman's confused at this. "I can't tell you that, Blue. It sounds like a memory. Does it feel similar to the memories you have of the time since you came to?"

Blue hesitates at this, looks out the window. Outside, the snow is starting again, blowing in gusts from the sky.

"I guess so," she says. "But it's different, too. I can't describe it. I don't know," she says, and her voice trembles, and tears fill her eyes.

"What's the feeling that goes along with it?" he asks her, and she shakes her head. "I'm confused," she says. "I don't see how I'll ever get out of this."

The rest of the session is spent on this feeling, on Blue's frustration, and Blue at one point thinks of telling him about the other memory, the woman's voice, the snow angel memory as she's come to think of it, but she doesn't tell him; it's as if this memory is fragile, as if uttered out loud, it will splinter and split.

After Blue leaves, Reichman sits at his desk, leans back in his chair, looking out at the snow. Is it possible there's something in her past, her distant past, that could keep Blue from wanting to remember? Is it possible she doesn't want to remember, so she won't have to go back? Is it possible he doesn't want her to, doesn't want her to leave?

He sees the clock hands approaching five, and goes to the office door. "Tony? Come on in," he says, and another session begins.

⌒

In the early mornings of December, Blue wakes in the apartment cold, but she soon hears the radiator start to clang, hears the hiss of steam and smells the dry burning of the iron pipes. She lies in bed for a couple of minutes before getting up, the pup by her feet, and every morning she waits for another memory, but none comes, and so instead she thinks of her memory, of the carpeted hallway under her bare feet, the little courtyard below covered with snow.

One mid-December morning she wakes like this, and she doesn't remember a memory, but she remembers something she once knew, something she remembered when she woke up in the night, and she thinks of how she woke in the dark, the streetlight coming through the window, and she thought: winter is the time for solstice. Awake in the center of the night, her anxiety rose inside of her, her loneliness a hot coiled wire lodged in her chest. She didn't cry; it was as if her eyes were pried wide as the sky, and no tears would come through. *Is this what hopeless is?* And then, to lull herself back to sleep, she pictured the planets orbiting the sun, the earth pulling further and further on its tilty axis, pictured the maps Dr. Reichman has shown her of the world, and so she slept again.

Now, in the early morning pale dark light, she pulls up the window shade, looks out at the river.

She likes checking it every morning, and she's watched the river turn from the roiling snaky brown of November to this, a solid length of ice. Now, before the snow gets too deep, in the afternoons the school kids meet down at the pool along the path, sit on their parkas, shuck their boots, pull on extra socks and skates. Sometimes from her window Blue can see them, bright spots of color, gliding across the ice, or holding hands to form a whip. It's that cold here—so cold that the river, even flowing fast, can't outrun the freeze.

In the mornings of December Blue looks out at the ice, at the snow covering the riverbanks. If she's on the late breakfast shift and doesn't have to be in until 7:30, sometimes she lies there as long as she can, which means until the pup stirs, sees her awake blue eyes, nuzzles her hand, wiggles insistently. She lets him out, stands shivering at the back door, watches him scamper down the steps, then looks up at the sky.

On this morning, December 21, the sky is pale, mottled, rose and cream and blue. *It's like . . .* she thinks, but doesn't know what. *It's like . . . like something,* she's sure. *Something you wouldn't think it's like. Not like the sea, or another kind of sky.* Blue shuts the door, puts on the water for coffee, comes back, stands at the storm door again.

It's like paper flowers, paper flowers that blossom in water, Blue thinks. *Yes.* She sees then a wide-mouthed glass, a heavy glass with a green rim. She's holding a shell, a seashell, and she drops it into the glass, and the flowers balloon out, fully formed, transformed from little paper squares, yellow and pink and pale, pale blue, blooming up to the surface of the water in the glass.

At this memory, she scrambles to do everything: finds the notebook, writes the vision down, not caring if she gets so deeply in that she'll be late to work. She sits at the kitchen table, trying to name the feeling properly, but all she thinks is, *calm,* until the coffee water shrieks in the background, and she gets up. Like the paper flowers, the memory is fully formed, distinct, with no surroundings, no background, no context. Just the glass, the flowers. Her own hand, her adult hand. No table the glass sits on, no room she's in, no one with her, no view to garden or ocean or city. Just the paper flowers blooming in the glass.

Finally she takes the water from the stove, burning her fingers. *I want to know,* she thinks, but even as she's thinking it, she feels the wire going hot in her chest: *knowing means missing.* If she doesn't remember, she won't feel *the heart's rue for that which it had scarce possessed, and yet had lost.* Regret. Maybe it's better not to be able to ask the question that she knows hangs behind everything that Dr. Reichman says: *What happened? Why now?*

As she's pouring the water over the coffee grounds she hears the pup at the door, scratching, and she lets him in, bends to rub his head, but he isn't having any of it; he wants his breakfast, and, disappointed, *slighted,* she pours the food into the bowl for him.

Outside, it's colder than it's been yet, and Blue lets her car warm up before pulling out of the frozen parking area and heading to the Intervale Diner. Today she's wearing her cardigan and a heavy sweater over her thin nylon uniform, plus the bulky down jacket the social worker instructed her to buy, but still the wind has gotten to her skin, and she shivers all day, all day thinking of the frozen river, thinking of how cold everything is beneath the ice, the fish and—*what else lives in a river,* she wonders, but there's no one to ask. She knows that asking such questions of her co-workers brings on exasperation, although she hasn't regained the *what-she-knew* of other people enough to understand that their exasperation comes from their own frustration with their own not knowing.

She makes it up in her head as she moves from the customers at their tables to the window of the kitchen where the steaming plates appear: how cold the fish, the rocks, the little bits of algae and the stones, all submerged beneath the ice. How all winter long the fish swim up and back, looking up at the thick length of ice above, knowing that they're trapped below.

~

Rita pulls into the freshly plowed parking lot of the diner just before four on a Monday afternoon, the winter light paling into dusk. She sits in her truck, waiting, the window rolled down part way, even though the air is so cold that Rita shivers, sitting there. Waiting. She doesn't want to light a cigarette, afraid that if she's holding it when the time comes it will slow her down, but she picks up the pack the from the dash, raps it against her knee, puts it back down again. She's ready.

Finally, the back door swings open, and out comes a girl with hair that billows behind her head, pulled back in a toothy pink pony clasp, laughing to an older woman who follows her out. They cross the parking lot toward the back, where the employees keep their cars, and Rita slouches down low behind her steering wheel, but they don't look her way, don't see her there, just get in their cars, pull out of the lot.

The door remains closed then, the parking lot darkens, and Rita can see the lighted sign that says INTERVALE DINER switch on in its yellow and blue. Where is she? What if Rita got something wrong, and she'll never see Blue again? But then, the door opens, slowly this time, almost as if it's hesitant to let whoever is in there come out. Here she is, looking down at the ground, not looking around, not looking up to watch the snow starting to fall.

Good, Rita thinks, she won't see me. She watches Blue get into her car, notes that she hasn't kept it locked all day, just lugs open the door and starts it up. Blue sits for a moment, and Rita thinks, maybe she's lighting a joint, or tuning in a station on the radio—the kinds of things Rita would do, if she were leaving work now, if she were Blue. But no, she can see even from here that Blue's just sitting in her car, as if waiting for something, looking straight ahead.

Finally, her headlights wink on, and then she pulls out, and Rita follows behind, careful, feeling the excitement quicken her heart and weaken the strength in her hands.

She follows Blue back down Pasture Road and on into town, up Main Street, past Rita's own building, and onto River Road. She must be going home, Rita thinks, and sure enough, Blue turns left, then right, then left again, and finally comes to a stop in front of the worst-looking row house on the street. Is it Rita's own house, one of the places she and her mother lived when she was a kid, maybe the summer she was seven? She isn't sure; there were so many places it made her head spin.

But this house was one, she's sure of it now: she remembers the maple tree in the yard, how she tried to rig up a swing to hang from its thickest branch. And the bullies on this block, they were the worst, she remembers. There was a path down by the river where she'd walk sometimes, where she'd look for the wolves, where she'd look for her twin.

Rita slows, but keeps driving; by now her excitement has turned to a chill, even with the window rolled up and the heater turned on. In the rearview mirror she can see Blue leaving her car, walking up the half-shoveled path to the row house steps.

At the first stop sign where she's sure she won't be seen by Blue, Rita stops, taps out a cigarette, lights it with trembling hands.

What could this mean, that Blue lives here, in one of Rita's old homes? Only one thing, Rita is sure, and she drives herself home, parks in the lot, and slowly walks up the long flight of stairs.

Inside, she stands at the window, looks over the plunging waterfall that appears to be so far below. Down by the horizon, the sky is all pink, but high up above, it's nearly black. Now that she knows which house is Blue's, she could easily approach her, stop by, introduce herself, couldn't she? But she'll frighten Blue off, or Blue won't remember her. In the kitchen, Rita pulls open the drawer where she keeps the pot, along with scissors, tape, and string, and slowly, carefully, rolls herself a joint. She's got to do something. She's got to think.

~

It isn't easy, packing up the house in Brookline: Reichman's dad is little help, fluttering around him, telling him how to wrap up the glasses that will go to the Jewish Community Center to sit in the basement for six months waiting for the annual rummage sale. The house is slowly falling away, falling into the boxes marked "JCC" or those to be sent to England, labeled for his sister, "ROZ." Only a few are marked, "TAKE TO MAINE," and Reichman has to urge his father to bring more things with him, saying, "Dad, don't you want your books?" or, "What about this old globe?"

What Reichman's father really wants to take is his memory, the way it was back when it held his whole life, the memories of the big occasions and the memories of the details, too. Back when it was complete, intact. He wants to bring that perfect recollection he had for names, and dates, the way could match face to name for all the students in his university classes, at least until the classes swelled up beyond thirty-five students at once. How he had so firmly in his grasp the properties of electricity, of gravity and sound, and how carefully he doled this information out to the students, eager or bored as they were.

Most of all he wants to take with him to his son's house in Maine his memory of his wife, when she was young, before the children came, when she

was a young girl, with her bobbed hair and her smooth, olivey skin. He didn't
let on then, early in their marriage, how he'd secretly watch her doing things,
how he'd look out from the kitchen window to watch her hang the laundry
on the line, how he saw her in all her habits, and how he loved to watch her
doing something simple, planting flower bulbs or feeding the baby. He
watched her once, from the car, while he waited for her to come out of the
market, and through the glass he could see her smiling at Sam as he tallied up
her purchases. He wasn't jealous, then; he was proud, and could imagine,
sitting in the car, the way she'd make a joke with Sam to make him laugh.

He even wants to remember what he's spent a lifetime trying to forget,
the memories that have dogged his steps since he was a little boy, being
lifted into an uncle's arms, waving over the uncle's shoulder at his mother,
as the train pulled away.

Now, all this packing to do. He wraps the Shabbes candlesticks carefully in their soft brown cloth. These he'll take; they *are* Miriam, to him.
His son is upstairs, in one of the children's rooms, and for a moment, he
thinks Miriam's here, with him, in the next room, out in the kitchen, and
he slips from his increasingly tenuous spot of *where he is,* and, "Mimi," he
calls, for a moment not remembering the reason they're packing, where they
are going, or that she's already left.

Upstairs, Reichman doesn't hear his father call out his dead mother's
name. He's stacking books in boxes, his old Hebrew primers, his collection
of comics, his textbooks from high school. Why did his mother keep this
stuff around for so long? What use would it come to? The only thing to be
done with it is to cart it all off to the JCC rummage sale, where no one will
want it. *History of the Jews* with its line drawings of Moses and David, a hip-
pie version of a Haggadah he brought home when he was seventeen. *Frannie
and Zooey,* old unused coloring books, the set of outdated encyclopedia.

Sitting in the midst of the books and mementos, Reichman is filled
with a single feeling, a clear bell of emotion, of melancholy, of loss, of missing his mother with such an insistence he fears for a moment that he'll stop
breathing. "Mom," he says, out loud, under his breath.

⁓

*I wanted to tell that doctor who doesn't look doctory all about the tent. Its win-
dows. Its wholeness. The little stitches creeping all around the hems, all in order*

like they should be. How big it seemed sometimes. How I found it that time in that park, so long ago, when I first started out, when I first hit the road. But I wouldn't tell her how I lost it, that night when I lost everything except the packet of my special things, because back then I never let the packet go.

But she was gone, next time, that doctor with the three braids back of her head. Next time a man, a big man, Right Man, he said. I'm Doctor Right Man, he said to me. Yeah, right, I said back to him, scaring him, I could tell that.

I couldn't tell him about the tent, so I waited until the nurse came through the door, tried to run out, but they grabbed me and sat me.

Later, the Doctor Right Man asks me where I'd go if I left. Stupid. Now I know he's the real doctor. I don't want to tell him about going, I want to tell him about the tent.

I'd get a tent, I say.

He writes something down on the pad. His eyebrows go up, then down, meaning he's confused.

The reason I ran out is I wanted to tell about the tent and about the river. I wanted to tell about the wolf and how I wasn't scared. About rabbit chewing on the grass that time, and Kitty curled into my bed there by the river, where I had my camp, where I made my home.

But when I crouch in the chair to show the rabbit Doctor Right Man says he can tell it's been a long day for me and puts the lid on his pen and stands up.

And then what have I got? before, I had my rabbit and my cat, my tent, my packet, and my riverbank. My little basket I sent downriver just like Miriam sent Moses. And now? this room, with its stiff bed, its door locking shut.

—

Down at the roadhouse Rita tips her cue at the corner pocket, pulls one hand back for the shot, then snaps her wrist, clattering cue to eight ball to the side, and the ball shudders into the pocket, just as she wanted, just as she predicted it would.

She allows herself a small smile, but Rita's not the kind to whoop and giggle when she makes a shot. Instead, she's cool, and calm, and barely seems to notice sometimes that she's done exactly what she wanted to. Besides, tonight she's aware of the guy standing off to one side, the guy she's never seen in here before—has she seen him *anywhere* before?—who has written his name, "Rick," on the chalkboard, waiting to take his turn at the table.

On the next shot, she misses, hitting a little too hard to the right, sending the ball to ricochet from one edge to the other, giving Bart a perfect opening, and while he shoots, she lights a cigarette, cupping her hand around the match. Anyone watching her who hadn't already seen her a hundred times before would think she looked like someone in a cigarette ad, the Marlboro Man, or more accurately, a woman playing the Marlboro Man, in her tight jeans and fuzzy pink sweater, her leather jacket slung over a chair back, always where she can see it.

She pushes her hair out of her eyes. Across the pool table, Bart misses his shot, then winks at her, losing the game on purpose so that Rita can play the next game against Rick.

Rita stays cool, smiles a little at Bart in thanks, and sets up the new rack. She could, she knows, let her interest in this guy nerve her out, could succumb to her wanting him, and could let her desire make her fingers quiver on the cue, make her misjudge her first shot and miss the rebound, lose the game before it even begins. This could happen, but Rita won't allow it, won't allow her sight down the cue to waver, won't get distracted by her self-consciousness of her ass tilted in the air as she leans in for the shot. It's all game now; clack and clap of the balls and sticks.

And when it's over, she's barely won, just won by a bit, she hasn't trounced him, and here he comes, hand extended, wide smile, shaking her hand.

"Great game. Can I buy you a beer?" he says, and Rita thinks: here we go. She says, "Sure, Miller Lite," and he nods and goes off. The next game is hers, if she wants it, but the next player up is Sandy, and Rita knows precisely how Sandy will play it, how she'll shift her weight foot to foot about a million times before making her shot, and anyway, Rita thinks, she's got a shot of her own here, she's got a shot at this guy. She hands her cue to Sandy, and Bart starts setting up the rack, and by the time they're done teasing her, the new guy is back with her beer, saying, "You're done playing?"

"Oh, just for now. I get sick of it after a while," she says, leaning against the post that holds the ceiling up.

"Want to sit down?" Rick says, and Rita puts out her free hand again, saying, "I'm Rita," and they shake again.

"I know," he says, and she looks confused, and, for a moment, scared. "I heard your friends calling you," he explains. He's got a nice smile, she thinks. He seems like a nice kind of guy, and maybe he likes her. Maybe he likes what he's seen so far.

"Oh, yeah," she says, nodding, but now that he's made the dividing line clear—she's a regular, he's not from around here—she's getting nervous again, wondering how to make a good impression. "Let's sit down," she says, and walks toward a booth, the only empty one left, up by the window in the glow of the neon lettering spelling out "HIGHER GROUND" in the window.

"You live in Intervale?" she asks when they sit, even though she knows the impossibility of this.

"No," he says, "I'm just visiting. Just passing through. Actually, I've got a job interview at the hospital."

Three months previous Rita wouldn't have thought anything about this; now, the word *hospital* makes her think of Blue, and her interest, already beginning to rise, piques. So what if Blue's long since moved out of the hospital and into the town?

"What sort of job?" she asks, then says, " You mind if I smoke?"

He waves his hand, no. "I'm a phlebotomist," he says, and Rita thinks, well, she knew he wasn't going to say he's a doctor, not with that gangly skinny body, the same cheap jeans and rumpled T-shirt all the guys she knows wear.

She's seen this job advertised in the want ads of the *Intervale Gazette,* and asks him what it is, listens as he talks about drawing blood and tourniquets, leaning in to band his hand around her arm while he explains, letting his finger trail over her skin.

Another beer follows, another round of pool, more time sitting in the booth, shots of lemon drops, and then, Rita's outside with him, and outside, Rita wants everything, there under the sharp stars littering the night sky. She wants him to take her in his arms, to tilt her face to his with one gentle fingertip, wants him to kiss her on the lips then, softly. She wants him to lean his palms against the car, with her between his arms; she'd feel protected then, and safe. If she could have anything, she'd have him stand like that, his back to the cold wind, and standing like that with him, she could pretend anything, pretend she was anywhere in the world: in the desert way out west, with dust devils swirling in cloud-forms around her, surrounded by cacti growing up into the night. Or on a beach, maybe in California, with the surf in the background, and here Rita imagines that the sound of the cars out on the interstate is the sound of the surf stacking in, remembers the surf's rub from the one year she and her mother lived at the beach down in Wells, a cold winter in a cottage intended for summer use, but her mother had gotten a good deal on it, and convinced Rita that it would be charming, cozy by the fire: "Where else can you get beachfront property for a price like this?" When the wind rustled in between the flat boards of the bedroom, her mother hung blankets up along the walls, and Rita pretended she was an Indian in a teepee. She remembers how the surf sounded; that's how she conjures it now, for this fantasy of what could be.

That's what she wants. Something romantic, for crying out loud. What she gets: another dumb mistake, another fuck-up, another guy at the road-house out on Route 3 fumbling her against his car. The front seat is littered with parking tickets, some spare car parts, wrappers from fast-food restaurants, and in here it smells bad, of old food and motor oil. What she gets is his mouth on hers too soon, immediately, his rough cheek on her face.

But this isn't rape. Rita's into it: here's her hand snaking down between his legs, here she is kissing him back, here she is pulling down her underwear for him, *helping him.* All the time, she's thinking, maybe this could work out. If she just had an hour, she'd have that car clean, and men can be trained, she still believes, trained to love women and to treat them okay.

He doesn't say he loves her; how could he? Instead, he says, "You're a good fuck," and in her head, Rita translates this to mean that he likes her, that he'll want her again, that she's good.

Later, she wobbles out of his car and into the parking lot, and he kisses her on the top of her head, saying, "Thanks, that was great," and she knows she shouldn't say it but can't resist, says, "I hope you get the job. Give me a call sometime," and then he's turning to head back into the roadhouse, and she's heading down the slope of the parking lot, downhill, toward her truck, in the dark dirt lot, under the stars.

As she walks, a few bits of snow begin to glitter down from the dark sky, shimmering in the light from the roadhouse, making the world seem, to Rita, in her beery haze, magical. Anything is possible in a winter wonder-land. She thinks of her twin: *where is she now?* Is her twin really Blue, or is she wrong about this, and instead her twin is living in some nice house on Hospital Hill, with a loving husband and well-brushed kids, a pool in the back and a lawn in the front. She imagines her twin looking out the window of her clean home, watching this same snow begin, wondering to herself, where is her twin?

Or is she still with the wolves, a wolf-woman wrapped in hides and in skins, fur boots tied onto her tough feet with string, the only upright creature among the animals, following the pack across the snowy meadows, all of them loping together, a family, through the forest of the night? Is she unspeaking, knowing not the language of humans, knowing only the language of wolves?

Her twin must be Blue, Rita thinks as she starts up her car, shivers with cold, pulls out of the parking lot, and tries to focus on the black road under the wispy shifts of snow.

When she crosses the bridge, instead of going straight into town, she turns right, follows the street down past the school and the park, down to the street where Blue lives. River Road.

Here they are, the broken-down row houses, a string of wooden matchbox structures, all of them looking as if they'd collapse at the first strong wind, their backs to the river, their fronts to the street. Rita parks midway down the street, sits in her pickup, engine running, lights off. Most of the apartments are dark. Rita checks her watch: 2:30 A.M. Through one window she can see a TV's flickering grey and blue glow, and in an upstairs window, she can see that someone's left an overhead light on in a kitchen. But that's it. The rest is all dark. Which apartment is Blue's? she thinks, and feels a panic start in her chest. Somewhere in there Blue lies sleeping, wrapped up in blankets, warm and safe and dry. Not like her at all: not sore from Rick's insistence that she wanted to take for passion, not reeling with the beer, and shots over her limit again.

Rita scans the buildings once more, but nothing is happening. This is getting her no place, fast, just as everything does, *same as it ever was*, she hums under her breath. She switches on her headlights, and as she pulls away, a fat orange tomcat trots across the street and into the snow. For a moment, she slows, watches its eyes glow green against the dark, and then she heads home.

~

Blue can't shake the idea that Intervale is like the glass ball with snow inside that Dr. Reichman keeps on his desk, only instead of holding a little

Austrian chalet, the Intervale ball is crammed with everything that makes up the town: the solid colonials and Victorians that line the hill to the hospital perched up top, the rickety row houses where Blue herself lives down below, the highway sweeping along one side, the river cutting across the whole scene, all of it held tight, suspended, under the domed glass sky. Sometimes when Blue wakes in the night and can't sleep she imagines the town as if from high above, as if she could soar like a bird over it all, and in her head she maps out the streets and houses and roads.

But this mid-December night Blue can't sleep at all; the memory of pulling out of the parking lot, the pickup truck following her all the way through the town and down to her own house keeps her awake. She's seen that truck before, somewhere, but can't recall a place or name. This frustration in not being able to remember feels different to her. Feels newer. Truer? She can't say, but she knows she wasn't frightened by the way the truck followed her; she felt safe, not afraid.

Hasn't she felt this kind of thing before? Yes, she's sure. Where, and why, and when is the mystery.

When she first opens her eyes in the middle of the night, she can't tell the difference between *eyes open* and *eyes shut,* the room's so dark, all the electricity of Intervale knocked out by the snowstorm that's swirling all around her row house. The pup is sacked out by her feet, but she lies on her back, hands clasped behind her head, looking up. The dark is like her amnesia; what difference would it make if she could remember? What difference would it make if she could see?

If I could remember, she thinks, I'd float into a child's bedroom, looking down from the ceiling, and see a little girl sleeping in a child's bed. She thinks of the hallway, the courtyard from her single memory. What difference would it make if she could remember waking in a painted iron bed in Michigan or in a bottom bunk in California, or even in a sleeping bag in Arizona, the walls of the tent like green slate in the morning sun? What difference if it's a pink-canopied bed in a big apartment in Manhattan, opening her eyes not to the still, silent dark she wakes to now, but to the light in a ribbon under her door, the soft notes of clarinet playing on a stereo?

And then, she remembers more of the room, remembers waking in the night in her child's bed, balancing on the balls of her feet to the door, peering down the carpeted hall. The smell of stale pipe smoke coming from the living room, the soft umber light of the lamp, and she can't see from her stance in the hall but she knows her mother is sitting there, listening to the ruby clarinet notes from the stereo, not reading, just sitting and watching the lights out the window, the lights down below. A glass, with an inch of amber liquid, in her hand.

This isn't a new memory for Blue; it's part of the same first memory— *snow day*—and she doesn't try to write it down, knowing that in the pitch dark of the blackout she'd just scribble back over her own words. Instead, she lies like that, waiting, and soon, the shapes of her room, of this strange room, make themselves known: the hulk of the dresser, the closet door partway closed, the laundry basket holding her scant soiled clothes.

Lying in the night like that, Blue doesn't want to wake, doesn't want to sit up, can feel the ticking in her chest: *alone, alone, alone,* and this she knows she knows from long ago, this feeling of cold squirreled deep inside her bones. *Little bones,* she thinks, the little bones of the hand and feet: *scaphoid, lunate, navicular, cuboid, talus.* How does she know these names? But even as she wonders, she knows without a doubt they're right. She doesn't remember but sees like a vision a little girl lying in a bed, just the way she's lying now, but under a spreading pink sky, the sky a dome like the glass ball's dome, and under the dome just one little girl, lying in her bed alone.

⌒

After Blue tells Reichman about the new memory, or the expansion of the first memory, Reichman brings to their next session a tape of clarinet music, *Mozart's Clarinet Quintet.* Maybe if he hits it right, she'll hear a piece of music that had been familiar to her when she was a child, when she was girl, and maybe the music will open up a pathway that's been blockaded until now.

Blue takes the tape with her usual lack of affect, saying, "Thanks," slipping it into her coat pocket, and Reichman's hurt by this, wants to tell her the trouble he went to for that tape, how, during his last trip to Boston, he'd detoured from dropping off some boxes at the JCC and stopped in at the big classical music store, where he clacked through the rows of CDs until he found what he thought were the most likely candidates for Blue. Once home, his father settled in the guest room, Reichman had asked his father to make a recording of the CDs onto cassettes, thinking this would give his father something to do, something instead of dozing, reading, or staring out the window at the sky as he'd taken to since moving in. And his father had made the tapes, neatly and perfectly labeled, as if nothing was wrong, as if he were fine. Now, Blue's lack of interest is like stone in his shoe, and he finds it hard to concentrate when she does finally start to speak.

For her part, Blue's got other matters on her mind today, a brittle exchange at the diner, something superficially complicated but in Reichman's analysis, simple. It seems Tiffany was jealous of the attention Blue was getting, and Blue mishandled the situation. The problem, Reichman thinks but doesn't say, is that Blue, somewhere back there, received an education that was so good her mind is trained to skip ahead, to wonder, to analyze, and Tiffany's mind is stuck in the track of accepting what's handed to her, never questioning or arguing an idea. To Reichman, Tiffany sounds like many of the women he's met in Intervale, frustrated with their predictable lives, doing what they're told and then hating the world for not demanding more of them.

Reichman doesn't get bored easily, but he finds his mind drifting away from Blue's long story, and catches himself wondering if his father's okay, this first week in Reichman's home. He checks the clock: fifteen minutes left to go. Maybe Blue needs this break, needs a session in which she doesn't focus on her nascent memory. He won't push her on it, not today: today, he'll advise, assure, support.

By now, it's late afternoon; they've calibrated their schedule to Blue's work times, and when they meet in his office on Elm Street their session spans the cusp of afternoon to early dusk. At ten minutes before the hour is up, Reichman switches on the lamp, thinking this gesture is too symbolic, thinking he has to remember to turn on the lamp at three, before his later patients arrive. And then, "I might have remembered something else," Blue says. Reichman tries to conceal his interest in this, tries to maintain the placid, slightly bored look on his face. "Oh?" he says.

"Well, I don't know if it's remembering, really," Blue says, feeling that whisper inside her head saying *back off*, saying, *not so fast*.

"It was more like a feeling," she says, but she doesn't want to say more, doesn't want to tell Reichman about the pickup truck following her home. What would she say, anyway? That there's something there, something she remembers. She doesn't want to tell Dr. Reichman the pickup truck reminds her of *tenderness*, reminds her of *love*.

"What was the feeling?" Reichman asks in his quietest voice.

"Well, it was like. . . ." Blue looks out the window, as if the answer will be there, floating by with the dark clouds promising snow. "It was like I cared about someone, and I wondered if maybe someone cared about me."

"Do you mean now, or in the past?"

Blue's lips are pressed together, tight. She nods, yes, meaning both. Before: *didn't someone care for me?* And there, in Reichman's little lamp-lit office, sudden and insistent, comes a memory, she's handing a plate to someone, someone she can't quite see, or she's looking the other way, handing the plate without looking, so sure she is that the person on the other end will take the plate from her hand, will touch her fingertips resting along the plate's green rim.

Blue's closed her eyes, put her fingers to her head. "What's going on?" Reichman asks, but the sadness welling up in her is too great, and Blue just shakes her head, no. "I've got to go," she says, and gathers her scarf and gloves and coat, the tape pocketed in there like a secret, in its flat smooth box.

~

It's just evening when on Thursday Blue leaves the restaurant, calls goodbye over her shoulder, trying to lift her voice into the high, casual tones the other waitresses use. When she came to work this morning the sky was just the same as it is now, but seen at the opposite cusp, at dawn; now, at dusk, the clouds are washed rose and blue and crouch low to the horizon, the mid-winter darkness punctuated by a few lights switched on in the houses Blue drives by, where now a mother receives her children from the lumbering yellow school bus. The orange warning lights pulse on, the little red stop sign flips up, and out, and Blue stops, watches the children disembark, then moves on.

Main Street's become a river of light, car lights coursing through the town, not at all the Main Street she's seen on her way to the breakfast shift, when the storefronts are blank windows laid flat against the morning, even the traffic lights switched off for the night, just a single orangey-yellow blinking in the dark.

Now, as she comes down the hill, her little car spluttering with effort, she sees the street is jammed with cars, with people and with lights, and she feels as if now she's part of something she's wanted her whole life to step into, as if now she's part of something exciting, something real.

Once she parks, and starts walking up the block, Blue smells *holiday* in the air; there's a bustle in the crowd particular to December nights, palpable, red anxiety and green excitement charging the air like electricity, the shop windows decorated with snaky swaths of fake evergreen and lengthy streams of small white lights.

Across the street and down, Rita walks in the cold dusk from her building down to Hansen's Variety, happy just because of the excitement in the air. The bell over the door of the variety store chimes as Rita comes in, stomping the snow from her boots, looking around, making a quick assessment. What's she here for, anyway? She's unsure. Something Christmassy. She's already got her tree, having brought it home in her pickup truck from the supermarket parking lot where the 4-H sets up each year. She dragged it from the truck into her building, its pointy tip cutting a swath through the snow, trailing snow and pine needles up the stairs and into her apartment. It was too tall; but what else is new? She's always chosen wrong, the wrong tree this time, and she had to borrow a saw from Mr. Lurie at the hardware store down the block and labor at cutting through the bone.

But now, the tree is up, standing straight and tall, its branches spreading out below, right in the window. The night after she got it home, Rita told Bart to come over, and together they drank eggnog doused with rum, looped the lights around the branches of the tree, then hung the ornaments, the few glass balls that survived Rita's childhood moves, and the new ornaments she's collected, glistening on the tree red and green and gold.

Now, she wants something more. She selects some gift wrap, and for Mert, whose name she got in the Secret Santa grab bag, a windup Santa holding an accordion that plays "The Beer Barrel Polka." She looks around for something nice for Bart, to cheer him up. A Make-Your-Own wreath kit, complete with evergreen, ribbon, and bells. They can put it together on Christmas Eve. But there's something more she wants, for her own place, something *Christmassy* is all she can think, and so she walks out among the things of Hansen's Variety, the rolls of tape and the squares of felt shingled in all their colors. The skeins of nylon yarn, the tinsel lying in the tinsel trays like pretty rope, or silver hair.

Rita doesn't see what she wants—whatever it is, it isn't here—and chats with Becky at the register, about Christmas plans and what a busy time of year it is. She pretends to be happy—after all, it's Christmas!—but even as Becky's handing her the change and her receipt, she's scanning around, looking for something. Something else. Something more. The bell at the door chimes, the door clicks open, and Rita looks up, and there she is: Blue.

She feels like there's something she should say, as if she's running into an old friend; she's known the mystery woman so long, now, lived with her newspaper photo clipped to her fridge, thought about her, followed her. But she's scared, too: what if Blue saw her tailing her from the diner that night, following her home? What if she thinks she's following her now?

Her sister, her twin, she's sure of it now. Look at that face: the eyebrows too heavy—Rita's would be, too, if she weren't careful to pluck them every few weeks—and those narrow cheeks, the dark hair falling into her eyes. So what if they weren't identical twins? Rita knows that the other kind, *fraternal* they're called, are much more common anyway. And if Rita styled herself differently, didn't so carefully make up her face, she'd look more like Blue, look more like her twin. She would. Wouldn't she?

Rita smiles at Blue, but Blue, on her mission, doesn't see, just walks on into the store. Rita turns back to Becky, prepared for Becky to say, "Gee, are you two related?" but Becky's gone back to reading her magazine, and Rita's left there, alone, holding her purchases in the plastic bag with the holly design, the rolls of gift wrap awkward under her arm.

Becky's so distracted that Rita sees she can slip away, but just in case, to cover herself, she snaps her fingers, says under her breath, "Darn, I knew I'd forget something," and heads back down the aisles of goods, just a few steps behind Blue.

Rita's not too concerned with her cover; she knows Becky isn't paying attention, and besides, who cares? But she doesn't want to arouse Blue's suspicions, and so she hangs back, dawdling, fingering the hair barrettes in their neat plastic-wrapped stacks.

There she is, up ahead, running her fingertips across the felt squares. Is she touching them the same way that Rita does? Rita thinks so. Yes. There's something in the way she passes her whole palm over the square that's similar to Rita's own hand motion when she's looking at something, letting her mind wander, when she's in that dreamy state of wanting something, but unsure what it is.

Rita hangs back, and Blue doesn't see her, but Rita's watching, watching as Blue makes her way to the stationery, then passes and stops at the tape players and radios.

Blue knows what she wants; she's just been waiting for enough pay to ensure she's got the rent covered, but even so she wants to wander, wants to see all the goods for sale, to touch them. She walks up and down the aisles, running her fingers over the packages of colored yarn, the poster paints and clean metal bowls, the tinsel lying smooth and shiny as fish scales in the plastic windowed packages. When she finds the radios and tape players, her choice is easy; she'd like the cheapest, please.

As she carries the box back to the register, she looks down the stationery aisle, sees Rita with her bagged goods and her bulky gift wrap, turned now as if engrossed in examining the paper clips and pens, and Blue feels a flutter of recognition, thinks suddenly of the night on the bridge, *the night I was born,* feels the rain and cold, wants to say, "Do I know you?" then shakes her head, and takes her purchase to the register.

At the register, Becky punches in the price, then says, "Is this a gift?" and Blue is momentarily confused: what kind of question is this? But then she thinks, *remembers,* they always ask this at Christmastime. She starts to shake her head, no, then says the first thing she thinks: "Yes, it's for my brother." *Liar.* But she can't help it; she's mesmerized by the girl's name tag, spelling out "Becky" in plastic letter-gun letters, with a tin and cloth corsage of red poinsettia jiggling just above the curve of the girl's left breast. *Too high to be resting over her heart,* Blue thinks. *How do I know that?* and then she's caught in a feeling of memory, a feeling with no images, just the question: *how do I know,* and the words: *systole, diastole, systole, diastole* spinning in her like soapsuds going down a bath drain, until she realizes she's just standing there, dumb, staring at the girl's nametag.

"Sorry," she stumbles, righting herself quickly. "That's such a pretty pin you've got," she lies.

Becky self-consciously touches the cloth and tin with her fingertips, as if to remind herself of how it looks, then smiles. "Thanks. I don't really like it, you know, but they make us wear them. Do you want me to wrap this?"

Blue, pleased with her quick recovery, says, "No, that's okay," and emboldened by her discovery that she can lie so well, adds, "I've got plenty of gift wrap at home," and she pays, and leaves the store with the package in her arms, pressing it to her chest like it's a baby or a small animal that's in distress, and she can feel nestled deep in the pocket of her jacket the tape that Dr. Reichman gave her, resting there like a passport, or an emergency dime.

Rita waits until Blue's made her exit, then languidly comes back to the register. She's seen and heard the whole exchange, the tape player purchase, the gift wrap offer. It can't be true that Blue has a brother somewhere, can it? Then who is the tape player for? Does Blue have a friend? Rita tosses a handful of ribbon onto the counter. "This too, I guess," she says. She's so mad and hurt now, hurt that Blue has some *other* friend, that she doesn't even notice that Becky doesn't mention the resemblance, doesn't even wish that she would. She just takes her change and leaves, no longer in search of something Christmassy, no longer in search of anything.

⌒

Blue carries the package up the steps carefully, as if it's precious. Maybe this will be it, maybe Dr. Reichman has found the music that will crack open her memory, bring her home. Inside, she switches on the light, strips off her gloves, acknowledges the pup with a rub to his head and a shoo outside, but she can't wait anymore than that, and still in her down vest and boots she tears open the cardboard box, pulls the player from its plastic sleeve, then from her pocket takes out the tape: *Mozart's Clarinet Quintet* is written on the tape in scrawly letters. When Dr. Reichman told her to play it at home, he wasn't thinking that she of course had no means for playing it. Now she does, and dutiful, hopeful, Blue slips the tape in the slot, presses the button marked "PLAY" and lies on her back on the rug. Through the window, she can see the tops of the bare trees, and the sky lit orange by the streetlamp.

What comes out is clarinet, pure ruby notes slipping up and down the scales, slow as water dropping on a roof, then fast, then slow again. Blue closes her eyes, waiting. *This has to be it!* but although she feels the music pulsing in her, although she feels it in her so clearly that she slips her hand beneath her left breast to feel the kick of her heart against her chest as it rises, then drops, rises, then drops, she remembers nothing.

Blue, who are you? she thinks, and the lost woman, lanky, straight hair falling to her forehead, face too angular and strong to be called pretty, eyes the color of the watchet autumn sky, long fingers pressed against her ribs as if reading Braille for her own, true name, lying on her back on the battered rug patterned white and blue and rose and green, in some apartment in some city at this particular crossbow of longitude and latitude, nameless, past-less, closes her eyes, and without a sound, finally she cries.

If the notes of the clarinet could call her back, if the music could dredge memory's deep waters and cull something, some scrap, Blue would remember this record spinning, flat and black and perfectly grooved clarinet notes tumbling from the old stereo speaker in its wood box.

The dark pulls down quietly, and with the dark comes snow, as if the dark is a shade pulling the snow down behind it, and Blue watches without turning on the lights, and she thinks, *snow feels like an anagram for home.*

In her bed that night, she dreams a memory, dreams a beach house, settled into the sandy path, and she likes the hot sun and the feel of the cool hard sand under her feet down by the water's edge. She likes packing up everything for the summer, carefully putting her favorite books and games and her stuffed rabbit into the cardboard cartons. She likes the excitement of piling it all into the car borrowed from Grammie Martha, of riding in the backseat with the window down, Random, her English spaniel on the opposite side of the back seat, each of them looking out their respective windows, feeling the air go cooler and saltier as they exit the city and near the beach.

She likes their arrival, her father fumbling the key into the lock, her mother saying, "Ezra, come on, what's the matter with you?" She likes the musty smell inside the house, how dark it is, the windows still boarded up from last year, her father switching on the lights. They set about cleaning, her mother pouring ammonia into a bucket, mopping the floors, the smell is so strong and bitter that she's afraid she won't be able to breathe.

One summer, she walked into her dark bedroom and stepped on something, something soft, and she thought at first it was an old swimming suit she'd left the year before, and reached to pick it up, then screamed when she felt the fur. Her mother came in with the flashlight, shined it onto the animal, a grizzled thing, a muskrat, its scaly tail sticking straight out in one sure line, and her mother screamed, too, then laughed out loud.

The first night at the beach house, her room is dark, and it's funny to have the room so dark and hear such a big silence, only the relentless heave and suck of the tides.

Here's their first party of the summer, and everyone's loosened up from the day in the sun, the day broken only by a break for lunch in the cool of the porch, sardines and sliced tomatoes and for the grown-ups, vodka tonics. The first weekend at the beach, and by nine at night the grown-ups have tired of their talk of art and politics, and they need a distraction, and somebody says, "Let's go for a swim." They traipse down the beach, the women in their dresses, men in their khaki pants, everyone shucking shoes and belts as they go, toward the water that lies out there like a reversed night sky, moving in its slow night waves.

And here's the girl, coming into the living room, forgotten, unsure what to do. Is the party over? The clarinet music is still playing on the stereo, the music that makes her think of birds in the woods. The grown-ups have left the candles in their storm cups lit, and one tall tiered lamp is on, and when the record player's arm clicks up and back, she can hear the laughter and the calls from out on the beach. If anyone were to turn from the laughing group of adults on the beach and look back at the little house, he would see the glassed-in front room, see through to the living room like a set on a stage, the clutter of plates with their chunks of cheese, crackers strewn out on a cutting board, glasses standing empty, or partially filled, ashtrays littered with cigarette ends: the evidence of life, the girl thinks, remembering a line from the museum she visited with her class. Anyone watching would see her in the celery-green Chinese summer pajamas her Grammie Martha gave her on Memorial Day, with their elaborate cloth buttons and a big chicken embroidered on one side of the chest. Anyone watching would see her stand for a moment at the windowed wall, looking out toward the beach, toward the black sea, and then he'd see her start to move around the room, picking up dishes in a big stack, blowing out candles in their round glass cups.

In her kitchen on Christmas Eve, Rita pours herself an eggnog and adds a shot of rum, then takes the wreath-making kit out of the box. After all, it's Christmastime, she thinks, and puts the radio on, tunes in to the WKID Christmas special. Stupid Bart with his job in the sound room at WKID, agreeing to work Christmas Eve, after she got this wreath, thinking this would be something fun for the two of them to do together.

She's found something Christmassy, this wreath-making kit, and she's found more than that, more than she'd hoped for: she found Blue, there at Hansen's, opening the door. If Bart won't come over to help with the wreath, she can give it to Blue, leave it at her apartment door. Perfect, she thinks, playing again the scene at Hansen's in her head, remembering Blue coming into the store, and each time she remembers she forgets a little more the bruise of hurt at the way Blue seemed to look right through her, or at hearing Blue say she had a brother. *Liar.* As Rita remembers and drinks her eggnog, the scene slips and shifts into a scene from long ago, an apartment she and her mother had on Elm Court when Rita was eight, the left half of a duplex, "a whole house to ourselves," Rita's mother had said.

On Christmas Eve, her mother not home yet, Rita tidied up the apartment, the *house,* got out the cleanser and scrubbed out the sink. There's the tree in the living room, standing straight and tall, branches still bare. "We'll decorate it tonight," her mother had said and so Rita finds the box of things, *"ornaments"* she's learned to say, except she says *"orma mints,"* making her mother's new boyfriend, Ed, laugh and swipe at her head with his big meaty paw.

Ornaments, ornaments, she says to herself, over and over again, while she waits, sitting on the sofa, watching *Christmas in Vienna* on TV, the box of glass balls and trim on her lap. She doesn't dress the tree; she knows her mother would be mad if she started without her. Is Ed coming tonight, too? Rita feels a burning in her chest, and if anyone asked, she'd say she wants him to come, she'd say that she likes him, but really, she'd know this wasn't true; she'd know this was a lie.

The living room's nearly empty except for the tree, the TV and the sofa, and Rita falls asleep like that, on the sofa in her red dress and green tights, with the box of decorations on her lap, the piney smell filling the room, as if she's asleep in the woods, as if she's been given up in the snow for dead.

She wakes, and here's her mother coming in, laughing with Ed, Ed's big horsey laugh following her in. Rita shakes herself awake, and her mother says, "Sweetie, I didn't know it was so late." She turns to Ed, "Will you pour us a drink, Ed? Let's trim the tree." Rita's so sleepy as she stands she can barely keep her eyes open, and it doesn't seem real; it seems like a dream.

Her mother turns off the TV, puts a Christmas record on the stereo, and while they hang the decorations, her mother hums along. But then there's a sad song, and her mother turns away, leans on the wall, rests her face in her hands. Ed puts his hand to her shoulder, saying, "Colleen, what is it? What's wrong?" and she shakes her head, saying low, "It's just at Christmas that I always think of *her,* and what a terrible thing I did," and Rita turns away, tries to make herself invisible so she can hear.

"What did you do? Baby, you couldn't do anything wrong," Ed says, then starts kissing her neck, and Rita knows this is her cue, her time to go, and she quietly exits the room, goes to the bathroom, brushes her teeth, and by the time she crosses the hallway to her bedroom, she can see the tree, lit, the living room dark and empty now.

Now, in her own tidy apartment, Rita thinks maybe it's the piney smell that pushes that scene into her head, or maybe it's the same feeling of sitting alone in the living room, Christmas Eve, drinking an eggnog and trying to make something pretty and good with her hands. For a moment, she puts the wreath things down, and picks up the Christmas gift Bart gave her, admonishing her, "Don't open it without me, just keep it so you'll have something under your tree."

She can tell just by looking at it what it is: a new learn-a-new-word-a-day calendar, but still, she holds it for a minute in her hand, then puts it back under the tree.

Is it just that she's stupid, or is it that the directions for making the wreath aren't that great? On her living room floor, Rita jams the twigs into the metal posts. Soon, the thing looks like a mess, all tangled and buckled, too much green bunched to one side, the other side bare.

So much for her attempt at Christmas creativity, Rita thinks. She'll have to do something else; she can't give this thing to anyone, especially not to Blue. Hell, she can't even hang it on her door, and she went and paid $14.99 for it, for this, for what? For nothing. For a big pain in the neck.

But while she cleans up the mess, pushes the wreath into the trash, she thinks about how she wanted to give it to Blue. She thinks Blue needs a Christmas gift more than anyone, and she pulls on her jacket and boots and goes out into the cold, out to the parking lot, starts up her truck.

Even this late on Christmas Eve the 4-H lot is busy, the lights swinging in the cold wind, fathers clapping their hands together impatiently, kids dawdling, saying in their mock-adult tones, "maybe this one," or squealing, "here, here, here!" Rita takes her time, too: this time, she'd better get it right. Round and full and tied with a bright red ribbon, no, a plaid ribbon, that's more cheerful, Rita thinks. She pays, less than she paid for the kit, because this is after all Christmas Eve and all the prices at the lot have dropped, have *plummeted*. Why doesn't she ever wait until the night before Christmas to pick up her tree?

Rita drives across the excited town, crosses back over to Main, and heads down River Road, turns, and turns again. Here it is, the yellow peeling row house. It looks awful, she thinks again. Rundown. Like a *tenement*.

The lights in Blue's apartment are all out, and Rita then remembers the diner's open late tonight, and who better to take the shift than Blue, and she trudges up the stairs, quietly, on her tippy toes, careful not to make a sound, just in case. At the top of the stairs, she fumbles, realizes she hasn't brought anything to hang the wreath with, she's got nothing in her hands, but on the door there's an old nail sticking out, probably used for just this purpose in years before, and Rita hangs the wreath there, for a moment presses her fingertips to its spiky green, and just as quietly as she came, she leaves.

The policy at the Intervale Hospital is to allow the patients to keep whatever mementos they want in their room, provided the items can't be used for cutting, bullying, or suicide. No jewelry, no cash, nothing sharp and dangerous.

In Annie Blaze's room, she's got a bed, walls painted yellow, a night table and a dresser. On the dresser, she's laid out her things: her stuffed toy cat and the photo from the magazine of her friends at the beach. Someone, some aide with a sweet disposition who remembers being a girl, has washed out the toy cat in the sink, and now its white fur stands out in somewhat clean tufts. It looks a little startled. Every morning Annie goes to the photo and to Kitty and touches them, as if at an altar, as if saying her prayers.

In late December the Christmas decorations come in, igniting once again the annual debate over whether it's more depressing or less to have the halls festooned with happy cardboard Santa faces and swaths of plastic red and green. And there's the annual problem of visiting families and requests for leaves, and for Reichman, the complaints from staff about the holiday schedule, the arguments and injuries over who has to work Christmas, and who pulls Christmas Eve.

He goes some distance toward solving this by coming in himself throughout the Christmas week, making a quick foray back home just in time for the meal his father has made at Reichman's direction. On the kitchen counter, every morning Reichman leaves a note, which at the top gives the day and the date. At Hansen's Variety, he bought a big battery-powered clock with hands, and he sets the feet of the clock on top of the note, anchoring it, as if this will also anchor his father to time and place.

The note instructs his father what to do with his day, and what and when to eat:

12 NOON: lunch, make turkey sandwich.

1 P.M.: nap

2 P.M.: Antiques Roadshow on.

3 P.M.: snack: applesauce and half a bagel.

After snack, *daven Mincha.*

5 P.M.: put casserole in oven, turn oven on to 350 degrees.

6 P.M.: Bobby comes home.

All of Christmas week, he leaves home again right after supper, and must amend the note, and this disruption, he knows, rattles his father. "Where are you going?" his father asks, as Reichman puts on his coat, picks up his keys. "I'm going back to the hospital, Dad, back to work. All this week I have to go in each evening," he says, again, and his father nods. "Oh, yeah, that's right, Bobby," and he waves his hand as he shuffles back toward the easy chair, switches on the TV with the remote.

On New Year's Eve Intervale is lit up bright, the restaurants and bars festooned with lights and "HAPPY NEW YEAR" signs. The big theater's marquee is glowing white, announcing the annual holiday production, which this year is *Man of La Mancha.* At the hospital, the skeleton staff is glad to see Reichman show up, glad he's good as his word, and he knows that by coming in on holidays, he's going a long way toward keeping the peace, and it's worth it. Besides, what else would he do tonight?

The ward is nearly full, with some patients having special New Year's Eve visitors, a treat Reichman has approved for many of them, and others holing up in their single rooms, pressing the pillow over their heads, crying into the balledup sheet in the fist. Reichman's always faced with the problem of families at this time of year, families wanting special visits or adamantly refusing to visit the patient.

Annie Blaise is the exception here. The hospital hasn't yet turned up any information about where she's from or where she might belong, and she doesn't seem to care. The search for fingerprints has yielded nothing in Maine, and now the search is extending into the rest of New England. Apparently, she's been a wandering lost soul for so long, no one's coming forth to claim her, and even now, after the medication is starting to work, there's nowhere she seems to want to go but back to her encampment at the riverbank.

He raps with his knuckles on her door. "Annie?" he says, striving as always for a tone of confidence he doesn't feel with the more psychotic patients. As he expected, there's no answer, and he goes in anyway, sees her sitting on her bed, legs crossed, making pictures with the crayons and papers she's been allowed.

"Hi, Annie, I just came by to see how you're doing," he says, and she still doesn't look up, but says, "It's about time someone dropped by, because I started to think dropping by was just another pie in the sky."

"Mind if I sit down?" he asks, and she shrugs, and he sits. He knows she won't look up at him, knows how unlikely this is.

She keeps coloring on the pad, with her burned left hand, even though the fingers are still bandaged and crimped, and Reichman peers down: yellow and orange and red, like flames. She's painstaking in her work, making tiny marks on the page, all the color scrunched down in the left-hand corner, the rest of the page big and open and blank. Somewhere she learned there wasn't much room for her, he thinks. Someone told her she wasn't worth much.

"What are you drawing?" he asks, and then waits, and she says, very softly, "I'm drawing the fire. The fire of my heart's desire."

Even though her words slur around her cleft lip, he understands her. "Where was the fire?" he asks, and she doesn't speak. Eventually, he gives up, says a few reassuring things, and leaves, sighing as he exits the room, wondering which drug to try next, wondering which combinations of agents will worm their way up into her brain, so that at least she can communicate. As long as she's talking this way about the fires, he's justified in keeping her here, he thinks as he heads down the hall.

The fires were the fire of my heart's desire, and down in the riverbank I had what I needed, had everything my greed saved for me. My heart's desire the woman in the night lying to me telling me everything would be all right, but it wasn't all right, no, it was all wrong. Wrong, wrong, the wrong song of sixpence.

They want to know where I came from, where I belong, but they can't see
I'm just a wanderer, I'm the traveling Annie, Annie Traveler, that's me, home to
home and room to roam. Don't they know how I was just thirteen when the
travel bug bit down hard on my lip, and before I knew it, I was in shit? The
money changing hands over my head and between my legs.

Now, I can run my hand down into my pants and still feel the scar there
risen like bread, scar of my desire, scar of my fire's deep heart's desire. I can feel
the tip of my lip where it bends into my mouth, the cleft in the palate like the
cleft in the rock where Moses hid. Don't look at my face, God shouted.

Where'd that doctor go to now? I bet he wants some, I bet he'd like a little
taste. I'd give it to him, too, if only he'd let me out for a time, a minute or a
mile, and I'd be down by the river, then out on the road. Where's my rabbit I
left behind? How will she survive in the cold?

New Year's Eve, and the staff doesn't grumble; most are glad for an
excuse to leave their family obligations early or to come home late, and
besides, working New Year's and Christmas you get a bonus; plus, there's a
party atmosphere on the ward, even if only among the staff, and at the nurses'
station they talk about matters other than what's happening on the ward, and
pass around the snack plates they've brought in. Reichman reaches for a pig-
in-blanket, then pulls back, unsure, really, why, but thinking of his father. At
midnight, they have a toast of eggnog, and down the hall, Annie Blaze runs a
finger along the photograph she keeps, mutters to herself, then sleeps.

~

Since she began following Blue, Rita's let her hair grow out, and it's growing straight and thin and not fluffy and curly the way she remembered it
when she was younger, "like a hundred years ago," she says to Bart when he
comments on it.

"I have a picture of me with it longer, and it was completely different;
you wouldn't recognize me," she says to him at their regular booth at
Bodeo's one Sunday afternoon in early January. The Christmas decorations
are still up, but are looking worn, the Y in MERRY starting to fall, the
sparkling glitter showering down from the sign every time a tall man walks
underneath.

"Oh don't be silly. It looks fine. But why are you letting it grow?" he
asks. "Let's see, who would you be trying to please with that. . . ."

"Exactly no one," Rita snaps. Bodeo's in the daytime has a wholly different feel than Bodeo's at night, everything showing up more in the pale light from the plate windows, the carpet, once a handsome red and black pattern that looked like Christmas decorations, now muddied and stained to a murky darkness; the tables at the booths polished and washed of their sticky rings and spills. The smell of stale beer and cigarettes hangs heavier in the air on a Sunday afternoon.

From where she sits, Rita can see the street, Lower Main, through the letters spelled out in neon: B-O-D-E-O-S, the O and S smaller and cramped to fit, and she can see the snow just beginning to drift down from the sky gone white with clouds. She drinks her coffee, and dimly hears Bart talking, going on about his own hair, or the increasing lack of it, and yet she's drifting too, thinking of Blue, wondering what she's doing now. She imagines Blue looking up at the snowy sky, imagines her wondering too if she's got a sister somewhere, a twin, maybe even somewhere near.

"Hey, let's go up to the diner," Rita says, suddenly, suddenly realizing that if she goes with Bart, it won't look so suspicious, and Bart, mid-sentence, is caught off guard, but he doesn't say, "Hey, I was just starting to tell you about the commercial I saw for E-Z hair." Instead, he says, "Huh? Why do you want to go there?"

She's got to scramble, and conveniently, the truth fits in. "I'm starved. I haven't been to the IGA in weeks."

"Well, maybe that's where we should go," Bart says, always practical, like a mother.

Rita makes a face at him, twisting her lips into a sneer and bobbing her head. "Look, I've already got a mother," she says, even though both she and Bart know this isn't true; and even before her mother died, this wouldn't have been a convincing argument. In her head, Rita sees Bart dressed as a mother, a mother from a 1950s sitcom on Nick at Night, like what's her name, like Donna Reed, in an apron and a wig.

"Come on, Bart, wouldn't it beat sitting around in this dive? I mean, look at us: we're pathetic."

"Okay, whatever you want, Princess. But we're taking my car, unless you've surprised me by getting that exhaust fixed on your truck."

"Oh, get off my case," Rita says, more gently now that she knows she's won, now that Bart is pulling on his jacket, carefully winding his striped scarf around his neck.

The diner's nearly empty when they come in; Rita knows she's got to pretend, she can't let on to Bart what this is really about. Or, certainly, to Blue. At first, Rita looks around the diner thinking she's made a mistake; what if Blue isn't working today? But then, the kitchen doors swing open, and here she comes, carrying a tray with steaming plates, her face seeming to steam up too in the exhaust that rises from the hot food.

"Table for two?" Eleanor asks, and Bart and Rita nod, follow her in. She hands them menus, oversized laminated things, and hidden behind her menu Rita tries to look as if she's scanning the list of drinks and foods while looking for Blue from the corner of her eye. She knows what she wants, anyway; it isn't as if she's never come in here on a Sunday before.

"What do you want?" she asks Bart, hoping he won't notice how her voice shakes.

"I don't know. Do you think the chicken salad is any good?"

"Bart, this is the Intervale Diner, not the Ritz. Sure, it's okay. They probably whipped up a fresh batch just last month."

Bart wrinkles his nose, squints up his mouth in distaste. "I think I'll just have a regular salad," he says.

"Dieting again?" Rita knows what the answer is; it's always yes, except for those times when Bart sinks down into his depressive hole and eats Little Debbie cupcakes from the box for days on end until Rita shows up, bangs on his door, and drags him out again.

And then, here she is, standing by their table, pad in one hand, in the other her pen, at the ready, saying, "Do you know what you want?" in a flat monotone, as if she's never wanted anything, herself, as if she really doesn't care.

Rita speaks first, quickly, nervous, afraid to look at Blue while she gives her order: the Hungry Jack special, with the eggs over hard, and sausage, not ham. And then, as Bart orders, she watches his face, looking for any trace of evidence that he's recognized Blue. Recognized her own face there.

After Blue leaves, Rita can't wait, and leans across the Formica table to Bart, conspiratorial, whispering, "I think that's her."

"Who?" Bart asks, looking down at his nails.

"That waitress. That's the amnesia woman from the paper. You know."

"Oh, you think so?" At this, Bart looks up, scanning the room.

"Bart," Rita whispers, a little too loudly. "Don't stare, for God's sake. Just wait 'til she comes back with our order, then look."

"Okay, okay," Bart says, whispering now, too, but rolling his eyes.

Blue comes back with the food, "Hungry Jack Special," she intones as she's been trained, and Rita puts her hand up, palm out, says, "Here," as if she's a girl in grade school, and watches Blue's hand as she slides the heavy plate down onto the table. Is this hand like her own? Long fingers that tip out at the ends, but her nails aren't painted, they're just plain, and short, making the hands somehow look not as stubby as Rita's hands do.

After she leaves, "Well?" Rita says, cutting into her pancakes.

"Yeah, I guess that is her," Bart shrugs, drizzling the dressing over his lettuce. "I don't know how you could tell that from that newspaper picture."

It's clear as anything, at least it is to her, but then, she had the advantage of seeing her first, in person, that night on the bridge. And maybe she has the advantage, too, of genetics: what moron wouldn't recognize her own twin?

Besides, Bart's just about the least observant person you could find in all of Maine, except when it comes to himself, and that's why he didn't notice the resemblance, that's why he didn't say anything. Rita sighs then, and with one finger nudges her plate toward him across the table, and he smiles at her, pushes the skimpy pale salad away, and takes a big forkful of sausage and egg.

~

Blue slides the dirty plates off her tray and onto the shiny steel counter. *There,* she thinks. *That'll show them,* as if she's stamping her foot. She knows this is some kind of memory, knows she should stop at this feeling and make some kind of note, but Eddie is tapping the counter bell, calling out "order up" and then she's just mad, mad at Dr. Reichman for not understanding that she can't just give up what she's doing every time some glint from something called *the past* passes through.

He acts as if the past is better than the present. What's wrong with this, with what she has now, with who she is? Nothing. Blue imagines slamming her fist on the doctor's big desk. *There's nothing wrong with this,* she'd say.

Except for the loneliness, she hears in her head, but she turns away, picks up the plates from the counter, two identical steaming slabs of corned beef, each with a scoop of sauerkraut, tangled like seaweed out on the beach, and the tang of the sauerkraut steams up to her, and she sees the messy ribbons of green lying on the firm, wet sand. What is the past, anyway? It's just some place, some place like this, a collection of people, a job, a home.

She looks around, but the woman she's seen lately, staring at her in Hansen's Variety, driving around in her pickup truck, following her as if she's some kind of freak on display, that woman and the man she was with have gone. Good. *Good riddance to you,* she thinks.

As she slides the plates onto the table and the customers, a fat mother and fatter daughter inhale their "ohs," Blue thinks, what's wrong with Dr. Reichman? Isn't it his fault she still hasn't remembered much? Isn't he to blame that she still can't say where it is she's from, or form her own, old name, whatever it was?

⁓

I wanted to tell the doctor about the tent, but not the rabbit or the bridge woman yet.

After the tent where did you stay, Doctor Right Man asks this time. This time he's got a green tie around his neck. I smile, I'm so happy he says the tent because to say the tent you have to see the tent because seeing is believing. He must believe the tent and maybe he even saw it somewhere and maybe he'll give it back to me if he has it, if he can, if I'm good.

I'm so happy he said the tent that I let myself look up and out the window, and there's the snow icing down like the white stitches on the tent's rim.

Annie, he says. He says that because that's the name I gave when I came in. Now it isn't Annie, but he can use Annie even though I want to say, could you please use Sugar now instead, but he can use Annie if he wants because he saw the tent.

Annie, he says. After the tent where did you live?

On the beach, I say. If I turned my back the other way, I couldn't hardly hear the trucks and cars out on Route 1. There were white birds and the smell of the ocean and a lot of wind there, on the beach, whispering in the grasses.

Why did you light the fires? Now, he's skipping ahead, he is, the fires weren't lit on the beach, not at the ocean, not at the sea. He must know the fires because he knows the tent, and what else does he know, the secret of the baby bones, the baby that was grown and died in me? Does he know the red beads in the chain I made across the rabbit's skin? Does he know how I lived and what I did? I'm hoping he doesn't know, and hoping he does, that much is true.

Why the fires, Annie, he says.

To get food, I say.

I know this isn't quite the right thing, but in its way it's true. I was cold, that's it, and the cold went along with wanting food, and I knew it must be time to go inside and leave the tent and leave the cat and rabbit and the beach, but who could do that? Not little Annie, no, not me.

I carried my tent to the rivery beach and set it up in the mist, under the bridge, the Bridge of Styx, out among the baby bones. Sometimes I slept with Kitty curled on my feet, and sometimes I did not. But after the bridge woman came and the man with the teased cock, I said it's time to go, so I lit the fires because you know how fire attracts moths, how they fly right into the burn like they know where they're going and want to get there, fast. The sizzle of their mothy wings.

I'm thinking about this when I look up, and there's Doctor Right Man, still there, and I move for the door, and he says you can't go, but I didn't want to go, I just wanted to see if the tent came back, if the rabbit did live, if the beach fires were still glowing orange and the stars in the night sky like I'd always been told.

———

Whenever the doctor tries to dive into her head, Blue feels undefended, vulnerable, like she's the ground and a well is being dug. He acts as if there's a well already there, but there isn't, Blue wants to tell him. There's just the solid frozen ground. Or rock. She can feel the incisions tearing the grass from the rich, dark earth, and then the spade going in. Hitting rock. The ice-rock of her past, the solid unspeaking rock of her heart. The place she thinks her heart would be, if she had a heart.

Mid-January and Intervale begins to thaw; there's a warm flush in the air, and the sky looks a little brighter, as the earth edges out of darkness and inches toward the light. The temperatures rise above the freezing mark, and on Main Street Crow turns off the heat, opens the door to Crystal 'N Sands to let the fresh air in. But the other townspeople laugh to one another, saying, "It's not over yet," and "Don't get too comfortable," knowing that the January thaw is just a tease, and by the month's end there will come another storm, another, deeper freeze.

It's on one such afternoon that Blue tells Dr. Reichman, "Maybe I just appeared one day. Maybe I have no past. Maybe I have no soul," and then the icy block breaks a little, and she feels her throat constrict, her eyes fill.

"Talk to me about it," Dr. Reichman says. "What is the crying about?"

In the weak winter light, the picture on the wall behind his head looks pale. Blue feels as if she's taking off in an airplane, the ground beneath her receding into a long sheaf of green and blue and yellow underneath her feet. Fingertips pressed to the doubled window glass.

"An airplane," she says. "I think I was in an airplane." She's crying now, the tears running down her cheeks, but making no sound, except to ask, "Why does this make me so upset?"

"What is the feeling?" Dr. Reichman asks back.

"Loss," Blue says, running her fingers back through her hair, pulling a tissue out of the box by her chair. "I think I lost something somewhere."

She looks around the office as she cries, scanning the room: the clock saying time is nearly up, the phone where Dr. Reichman gets his calls, the glass ball with snow inside holding his papers down. Even as she's crying, she picks up the ball, as if for comfort, tilts it slowly in her hand.

Goodbye. The feeling of *goodbye.* The paper flowers blooming in water, the water cold and clean. Wine spilling into a glass, a glass like the one with the flowers, with a green rim. Someone laughing. The urgent panic of "let's go." The smell of hot bread in a dry brick oven. The woman's voice: *make for me a snow angel.* The feeling of *goodbye.*

"There's just these little bits. Fragments," Blue says.

Blue cries herself out. If she's got no heart, no soul, then how can she have so much crying to do? Did she cry, *before?* In Reichman's waiting room, she loosely winds her scarf around her neck again, picks up her gloves, descends the stairs down to the street, but out here, in the warm breeze, in the sun, the sadness flushes through her again, and again her eyes fill. What can she do, now that she's lost everything?

It isn't until she's gone home, made her supper, taken the pup out for his walk by the riverbank, that she's sitting in the kitchen, looking through the day's news as told in the *Intervale Gazette,* and she picks up the heavy salt shaker she keeps on the table, thinks it's like the glass ball on Dr. Reichman's desk, and thinks then no, it's like another glass ball with snow inside, a glass ball standing on a little girl's dresser painted white with gold trim and a tiny rosebud centered on the front of each drawer. The ball is a paperweight, even though she doesn't know that's its purpose: she just sees that it's a glass ball with snow inside, and when she shakes it up and down, the snow scatters and swirls around and around, just like the snow outside, out in the courtyard.

There's a feeling here of return. Blue gets up, and the pup looks up from his spot on the braided rug, as if he knows something's up. She comes back with her notebook, and starts to write.

She has to make it up, and all she can do is describe in detail the glass ball, the rosebud on each drawer. And just one other glimpse: the hiss of heat steaming in the pipes, the snow swirling outside the window as she winds the curtain cord around her finger, looking down at the yellow taxis that pass with each switch of the light. The feeling: *waiting. Anxious.* Blue writes it all down, even though she knows as she's writing this won't get her very far. There's still no face she could draw for the police artist, still no name, no address to find. No one to find her, no one she knows.

Rita passes through Intervale on her newspaper rounds, crosses the bridge, crosses back again, drops off at the QwikMart. Today, she doesn't stop to buy a ticket or make a call; today, she's got two extra stops to make, as one of the paperboys called in sick, and later she'll say to Bart, "What a day." Out by the interstate, she swings into the parking lot that curves around the big bare apartment complex, passes the sign that says VERSAILLES, gets out of the truck, and walks building to building, dropping a small bundle of papers, each paper wrapped in its own protective plastic sleeve, by the mail-boxes just inside the door.

The January thaw is passing as the month shudders to a close, and now the snow's coming down wet and tattered, and as Rita steps inside Building 6, the smells of the dingy carpet and the cheap presswood, the smells of someone's bacon from that morning's breakfast, the dim light and the taste of oil sudden in her mouth swallow her into the memory of the winter she lived here, the winter she was twelve. It was in one of these "townhouses," a skinny apartment slapped between two others just like it, but her mother had said that it would be fine because it had a little yard out back. Was it number 11, or number 13? Rita looks around in the slanting wet snow, and now, she can't tell the difference: they all look the same, look just as they did twenty years ago, only worse for the wear.

This place gives her the creeps, she thinks. Thank God it isn't on her usual rounds. She hurries through her drops, all the while feeling that around each corner, something is lurking, watching, waiting for her. What's watching, what's lying in wait? Just her own memory, one that skits behind all the others, the one that rustles away whenever she approaches. If anyone had asked her, if she'd ever told, Rita would have said she hadn't known what she was doing that winter night, a night following a winter day just like this: in other words, she would have lied. But the truth was, she knew what she was doing, knew just what she was after: the attention of a man. Not a boy, but a man. Maybe even a kiss: she wanted her first kiss, and she knew this as she left her sleepless girl's bed and clicked open the door to the hall. Here, in this new place, this townhouse they're sharing with Derrick now that he and her mom have made up once again, her room is really just a big walk-in closet, with just one high, small window; the room is just big enough for a single mattress and a lamp that clips to the mattress' edge, and so she's glad to get out into the hall, glad to leave, to brush in her bare feet down the carpet that's the color of a root beer float.

She stands in the doorway, watching. On the brown Naugahyde sofa her mother got special for this place, Derrick's brother lies sleeping in his T-shirt, the old green sleeping bag smashed down to his waist, his mouth open, ashy-blond hair tousled, on his side so that the lower half of his face is collapsed against the pillow, while the upper half is still resisting gravity. To anyone else coming in the room right now, he'd look like what he is: a man, near thirty, who's been drinking too much most of his life, who doesn't often get out in the sun. A man turning to flaccid muscle too soon, who makes nothing happen, but waits for whatever will happen next. A grown man who still has to crash at his brother's girlfriend's place because once again his own girlfriend has given him the boot.

But to Rita, he's something other than this, as she watches him in the dim shimmer of the streetlight. Older. By day, since he came to stay last week, he's been nice to her, asking her grown-up kinds of questions, serious questions, asking her if she likes this new place. Not asking if she likes Derrick: he must know the answer to that, Rita thinks, standing in the doorway in her flannel nightgown, twisting a slip of the nightgown's soft cloth around and around in her finger.

I'll say I can't sleep, she thinks, and yes, this is what she'll say. She quickly scans her memory of the after-supper fridge: was there any milk left? Maybe he'll heat up some milk in the pan, and she'll pour in some Hershey's syrup, and together they'll sit at the table, drinking their warm milk, *intimate*. He'll ask her then what she thinks of Derrick, and she'll tell him, and he'll say he understands. He'll say he could tell she was lonely, say he knows that no else understands what she's thinking. There, in the warm kitchen, the late January snow swirling outside.

But he won't wake up, she thinks. *Why should he care?* and just as she's about to turn, to go back to her room, he shifts on the sofa, and she looks back, sees he's looking at her. Dead in the eye. "Hi," he says, and she says, "Hi."

"Can't sleep?" he asks, and she nods, yes, suddenly scared now that he's awake, now that it's real. *Is this real?* she thinks, and then thinks, *yes*, and she feels the flicker of something: it could be excitement, or it could be fear.

"I have that problem a lot, too," he says, shifting his position so his head is leaning against the armrest of the couch. He rubs his hand across his face, as if this will erase his sleeping face and make appear his wide-awake face. It works, pretty much, Rita thinks, standing now on one leg, leaning against the doorframe.

"Why don't you sit down over here?" he says, patting the couch in front of him, and she walks over there, thinking, he isn't really going to kiss her, she must look to him like a dumb kid. Thinking, this was a stupid idea.

She sits, and as she sits she realizes that he's naked underneath the sleeping bag; she isn't sure how she knows this; she can only see him from the chest up, but she knows. With one finger, he starts drawing on her nightgowned back, saying, "Here, guess what these letters are."

Rita scrunches up her forehead. "Um," she says, concentrating hard. "I can't tell. Oh, that's an 'R.'"

"Right," he says. Then, this is easy: I, T, A. Her name.

"I know something that will make you sleep," he says, and she thinks, now maybe it will be time for the hot chocolate, but instead, he says, "Lie down here," and he moves over a little on the couch.

Rita lies down on her back, next to him. She can feel his big body beside hers. Now what? Now he'll kiss her? No; instead, he keeps on talking, saying he'd like to take her away from here, take her to this cabin he knows out in the woods, teach her everything there is to know about love, and then set her free.

Love? Here's his hand, then, drawing letters across her chest, his finger tripping on the buttons on her nightgown. L, O, V, E. Then, his hand moving down her body, down to between her legs, and she's lying rigid and stiff and still as a thing, as a dead thing? no, she's lying stiller even than something that's dead.

"Relax," he says, "relax and enjoy it. This is the best way to fall asleep," and she tries to relax, and it does feel good, this does. It feels like nothing she's ever felt before, and for a moment she's scared her mother will come in the room. What if her mother gets up to go to the bathroom or something, and hears them, and comes in? And then for a crazy moment Rita only sees the light from the apartment complex parking lot glinting off the picture frame that hangs on the wall, a picture of a rose, and for that second she wants, more than anything she's ever wanted before, for her mother to come in the room, and it's almost like she's calling for her mother in her head: *come in, come in, come in.*

And then she's moving herself beneath his moving hand. She doesn't know why, and then he's taking her hand and slipping it under the sleeping bag, and she feels something there, his *thing*, rubbery and hard at once, like a chicken skin slipped over a bone, and he's saying, "Whenever you can, touch a man's dick. It'll turn him on, and it'll turn you on, too," and he moves her hand against him, and moves her hand faster and faster until her hand first hurts, then goes numb, and he makes a noise in his throat, and she thinks, *mom, wake up!* and then he jerks to a stop, everything stops then, everything, like the world is spinning, spinning, speeding up so fast it stops moving, and everything comes to a halt inside her, where it all just hangs, suspended in air.

"Now you'll be able to sleep," he says. He says, "This is our special secret. Derrick and your mom wouldn't understand; they still think you're just a kid."

Rita nods. Is this true? He quickly kisses her forehead, and then she sees he's falling asleep, and then his mouth falls open again the way it was when she came in, when she stood at the doorway, and she thinks for a minute she's still standing there, she never left the doorway, he never woke up, she never laid down on the couch. Then how did she get there, get to be where she is?

She gets up then, lets her nightgown fall back down, back to past her knees, where it belongs. She feels a little dizzy, standing, and she wobbles her way back to her room. Now, she's glad her room is so small, glad she just opens the door and leaps over the threshold and straight into her bed. It's safe in here, all hers, and she lies in her bed, unable to sleep, despite what he said, despite what he did. She replays what happened over and over again in her head. Finally just as she's about to sleep, she thinks of the cabin in the woods, imagines sitting there with her wolf-twin, drinking the hot chocolate. She sees it as if it's real, and half-asleep now it's as if she remembers going out to the living room, remembers him saying, *Come on, I'll make you a treat.* Her memory spins this up like cotton candy from a machine, twirls it around from nothing, makes it more real than the other thing was, the rubbery chicken skin, the onion smell of his breath hot on her face, and then, alone in her bed, in her coffin-sized room, finally Rita is able to sleep.

Her apartment complex rounds complete, Rita pulls out from the parking lot back onto the street, drives up Elm to her favorite stop when she fills in, the one she saves for last, the one she's been looking forward to while she trudged through the snow around the complex. She switches off the engine, goes in under the sign with the big Rx. As soon as she steps inside, she's enveloped by the perfumy smell, like all the perfumes in the world being opened at once, like beautiful music. A symphony, she thinks, a *fugue.*

Pleased that she's so quickly used her new word for the day, even if it's only in her head, Rita waits patiently as a horse for old Handy to sign for the papers. She waits for the two old ladies to pay their electric bills at the register, in their quilted nylon winter jackets, their handbags clutched in their hands. Even their shaking heads quiver in unison, as if they've spent so many years side by side they're operating on the same frequency.

Rita thinks about this while she waits, smiling to herself. She's forgotten the stormy snow outside, forgotten the memory jolted into action by her pass through the apartment complex. Now, she stands in the perfumy drugstore, the shelves all dustless and clean, everything white and gold, and inhales, as if this is where she comes from, as if this is where she really belongs.

On one of his late nights late in January, Reichman pulls in his long drive, sees the lights on in the living room, casting big oblongs of ochre across the packed snow. At home, his father's waiting, or rather, his father is there. Can his father wait for anything, now? Is it possible to wait for something, for someone, when you've lost the familiar track that winds around the day?

When Reichman comes in the door, there's his dad, standing at the glass doors that face out to the deck, swaying in the evening prayers. When he finishes, he turns, kisses the siddur before laying it down, then sits on the piano bench, not facing the instrument, facing the room. "Have a good day?" he says.

"Yeah, it was fine," Reichman says, standing in the doorway, unsure what his father can retain of whatever Reichman tells him, and so not wanting to bother with details. He doesn't say he's frustrated with his amnesiac's progress, or that he's worried he'll never get through to the psychotic with the burns who's taken up residence in the ward. He doesn't say he's tired of winter, that he feels as February limps to a start that spring will never begin.

Instead, he says, "Did you eat?"

"Let's see, did I eat? I think so," his father says, and Reichman glances through the hatchway into the kitchen, sees the oven still on but the dishes freshly washed, drying in the rack. "Cheese casserole," Reichman says, and his father says, "Oh, yeah, that's right, it was pretty good."

Reichman looks in the oven, sees the casserole still there, drying out, but very hot. He turns the temperature down to "warm," fixes a drink, and brings the *Gazette* with him to his club chair.

"Did you go swimming?" his father asks. Why is his father always in a mood for talk whenever Reichman just wants to sit and think?

"Yeah, I did. A mile and half," he says, looking at the front page.

"Your mother always liked to swim," his father says, and Reichman thinks, *Christ, if he's going to jump all over the place, I'm not listening. I'm not in the mood to try to keep up.* But, "Yeah, I remember," he says, still looking at the headlines.

"She wasn't afraid of the water, your mother," his father says then. "She wasn't afraid of anything." Reichman rises, goes to the kitchen, and returns with a plate of crackers and cheese as a shield against his father's rambling, which he proffers to his dad, then sets on the table as he sinks back into his chair.

"She wasn't even afraid of the Nazis," his father says, and at this, Bob Reichman snaps to attention. His mother had refused to speak of *what happened,* as if there was a thick curtain separating *what happened before* from where *we are now.* When, a few years before she died, he told her he was going to Austria for a psychiatry conference, she'd made a face of distaste. "I wouldn't go there," she'd said, "not if you paid me." And then, the night before he was to leave, she called, whispered into the phone the name of the synagogue where her parents had married. "Find it, Bobby. See if it's there."

Reichman says to his father, "Really?" striving for a casual tone, not wanting to scare his father off from the topic by letting him know how much he wants to hear. How much he wants to know, and doesn't want to know.

"Sure. Don't you remember that she almost even saved her sister, in the camp? Didn't you know that?"

Reichman just shakes his head, no. How can he remember a story he was never told?

And then his father tells him the story, about his mother, his own mother, once a girl, about twelve. His mother, a twin, with an identical sister. Birkenau. Mengele. At this, Reichman feels a twist in his heart, thinks for a moment, is this a heart attack, but knows that it isn't, and he listens, resisting the images that fuse together, then shatter apart.

But even though the memory loss has loosened his father's tongue, he's still the same reticent father of Reichman's childhood, and he doesn't give details, just says that Reichman's mother had a twin, and the twin was chosen for the experiments, and Reichman's mother was used as the control. She tried, somehow, at twelve, emaciated, ruined, to escape with her sister, but the sister, injured beyond repair, couldn't do it, didn't survive. Died.

"She told you that?" Reichman asks, and in that moment realizes in an entirely new way that his parents had a relationship solely their own. He feels like a child in understanding this so late.

"Sure, Bobby. A husband and wife share these things." His father remembers then the night she told him, just after they married, when they lay close together in their honeymoon bed, under the thin sheet, in the salty Cape Cod July heat. "I'd forgotten all about that," his father says now, remembering, meaning he'd forgotten how he had rubbed his thumb across her cheek, how her hair had spilled over the pillow, tangled as sea grass, dark and sleek.

Reichman shifts in his chair as his father talks, then stops. The two of them stare out the glass doors, out past the deck, to where night has descended, the winter stars glittering bright on the backdrop of black.

"You never said Kaddish for your mother, did you?" Reichman's father asks then, but not in the accusing tone Reichman would expect, more as if he's just bewildered, perplexed, can't remember.

"Well, yeah, Dad, sure I did."

"Not for a year."

"No, for a month. Thirty days," Reichman says.

"I did. Every day for eleven months, even though I only had to say it for thirty days. I guess I was saying it for you, you and Rozzy," his father says, shaking his head. "A parent wants to leave behind something good," his father says, and Reichman picks up his drink, sees his hand is shaking, what's left of the ice rattling a little in the glass.

Dad, he wants to say, *did that really happen to Mom? Was that how it was? What did that do to her?* But he doesn't say any of this, and his father signals that he's done by standing, leaving the room, calling over his shoulder, "Goodnight, Bobby," and Reichman calls back, "Goodnight, Dad."

Reichman sits in his chair, watches the moon come up over the tree-line. He imagines his mother as a little girl, imagines how she must have lisped even back then, imagines her in a nightmare hospital room, another girl—*his aunt*—her twin—on the bed beside her, the two of them looking into one another's eyes as if that's where they'll find whatever it is they need to stay awake, to stay alive.

Reichman hears the water running in his father's little bathroom, and knows this is all he'll ever hear of the story.

Just as well. How much more could he stand? Here's the moon, now fully risen, clearly a full moon, so full it's like a big balloon, and Reichman wonders if his father remembers the cycles of the moon, or if he's given up keeping track. If his father were alone now, how would he order the days of the week, the times of the month, the hours of the day?

Reichman rises then, too, goes into the kitchen. He so much can't bear to think of what he's heard that instead he takes out the casserole, sets it onto the cutting board, and without getting a plate, eats from the dish, standing up at the counter, as if he hasn't got time to sit down, as if he's a slave about to flee Egypt. While he eats, he takes his mother's story and buries it like a bone deep inside. His hands are still shaking, but he doesn't cry.

~

Blue tells Dr. Reichman about the glass ball, lifting the glass ball from his desk, tilting it up and back. "Austria," she reads, and he feels that cold rush spread through him that he sometimes, rarely gets, when a patient's progress intersects in this kind of small way with his own life.

Austria. *What happened there,* he thinks, but he just says, "Yes?"

She reads her description to him of her memory of the glass ball, standing by the window, watching the yellow taxicabs.

"Do you think you were waiting for someone?" he asks, and she nods, yes.

"Who?"

"My father," she says, and again her eyes fill, and then spill. Reichman has that flicker of feeling again, of how peculiar it is when a patient's course and his own converge.

"Can you stay with the memory?"

There's the ball in her hand, and when she shakes it up and down, the snow scatters and swirls around and around, just like the snow outside. Inside the ball, there's a snowy little castle, which she thinks of as the good princess' castle.

"He just got back from a trip," she says, "a month away, somewhere far away."

And then, she's standing at the window, looking down, down, to the street below, keeping watch. She has to go to the bathroom, but she's certain that if she turns away for a moment, she'll break the spell, the spell that will bring him back; her slacking vigilance will only delay his return, she's sure.

There's the hiss of the heat steaming through the pipes, the burning smell of the radiator coming on, the swirling snow out the window, swirling down, down, the snowflakes traveling so much farther than even the tallest building that just thinking about it makes her dizzy.

She watches the traffic, counts the yellow taxis that pass with each turn of the light; each time the light switches green a new flood of cars pulses past, and she watches them, tries to count all the yellow roofs of the taxis in each new wave, then looks up to the dizzying snowy sky. How will her father's plane land in all that snow? How will the pilot be able to see?

And then here it is: one yellow taxi slips out of the fleet, swings up to the curb. The passenger door opens, then the driver gets out, then her dad. It's him, looking up at the window, waving to her, and she shouts, "Daddy!" even though she's been trying, since she started school, to say "Dad" instead. She waves, vigorously, even as her father is helping the taxi man lift the luggage from the trunk of the cab, even as her mother is saying, "Is he here?"

Here's the elevator, here's her dad, carrying his luggage in his strong arms, dropping his luggage to pass one arm around his wife's shoulders, to loft his little girl into the air, high, high, high. Here's her mother, starting to laugh, then starting to cry.

"Sweetie, I have a surprise for you, but first let me talk to your mother," her dad says, and takes her mother into their bedroom, and here she is, standing again at the living room window, wondering if it happened at all. She looks over at her father's brown leather bags, standing like dogs at the hall door. She looks down the street, counts the taxis passing, as if still looking for that one taxi cab, the one that will stop to signal that now her real dad has arrived.

From the bedroom, there's still the sound of crying, then silence, and then her father appears again, tired now. "Let's make some supper, what do you say?" She nods her head. All through the meal, the cold leftover chicken and salad, a tall glass of juice, and then off to bed, she wonders, what was it? What was the surprise? Did he forget?

Telling the memory, Blue's nearly in a trance, her eyes fogged and far-away the way a patient's eyes are under hypnosis, even though the only hypnotic device at work here is her own memory. It doesn't take long for her to tell him the story, and as she talks he keeps careful track, watches for clues: a city, a big city. Winter. Boston? New York? Montreal? Chicago?

He asks her to stay with the memory, he asks if there's more, but nothing more comes of it: it's another stagnant moment holding little information.

At the session's end, she says, "What do you think about me? What's your assessment? Am I remembering?" and Dr. Reichman says, "Of course you are, Blue. This is good progress."

"But it's taking forever. I still don't have any clues. What do you think, really?" she asks, leaning forward, and with five minutes left in the hour.

"Well, one of my questions would be, why now?" Dr. Reichman says, at last, lacing his fingers around his knee. He's noticed that he makes this gesture whenever he's unsure, or more precisely when he's worried that he's pushing the patient too quickly, "pushing the river," as he likes to say, over these rocks and boulders, his rocks and boulders, not hers, not letting her find her own, slow way. But she asked, didn't she?

"Why now?" Blue repeats, squinting at him a little. She's left her hat on throughout the session, and Reichman notices this, wonders if it indicates a desire on her part to be ready to leave.

"Yes. Presumably before the fugue you were living a life somewhere, involved with a family, friends, a job. And then you left, and went into a fugue. The question this raises is, why now? Why not three years ago, or three years from now?"

He can tell he's going too quickly, and he clasps his hand more firmly around his knee, as if this action will slow him down. The question, of course, is what tripped her into the fugue, and he knows he shouldn't ask her that. Not now, not yet. Blue's scratching at her forehead where her hat meets her brow.

"But the more important question, I think, is what's happening now," Reichman says, and sees the relief flood into Blue's face. Wherever she came from, the air in the room crackles with this: there's something so electric in its risk that this young woman without a name can't yet begin to touch her fingers to the wire.

—

Doctor Right Man comes back in another day, a new day, and asks me more about my river tent, says he wants to know how it was living there, how did I live there, he says.

I lived by the river, by the wits of the river, I tell him.

How? he says. He doesn't understand much on his own, that I'm starting to see.

I scooped up my water in my tin cup, I tell him. I laid down at night on my pallet of drawn wood, curled into my little cocoon, and slept underneath the stars and the moon.

Was it warm in there? he wants to know.

It was warm until the end, I say. That's why I made the fires come and sweep me up in their hot arms, but I don't say the fires because to say the fires you must be a liar.

It was warm there in my little booth, my precious tent, real and bright as anything. Curl up small and no one will find you, no one will know.

What I saw there, down by the river, down in my bed, the rabbit and how it was that she bled. The river water turning red. The woman pitching down the rocks, tumbling like a pebble into the rain-wet baby bones.

I saw the whole thing, but they never believe me, no way, saying, Annie, Annie, just like the teachers said when I was small, trying to make my words come out smooth around the slit in my lip. They think I make up everything, think I'm in it just for play, but I'm not, and this is true, everything I saw, I saw with mine own eyes, everything two eyes can devise until my demise.

They say I make up everything, say it's impossible, but it was true, the blood on the wall and the baby coming out like a dead doll. But that was some time ago, wasn't it, dear? Now I don't tell anything. I won't tell them what I saw down by the river that afternoon, won't tell them what I found stowed away in the bushes like Moses in the bulrushes, waiting for his chance to lead the people out of Egypt and up into the promised land.

Here's my promised land: this room, trapped like a beast in its cage, four-walled in and warm, steam heater pumping, pumping into the air, like an animal wounded by a knife or a stiletto heel.

Heal, that's why I'm here, or so they all say. To heal up from those nights and those days by the riverbank alone. Living alone, living alone, that's what they say, but they never saw the cat curling up to the breast, the rabbit and how it brought the crows. And they don't know what it is I saw, and I'm not telling them. Not until they spill me out.

⁓

Night blueing out the horizon line while afternoon still lingers, and Blue lies on her back on the pretty, worn carpet, the tape of the clarinet playing again. Nothing there, no memory, and on this late winter night as the earth spins in toward early spring, she isn't melancholy, she's frustrated. Mad. If Dr. Reichman knew his stuff, wouldn't she be getting better now?

She lies on her back and fingers the carpet, then remembers Dr. Reichman's suggestion from her earliest days with him. Her earliest days *in his care,* she thinks, and gets out the notebook and pen, and lies down on the carpet, this time on her stomach.

This time, she starts with "If I could remember," then stops. "Make it up," Dr. Reichman says in her head, and so she does.

"If I could remember, I'd be jarred into memory by trauma, by the memory of trauma," she begins, and then it's as if she really is remembering, as if she can feel the rush of the elevator ascending, the thick smells of the apartment house hallway, of pot roasts cooking, and the trace of perfume in the hall. Then a switchback: a beach at dawn, the sand cool beneath her feet, her feet at first sluffing in the soft sand that's been combed by the cool night air, then stomping on the hard, wet sand down by the water's ripply hem. Down here, Random runs along the foamy tide's edge, runs off, then back, then off again, and she pokes at the rubble left by the night's high tide, looking for shells, looking for something pretty, or something her mother would like, something interesting, different, new.

On this morning, she finds a big piece of purple shell, what her dad calls "wampum." He's told her how the Indians used it as money, used it to trade with the first New Yorkers for food and fur and land. It was the currency then, and it's currency to her, too, because she knows her mother will like it, will put it up on a shelf in one of the glass-paned windows that look out to the sea. This is the biggest piece of wampum she's ever seen: it's nearly as big as her palm, and colored as if from the inside out, in a deep purply bruise, the color of a ripe plum, or the dark grapes that come at the end of the summer.

She sluffs through the soft sand, Random panting up to her, then running ahead, and she looks at her wampum, the light growing brighter as the sun comes up. Just before she reaches the path that cuts cut through the beach roses and sharp beach grass to their house, she sees that Random's nosing something in the sand, and then she sees it's a shoe, her mother's shoe, a single cloth espadrille, once striped red and white, once bright, now dulled with a half-summer's worth of soil, salt, and sand.

She picks up the shoe, carries it in her other hand up the path, up toward the steps to the deck. And here, and how could she have missed this on her way down, on her way out—here, in the long grasses to the side of the path, her mother lies, one arm draped over her head, her right hand lying over her chest, as if, were she standing, were she awake, she'd be pledging allegiance to the flag. She's in her tight peddle-pushers and her red silk blouse, just as she was last night, when she kissed her daughter goodnight, her breath sweet with booze, then ran after the others, out to the beach.

Here her mother is now, sleeping, bunched up in the sand, and in the moment she sees her mother lying there, she isn't shocked, she's ashamed. Not ashamed of her mother, ashamed of herself: how could she have walked right by on her way down the beach? *Selfish, selfish,* she hears in her head, and stands paralyzed for a long moment, shoe in one hand, bruised shell in the other, then goes to her mother, crouches down, shakes her chilled shoulder, shakes her awake.

Her mother comes around slowly, her eyes blurring in from wherever it is that she's been, from some place where there's sleep but no dreams. She lets out a little moan, as if she's hurt, as if she's one of the injured gulls they sometimes find on the beach, one wing bent back by a too-strong wind or a fight over a scrap of the human's food. And like those gulls, her mother moves away slowly, gesturing with her hand: *leave me alone,* as she stumbles up from grasses, wobbles up the path toward the house.

But the girl stays where she is, bent down by the grasses, where she found her mother. For a long time she looks at the impression of her mother's body, the grasses flattened, the sand pressed down and scooped around the negative of her mother's back and flank and thigh, the impression so deep that it's almost as if her mother is still there, almost as if her mother is real.

How will she ever tell Dr. Reichman this? Blue remembers the details, but to translate them to someone else would make it into a story; it wouldn't be a dimensional, detailed memory. It would be stripped down, laid bare: I remembered finding my mother passed out in the grasses at a beach house. *Colorless as a cadaver,* Blue thinks.

After Blue's writing has served its purpose, she rolls from her stomach onto her back, stares up at the ceiling, then turns her head to look out the window. From here, lying on the carpet, she can see the clear night sky, some of the stars obscured by the streetlights' glow, but high up, high above the town, the stars cluster and crowd. Blue thinks, she doesn't want Dr. Reichman to know this, how she found her mother that way. *How terrible*, he would say. Lying on her floor, in this strange town that is not her town, Blue closes her hand into a fist against her chest, as if she can in this way hold this memory close to her heart, as if in this way she can keep this secret of her own.

Part 3

Spring comes to Intervale slowly, after the winds and heavy snows of February and early March bring everything to a slow shuddering halt. Late winter, nothing happens in a climate that far north: the people, like the animals, burrow deep into their dens, their thoughts and feelings frozen, even their pulse rates seeming slightly slowed. When March begins its long melting, it goes unnoticed by most, until the snow's nearly gone and the air starts going soft enough so people say, "looks like spring's on the way" as they go about their business up on Elm and Main. As March ends, at night there's still a freeze, but by day the sun is strong enough that soon the steam emisses from the brick and concrete, soon there's the sound of running water, trickling down stone walls, rivering along the sides of streets, dripping from the bare branches of the trees.

Outside Blue's bedroom windows, the river ice separates in heaving groans. One night, after a day that's pulsed with the warm promise of spring, Blue lies in bed listening to the blocks of ice breaking apart, moaning as they rend and cleave. Like her memories, she thinks, and thinks maybe now that spring is coming, maybe now that the river ice is breaking up, her amnesia will break up too.

Her new memories are like the patches of water out there appearing between the blocks of ice, she thinks, and then she sleeps again, but by morning, the ice blocks have frozen back again, the river a bundled bunch of floes scattered from their proper places, the river slamming its door again to spring.

Through February, March, her pools of memory have become more frequent, but they're still unformed, and uninformative, too: a voice, a smell, a scene still-shot, not a whole movie running on. In the last of winter Blue added a few memories to her repertoire: sitting in a chair woven of leather straps, in shorts and a T-shirt; she's an adult, and the blue patio tiles are smooth and warm under her bare feet. In another memory, she's clutching a woman's hand—her mother's?—as they wait for traffic to pass in a busy street. Or she's a little older, and riding in the back seat of a plush car, next to an old woman who smells of perfume and powder.

Lying behind them all like a dog waiting to bite, the memory of finding her mother passed out on the beach. She isn't sure why she still won't tell Dr. Reichman this memory: because she's so ashamed of it, because she doesn't want to believe it, or because it might hold the most clues, and maybe, then, she'd have to begin leaving him, leaving her new life, and the past would become the future, too, and her time in Intervale, her *now,* her *here,* would be just an interlude. An interlude that's coming to an end.

Something happened to her, before, *back then,* something that she still doesn't want to remember, to which she still cannot return. And then, if that's true, something happened to land her here, some boot kicked her into this fugue. Into this particular city, here.

Still, here are her new memories, breaking up and floating together: an evening sky, purple and yellow and orange, seen as if Blue is lying on her back. A taste, sweet and sharp at once, that she still can't identify. The salty sea spraying into her face as she leans against the metal railing of a boat.

The earlier memories by now have become familiar to her, and sometimes, at night, lying in her bed listening to the ice break up and move, she mulls them over, like smoothing a stone in the palm of her hand, memorizing them so they won't escape her grasp again.

Out in the shed behind his house, Bob Reichman's got everything neatly arranged: peat moss pots for starting seeds, clay pots to fill with perennials for the patio, just as soon as the danger of frost has passed, and hanging from the wall, the tools, just as he left them when he put them away in the fall, cleaned and sharpened, his trowel and rake and hoe. In one corner stand the galvanized bins, lidded tightly against moisture and mice.

As he steps inside, for the first time since the fall, the smells of gardening and soil and spring engulf him, and he takes a moment to stand in the little shed, inhaling. The smells bring Amy back, how she loved to grow a wild tangle of flowers in a bed, letting the tiger lilies spread and the climbing rose engulf one whole side of the door. Well, he thinks, he'll make the garden his own, now, and he imagines how it will be neater, more orderly. How now he can work on cultivating the tall gladiolus that he loves.

Reichman picks up a pair of work gloves, and lets his mind reel out a long skein of netting. Today, the first fish he catches is Annie Blaise, the predicament she's placed him in: she's far better than when she came in, her burns have been treated as much as they can, and pretty soon, he'll have to discharge her; in fact, the state regulations will demand it. But Reichman knows that as soon as she goes, she'll most likely stop taking her meds, won't make her appointments, and will probably soon move on to another town, maybe return to wherever it is that she's from. Once released, she might, in fact, never come back.

But soon he'll have no reason to keep her under lock and key. Medically, she's fine, and she's more coherent now; plus, of course, there's the matter of how long he can legally keep her, if and when she wants to go. And there's the question of insurance and payment, matters the hospital administration simply won't let him forget. Digging his hands into a new bag of potting soil, he thinks, why not let her live out her days outdoors, talking to the animals that come to her encampment, scooping up water from the river as though it's holy, lost in her holy visions?

Annie Blaise is just as lost to her past as Blue is, isn't she? Both of them wandering, like the lost tribe of the Jews still wandering in the desert sands of modern life. In all the Diaspora, how many Jews are there who, like Blue, have forgotten all they'd been instructed to remember? Amnesic, wandering into their lives without knowing who they are, or who they could be? Like him, thinking now of preparing for Passover and feeling mostly guilt, not wonder or awe.

Reichman moves the galvanized tubs away to free the wheelbarrow so he can rake up the last of last year's leaves from around the house. The front wheel's a little stuck, always has been, and try as he has, he hasn't been able to fix it just right, and the barrow wobbles, pulling always to the left, as he backs it out the shed door, down the ramp, and heads across the lawn.

Each Jewish infant, Reichman learned as a boy, is born knowing the entire Torah by heart, but upon birth, an angel kisses the baby's mouth, and he forgets, and spends his whole life not learning, but remembering.

How we want to forget, want never to forget, have forgotten it all, have remembered everything, Reichman thinks, as he digs the rake into the wet leaves, turning them over to dry in the new sun. There, a cluster of crocus, determined, pushing their white and lavender noses up from the softening brown earth.

Back in the shed for the tarp, he hears a noise, and there's his dad standing in the doorway, silhouetted by the light. "Bob?" he says, worry edging his voice, but Reichman can't see his father's face in the darkness of the shed. What's going on, he thinks, what's wrong?

"Yeah, Dad—what is it?" he asks, feeling suddenly transformed back into a little boy, back to the child he was, awkward and worried.

"I just wasn't sure where you were," his father says. "I just wanted to know you were here."

<hr/>

I didn't want to talk about it, and I tried telling that to the doctor, Doctor Right Man. Of course by this time I'd come to my Right Mind, and I knew this wasn't really his name, Right Man. I knew, but I wanted to keep calling him that, like that would hold everything else off, keep it away, keep it at bay.

Black and grey, dappled and bay, all the pretty little horses. He keeps asking for my memories, my earliest memories, as if this will tell him something, as if this will say what it was that made me this way.

Little lamb, who made thee? What dread hand and what dread eye? I'd like to answer him this way, but I know he's serious; this is serious business here, and so I try to do what the doctor tells me, do what he says. I try to comply, but there are of course some things, some many things, I don't want to talk about, not to him, not to anyone, like the dream about—I don't think I can even think it to myself.

There are some things you would just rather not discuss. Doesn't he understand this? Every morning a nurse comes, slips the pill under my tongue. There's no hiding the pills, not with her; she's on to every trick I ever learned, and so I take my pill and swallow, and it's true what the doctor said, I do feel better now than I did when I first came in. When I first came to.

But I miss the river, I miss the tent and the rabbit, and now that it's nearly spring (I can feel it, can feel the quickening, even in here, even behind the sealed up windows and walls) I wonder, did the rabbit live? How could he survive the whole winter long like that?

Sometimes, at night, buried in my bed, hollowed in my head, I think about the rabbit, how he's underground like me, down in his tunnel, tunneling under, tunneling deep. I think about that rabbit, his softly softly fur, how he's underneath the frozen ground, safe and soft and alive and warm.

Sometimes, at night, I'm so afraid that I can't sleep, and inside of me, in my me of me, there's a yellow river of anxiety, tunneling under, rivering deep.

Goodnight, goodnight, I heard my mother whisper at my bed, the mobile of colored horses spinning over my baby head, wobbling horses all black and bay, dappled and grey, all the pretty little horses.

Would I tell the doctor how afraid I am, afraid all the time that I'm so flawed because of something I did? What if that concept could be understood?

In the summer bedroom, I slept soundly, without a sound coming from my head, without a sound like a color, a purple or red, coloring everything wild and free. In the summer, the sticky red heat, the father carrying me in his arms outside, out to the lawn, where the fireflies flicked off and on, the grass standing straight as a razor's blade, straight as if shorn, and over the rosebushes, over the hedge, the evening light leaking out, as if being squeezed from the big, round world.

Down by the river, that's what I think, down where I left my parcel of things, where I sent the basket for safekeeping downriver, that's the only place for me, perched on the brink, between the muddy bank and the watery smithe, the wailing wall and the terrific fast ride. Perched on the brink of disaster, waiting for the call back to the master.

⁓

Rita's new word for the day: *plexus,* a complex network, like nerves. Taking the calendar's advice and making a sentence with the word, using it in her conversations has worked on certain days, like the day the word was *hibiscus* and Ross brought one into the lunch room that day—nobody knew he was into plants—a coincidence that Rita marked down to fate. But *plexus?*

Besides, Rita's got too much on her mind this morning; she's got to hurry out the door and up to the highway. She's got an errand to run, and it's so nice out, she wants to walk. With the coming spring she's made a resolution to get some exercise; not that she needs to lose weight, she's too skinny as it is, but just to get out in the fresh air more, to be more of a healthy kind of person.

Rita walks all the way down Main, past the shops still shut up, not yet opened for the day, and in the April sun she follows Main all the way out until it becomes Pasture Road. It should be called Interstate Road now, as it heads not to open pastureland but straight out to the highway, passing what once were meadows and now are fields long-since mowed down, filled with wide-hipped apartment buildings jammed into complexes, Versailles, and Contra Costa, and The Wellington, cheap wooden structures with the cement showing in gaps beneath the shaky balconies.

One of these buildings was one of Rita's homes, but which one? From this vantage point, on foot, walking along the sandy road edge like this, it's nearly impossible to tell. Who cares? They all look the same any-way, and *what happened* with Derrick's brother on that night long ago barely bobs up from the waters of her memory, then sinks back down again like a stone.

Besides, she's on a mission. And here's the diner, looming ahead. She crosses the parking lot, walks in through the door.

Will Blue recognize her from that other visit, the one Bart was deter-mined to ruin for her, thank you very much?

"Just one this morning?" Eleanor says, then leads Rita to a table by the window. The place is busy at this time of day, and Rita thinks, *Shit, I'll never get a good look, never get to ask the questions I need to ask.*

But then, as she studies the menu, even though she doesn't need to, here's Blue at her table, saying, "Do you know what you want?" and Rita is startled, looks Blue dead in the eye.

"I want to ask you something," Rita whispers, and Blue, thinking this will be a question about making a change on one of the specials, switching biscuit for toast or sausage for eggs, bends to point at the little box at the bottom of the menu where it says right there: "No Substitutions."

But, "Do you think you could have a twin?" Rita says, blunt and bold as the day.

What can Blue say? At hearing this, she's filled with that lost feeling, that longing, that long cut of *I don't know.*

"I don't know," she says, letting her voice carry all of her hurt, her frustration. "Do you want coffee?" she asks, and Rita, put back in her place, ashamed, nods, and turns over her cup.

"Yes, and the pancakes," she says, knowing as she says this that it isn't really what she wants, it was just the first thing she thought of. As Blue walks away, Rita squeezes her eyes shut, squeezes her hands into fists until she can feel her nails bite into the soft flesh of her palms. *Damn.*

She picks up a fork, touches the tines down to the table. *Plexus,* she thinks, pronging four equidistant points into the white paper placemat. Of course Blue would say no. How stupid of her. Of course she doesn't remember if she has a twin, because of course her whole deal is that she doesn't remember *anything. How could you be so dumb?* Rita hears whistling inside her head: *stupid, stupid, stupid.*

—

April, and the wind blows at the bare tree tops in hard gusts off the river. The wind is strong, but the air isn't cold; it's so warm that Blue has opened her jacket, and she walks down the river path with her bare hands pocketed, watching for signs of life to appear. Everything smells dark, like mud and earth, and the river is a roiling pale brown, all the silt and melted ice stirred up and moving fast. The pup is excited by the spring, and runs ahead, chases a leaf, then stands still, nose in the air, smelling everything.

The river path winds along past the spot where in December the kids skated in their bright group; now, there's no ice left out there; instead, the river has coughed up a few pieces of debris onto the shore, wooden shards of the ice fisherman's shanties, a stray mitten, a paper cup.

Blue stops at her usual turn-around point, where the riverbank cuts a curve northward. All winter, the path has simply ended here; here, the path is less clear, more overgrown, but because the snow has melted back into the river, she can now pass through, clamber around the boulders that shoulder up nearly to the water's edge. She passes the curve in the path and she sees there, up ahead, the twin bridges clasped over the wide water, the railroad bridge and the bridge *where I was born,* she thinks, and then amends this: *where I was found.*

She would stop and stare, and maybe continue on up there, but the pup has found something in the muddied wet riverbank grasses, he's nosing at something in there, and she steps closer, feeling that shock of recognition at her memory of Random nosing up her mother's single lost shoe at the beach.

"What is it?" she asks, and the pup looks up at her, as if to say, "*I* don't know." It's a faded handkerchief, a bandanna, once bright blue, now smeared with mud and river silt, resting in a nest of twigs and reeds. Tied in a good knot, its top tied up tight.

Blue picks it up, and slowly works at the knot. Her fingers are cold, and stiff now that they're wet, and it takes her some time, takes using her teeth, to get the knot free. The river wind picks up around her, and she's careful, as the thing falls open in her hand, to hang on to whatever's inside.

It's a little pile of things, she sees, and at recognizing the first thing for what it is, she nearly drops the whole bundle: a rabbit's foot, a foot of a real rabbit, not a blue-dyed key chain conversation piece, but a rabbit's foot, hacked or chewed off at the ankle, the fur still on, still complete. But Blue's got a feeling, and she persists: there's a piece of paper, folded in quarters, nearly tearing at its folds because it's so damp, and a photograph. The bandanna nesting in her right hand, Blue picks up the photo, holding it gingerly by one corner. Two women on a beach, the colors of summer sudden and bright against the pale Intervale morning: the background's blue ocean and bluer sky, the daffodil-yellow tee shirt of one woman reflecting back the color of her hair. And, her chest pressing in now as if with a great weight, with fear, with *dread,* Blue recognizes her own face, her own dark hair, blue eyes looking at the camera. Looking at herself, standing there on the wet riverbank. A flicker of hope: *could that really be me?*

For a moment, the world goes still; for a moment, she can't breathe.

She looks around at the ground, looks for more, but the pup— *Random,* she thinks—has moved on, snuffled in the grasses, found nothing else. She kicks through the grasses, just to make sure, walks ahead a little ways, walks back. She doesn't want to lose this spot, this little beach of riverbank. She looks again at the parcel, at the blue bandanna holding its things, and sees looped around the rabbit's foot, a tiny heart-shaped locket, so small she missed it at first. Holding the bandanna in one hand, wrapping it around the whole mess, with one fingernail she pries open the locket: there's a lock of black hair inside, and at this, a frisson of recognition makes her hands begin to shake. Something slipping just beyond her reach.

She carefully places the parcel on the nearest rock, then lifts up the folded paper. She peels up one corner; inside, it's drier than she had thought it would be, and she peels back another fold, until it's open before her, and she has a sudden memory of cracking open a fortune cookie, the crumbs falling into her hands, unfolding the little slip of paper inside: *You will lead an artistic and happy life.*

It's a birth certificate. It's old, an old Xerox, black and white, the information hand-typed into the boxes. Stamped and sealed and signed.

Brenda LaPlatte, January 27, 1960.

Is this me? Blue reads every word on the page, peers in to see each word, no matter how inconsequential it seems, then looks up at the river, up at the sky. She can see the bridges quite well from here; they're not so far. Could she somehow have shucked this parcel from the bridge while she sat there, coming out of her fugue? Could it have tumbled down the river, to land here, muddied with spring, at her feet?

The sky is going grey, the handsome dark grey that means a storm is on its way, and Blue turns, calls out, "Random, come on," and quickly walks back in the direction she's come.

~

Reichman sees right away that Blue's got something with her today: a small brown paper bag that she carries with her hand clasped around the top. "Come on in, Blue," he says from the doorway, and she carries the bag and her jacket in with her, settles into her chair, and says, directly, simply: "I found something."

"Yes?" he says, with some trepidation. *What now?*

She opens the bag, and he thinks for a moment she'll pull out a bird's nest, from the way she's handling whatever it is that's in the brown bag, and he remembers with a short jolt Amy stooping down to the ground to pick up a nest that a big storm had blown down from the towering elm.

But it isn't a nest, it's a plain blue bandanna, muddied, with something inside. She opens the folds, and hands him the photo. Immediately he sees it's a photo of her, clear as anything, taken recently, a few years ago? Her hair is shorter than it is now, more in the style of when she was found.

And with her, another woman, her arm draped over Blue's shoulder, pulling her close. But despite all this, Blue's saying, "Could this be me?"

"Yes," he says. "There's no question." Then, as the importance of this photograph rises in him, "Where did you find this, Blue?" he asks, but already she's handing him the bandanna, saying, "Look."

He takes it in his hands, and at first he's shocked by the rabbit's foot: a real rabbit's foot, a little bit bloodied, severed, clawed. Terrible, with a cheap-looking, tiny heart-shaped locket tangled in the fur. He'll deal with that later, later he'll try to answer the question of what this thing is, where it is from. But now he puts the parcel of the bandanna down on his desk, lifts up the paper folded inside, carefully peels up the edges. A birth certificate, soaked and creased but fully legible, from the City of Boston, January 27, 1960.

Brenda LaPlatte.

Blue.

He looks up from the parcel, looks up at Blue. Here he sits, holding her photo, holding her birth certificate, and even as he thinks of the work still ahead, thinks of how long this could take, of the ambivalence she might feel, he feels immensely sad, and realizes he doesn't want her to go back, doesn't want her to leave.

Blue. Brenda LaPlatte.

"Could that be my birth certificate?" she asks, leaning forward. "Is this me?"

He comes back around then, comes out of his shock. "Look at the photo. Did you recognize yourself here?"

"Yeah, I guess I did. But is that birth certificate mine? Is that my name, Brenda LaPlatte?" She says this as if she's confused, as if the name is foreign in her mouth. But as she says it, Reichman thinks, of course; look at the date, 1960: the math isn't hard: now it's 1994, and he's always supposed Blue to be somewhere between thirty and thirty-five. And the mother's name, Colleen McGlew LaPlatte. Of course Blue has some Irish in her, with that black hair, those bright blue eyes. Of course she had some kind of an ID on her just before she was found on the bridge, just before she came to, even though the question remains, thudding now in Reichman's chest, of how this odd assortment of things came to be pack-aged like this. Where's the wallet with the driver's license and the cash that one would expect?

"Blue, this is you. Where did you find this?" he asks, and she tells him about walking down by the river, says Random found it first, it was all tied up like that in the bandanna. . . .

"Random?" he interrupts.

"You know, my dog, the pup."

"I didn't know you'd given him a name," Reichman says, marveling yet again at how a patient will leave out such important, telling details. To give a name to the dog she's insisted on calling "the pup"—the brown and white spaniel she's described to him—indicates tremendous progress.

"Sure," Blue hedges, still reluctant to tell him about the memory of finding her mother on the beach. And maybe now, she won't have to. "I found it by the river, not far from the bridge."

"Okay," Reichman says, thinking he'll just have to let this information go, for now; he has to pull them both back into the steady, sure stream he knows best, the suck of emotion. "I know this is a shock. It's shocking to me; it must be quite shocking to you, to find this. How are you feeling?"

"Scared, I guess. I mean, I don't know what will happen now. What will happen next," Blue says.

"Well, next we'll start searching the records to find out where you were from, where you lived."

"And then what? Can I stay here, in Intervale? Do I have to leave?" Blue's eyes fill with tears at this, tears that spill over and run down her cheeks.

"No, Blue, you don't have to leave. We just have to find out if anyone is looking for you, find your relatives, your family, and see if that doesn't help you remember more," Reichman says, trying for a note of reassurance. He knows, he's read, that often, in these rare cases of persistent amnesia, no amount of contact with the patient's relatives, or friends, will bring the person back. Sometimes, he knows, the patient just has to start over, has to reinvent herself.

For now, the important thing is keeping her calm, making any changes slowly, making any changes with care. He doesn't mention the rabbit's foot or the locket; the story behind them must be important, but it will come out in time, and since Blue doesn't mention it, doesn't ask, he thinks it's best not to push this.

"I'll start looking into this, and in the meantime, let's just continue as we are, okay?" he says, and at this, the tears stop, and she nods. "Okay," she says. They both look down then at the parcel lying on Reichman's desk, the two women in the photograph smiling up at them from their bright day of the simple past.

———

Now he's got something to go on in his search for Blue's identity, Reichman's a little unsure where to begin; with only a name and a place, where do you start to look for someone's origins?

First, he calls the state police, tells them about the birth certificate, and the trooper he talks to says of course, he'll run a search, but the machinery will only spit out information on her if she's been arrested, if she's got a record.

In his office, he flips aimlessly through his Rolodex of numbers and names. Who would know where to begin, who would know what to do? He remembers then one of the conversations at *kiddush,* how he stood at the edge of the group, and someone was saying he'd done some private investigating. Ira, or Al? Jacobson, no, Aronson, Ira Aronson, and he lifts up the phone.

Reichman's always surprised when a new acquaintance remembers him, as if he attends these get-togethers over *kiddush* as an invisible guest, and when Aronson says, "Sure, Bob Reichman," he feels almost as if he's got a secret that's been discovered. Over the phone, he learns that Aronson supplements his law practice by doing his own investigations. "It keeps me interested, solving the puzzles," Aronson says, and then Reichman tells him about what Blue found, the birth certificate, the photograph, not mentioning how, even as Blue found her little packet of things, he discovered that he's getting too attached to this strange case. He thinks, but doesn't say, that he's suddenly afraid he'll lose Blue just as he's losing his father, too. He doesn't say he acutely feels the unfairness of this, doesn't say he's had enough loss. He just says, "I just don't know what to do, or where to begin."

"You should be able to get somewhere," Aronson says, "acting on behalf of the person herself, but it will take days, maybe weeks," and gives him some numbers to call. "I've got a big divorce case right now," he says, "but give me the basics and I'll nose around when I can."

"Sure, great," Reichman says, but there's the elevator descent of disappointment, that plunge again in Reichman's gut, the feeling he had as kid that something was wrong but nothing was being done—something he's chalked up to his parents' status as survivors of the Holocaust. "Sure, thanks," he says, not believing at all that Aronson will do anything; why should he care?

But now he's got somewhere to start, and all afternoon Reichman wends his way through the portholes and slides of medical records and state agencies, phone pressed to his ear, swimming in the hollow echo of *hold*. Outside his window, a brief spring sun shower sends rain sparkling through in the air, glittering in the light.

It will take longer than days just to get the birth certificate confirmed. The medical records of thirty years previous have long since been boxed and stacked in the Boston hospital basement, and it will take finding someone at the hospital who has the time to search. Everyone he speaks to needs to speak with someone else for approval, and then there's the problem of crossing state lines. Reichman leaves his number again and again, and then, he settles in to wait.

If only he had someone to discuss this with. He thinks maybe he could talk to his father about this strange case, about Blue; he remembers how, as a boy, he would wonder about things with his father, his father positing ideas and theories about people and the world, about truths of physics and points of Jewish law. Together they'd have discussions that lasted months, the thread of argument looping through the days, Reichman suddenly saying at dinner one night, "But what about this. . . ." Now, he thinks, his father can't carry a conversation beyond a few moments, can't even stitch a morning to its afternoon.

Still, that evening he tries, as they sit together at the kitchen table, the window open to the soft spring evening. "I made some progress with an interesting case today," Reichman says.

"Oh?" his father looks up from his dinner plate; tonight, he wanted to order Chinese take-out from a restaurant, saying to Reichman, "Your kitchen's *trafe* anyway. What will it matter?" He checked too many choices on the paper take-out menu, fried rice and egg rolls and sweet and sour vegetables, asparagus in garlic sauce, General Tso's chicken. But Reichman, unable to say no, called the whole order in, and now, most of it still sits in the white cardboard containers, soaking grease into the placemats.

Reichman tries to eat more than his share, so his father won't feel bad, won't see what he's done. What he's become: an old man with barely any appetite.

"Yeah, I've got this patient who has amnesia," Reichman begins, even though his dad should know this by now; he's told his dad about Blue. "And this week she came in with her birth certificate, of all things, so it seems we might be able to figure out who she is now pretty easily."

"Is that right?" his dad looks interested, but vague.

"Yeah, she just appeared on the bridge last fall," Reichman says, feeling the now-familiar disappointment that he has to repeat this to his father, "Nobody here recognizes her, and she doesn't recognize anything; she just appeared."

"A stranger in our midst," his father says, and for a moment Reichman's confused: what's he driving at? But a moment later, his father says, "The Jew knows what it is to be the stranger. That's why we take the stranger in."

"What do you mean?" Reichman asks.

"I mean, maybe she's a Jew."

Reichman can't quite follow his father's line here; is his father sliding off the conversation again into some other conversation, or is he making a point? He tries to follow his father, thinks it's never occurred to him that Blue might be a Jew. Would it make a difference if she were? But now he knows this can't be true; not with a name like Brenda LaPlatte.

"I don't know," his father says, wiping his mouth carefully on his napkin, even though he hasn't eaten enough yet to make a mess. "I don't know. Let's see, most of your other friends were Jews when you were young, weren't they? Did you meet her at the synagogue?"

This time Reichman knows his father's lapsing into some parallel universe, where maybe they're having this other conversation, too. Is his father too fluid, or is it that Reichman's too stuck in one place?

Maybe his father's getting prescient, Reichman thinks in a crazy hopeful moment. *Maybe this means I'll meet someone at that Friday night service, a woman, a Jew.*

After he clears the plates and puts the food away, after he says "goodnight," to his dad, watches his father shuff down the hall to the guest room, Reichman stays up, staring out the big windows to the spring night.

The one he really wants to talk about all this with is Blue. He could drive over to her apartment—a thought so ludicrous it makes him smile. He imagines finding her, confronting her, but what could he say? what could he ask? *Where were you born? Who are you?* Blue's just whoever she is, and soon enough he'll know for sure. She's got a personality, a quick, educated mind, an easy laugh, a hesitant awkward way of speaking. What's the use in conjecture about what may have formed her former self, or who she might have been before?

Reichman sits in his red club chair in his big living room, all the lights out, and looks out over the lawn, out toward the dark woods. He smiles and shakes his head at his earlier thought that he might meet someone, might fall in love again: how can the human heart be so resilient? He's got to start getting out, he's got to make the effort to connect. Why didn't he ask Aronson to meet him in person, why did he settle again for using the phone? It's a bright half-moon, and the sky is clear, and he can make out the edge of the woods from here, the line of three pines to the left, then a space, then two pines to the right, like a doorway going into the woods, like an entrance. It's here he cut a path, lopping off branches to the left and right, clearing a trail that looped over his acres and up to La Venerie Ridge, but that was so long ago that now the path, he knows, just barely enters the forest, bellying out into young saplings and rocks.

Do anyone's origins matter, he wonders, watching the dark obliterate the woods, just the daffodils glowing almost white against the lawn.

⌒

As the forsythia burst open in their yellow blooms, and the sun coaxes the tulips from their beds of dark dirt, in the Intervale Hospital Annie Blaze begins to gradually come back toward the world of the living, the common world of the sane, and has taken to leaving her room, going down the hall to sit for the long hours of the afternoon in the day room. From here she can see the slope of Hospital Hill, the clusters of daffodils shrill in the daylight. Most days she takes the pad of paper and the crayons from the shelf and sits at the table, coloring, filling the whole page with tiny, meticulously drawn color.

There's a tangle of memories, memory snakes strangling together in their coil and hiss. I remember my dreams when I wake and remember my waking when I sleep, but I don't tell the doctor, don't tell him or anyone. Something's got to be just for me; something's got to be my own.

The doctor comes in the room, and now I don't call him Doctor Right Man anymore. He's just another doctor, just another man. I look away, look toward the door. All I want is for him to leave me alone. All I want is to just go home.

My little encampment by the riverbed is probably still there, isn't it? My parcel of precious things, my papers, my locket. Is the rabbit still there, or did I really hurt him the way I thought about?

I lie on the bed here, my heart in my head. Where has everything gone? I'm remembering a room, a room I've remembered how many times? How many times must I go back there? Haven't I done enough penance yet? Paid the price in full?

But here's the doctor. Father knows best. He always tries to look concerned, to look as if he cares. Why should he care? I'm just me, and there's no reason for him to get involved. Leave me alone, I'd say, if only I dared speak.

⌒

"But what about something more recent," Blue starts her next session, without even asking Dr. Reichman if he's found anything. "I mean, what about where I was right before this?" she asks, reaching forward, then tipping the glass ball upside down, watching the snow pool into the curve. "I mean, what brought me here?"

They've only approached this question obliquely up until now, and now, Reichman thinks, this isn't the time. There are too many traumas facing her now: learning about her origins—hell, even just learning her name, after a winter of struggling to remember just a few pieces and bits—that alone would be enough material for awhile.

Still, she's asking; her desire to know *what brought her here* is great enough that maybe it's an indication she's ready for whatever the answer is. Or at least, she's ready to start looking. And he has to remind himself, yet again, that it's up to the patient to direct the course of the river.

"Okay, let's explore that," he says, leaning back. "What possibilities come to mind?" He doesn't say that he's fairly sure it was the physical injury, evidenced by the bruises and the hairline fracture of her wrist when she was first found, that tripped the switch of her memory off.

Blue takes a deep breath, looks up at the ceiling. "I guess something traumatic," she says. "I guess something like an accident, or getting hit on the head. Some kind of injury," and here, her eyes fill.

"Okay, what kind of injury would it be?" he asks, maintaining his even tone, thinking maybe she's on the verge of remembering what happened just before she came to, and speaking as if she isn't starting to cry, as if she hasn't so quickly, apparently, struck gold.

"An injury to my heart," she says, as if in a trance, staring right into the glass ball she's holding right side up now in her lap, as if it's the crystal ball of a spiritualist, the snow sifting back down to the earth. "An injury to someone I loved."

It's not what he expected, but it's a good start, Reichman thinks: at least, it's more than they've had to go on before, and confirms for him one thing he's suspected since Blue first started remembering her fragments of her past: she loved someone, recently. This realization whispers to him: *hurry, hurry.* Doesn't this mean someone out there in the big wild world is looking for her?

After she leaves, he picks up the glass ball, tips it side to side. Could there be anyone out there looking for him?

⌣

Just a few days before the start of Pesach, Max Reichman sits back in the easy chair, the chair his son Bobby likes to sit in. It's pretty comfortable. Not bad. He puts his feet up on the ottoman. Let Bobby worry about making the house kosher for Passover. He's cleaned out his own room, not that there was much to do, and now, he thinks God will understand if he doesn't make a big fuss about it with his son. Better to keep family harmony, he thinks.

From here, he can see the spring garden starting to bloom. The yellow daffodils sing brightly against the greening grass, and the tulips, red and yellow, are beginning to balloon open. Maybe Bobby would like some help with his gardening, he thinks, then picks up the *Intervale Gazette,* folded open to the crossword puzzle he's been working on.

Let's see. He's got it almost halfway done; his memory's fine for things like the name of an old song or the Greek god of the sun. Twelve down: *braid.* He looks up, sees Miriam's braided hair, how she'd wind the braid up around into a bun at the back of her head, how he'd always wanted to touch it, smooth the rippling layers with his fingertips. Six letters, with a tricky "X" in the middle. *Plexus,* he thinks, and as he starts to write the "P" the pressure he's making with his hand in order to write becomes a pressure rising up into his head, a dark pressure suffusing him, and he knows this is it, and starts to recite: *"Sh'ma Yisrael . . ."* just as his lifetime of prayer has prepared him, just as he's hoped he'd be able to in the moment that he died.

Bob Reichman's gotten used to his routine, coming home, opening the door and calling out, "Dad," and this evening is no different, except that tonight maybe he's a little later than usual, having run into Joe Horowitz at the Y, having listened, actually writing down the time and place of the Havarah seder, this time saying, sure, he'll be able to go. He'll bring his father along.

"Dad," Reichman calls out again, coming in, setting his briefcase down on the hall chair. He continues into the living room, knowing even before he gets there. His father is dead. And then, there he is, in Bob's own red club chair, and Reichman laughs a little to himself to realize that his father's been coveting his own chair all along but letting Reichman have it for himself, or letting Reichman think that he does, except in the day, when he isn't here. Hasn't been here. His father is dead.

"Dad," Reichman says, crouches down by the chair. "Daddy," he says again, and knows, he can feel that the body is already going cold, the hands hanging limp in the lap, resting on the newspaper, the pencil fallen onto the floor. Reichman presses his cheek then to his father's face, feels the scratch of the whiskers the razor didn't catch. The tears well up so fast, he's unprepared. How can this be true? Is this right? The doctor in him takes over, and he lifts his father's wrist in his hand, presses his fingers to the hollow just below the pad of the thumb. Nothing.

Reichman stands, then panics. What does a person do? and he steps quickly to the kitchen, dials 911. "I'm calling . . ." he starts, then starts over again. "I think my father is dead," he says, and hears the hollow echo of his voice as he gives the directions to the house on Pequot Road.

While he waits for someone to come, he sits in the living room. He has no one to call, no friend. Amy? No. He sits in the living room with his dad, and finally, tells him everything, how he had loved Amy so much he didn't care that she wasn't a Jew, how he had hated his mother's long deep sorrow that nothing could touch. "I loved you," he says. Then, "I don't know what to do," he says to his father, as the evening light fades and the ambulance arrives in the drive.

—

"Schwartz Brothers Funeral Home," he tells the ambulance crew, tells them to call the Orthodox rabbi, as his father had wanted, as he'd arranged.

But then, after the ambulance attendants carefully pull a sheet to cover his father's face and take him away, Bob Reichman walks to the kitchen, and from under the phone book, in the jumble of papers and pencils and notes, he finds the photocopied booklet the Havarah sent him, with everyone's numbers and names. Numbers he's never wanted to phone. The Havarah leader, David Newman, an attorney whose attempts after *kiddush* on Friday nights to involve him Reichman has successfully dodged, is the one to call in case of death.

Reichman dials the number, waits for the ring, preparing to leave a message on the answering machine. When David Newman answers, he stumbles, unsure what to say or how to begin. First, he has to explain who he is, until Newman's memory is jogged. "The reason I'm calling," Reichman says into the phone, "the funniest thing—my father just died," and to his astonishment, he nearly starts to cry, but instead, swallows down hard, while Newman tells him how the arrangements will be made, tells him about what will happen next, now that he's called, now that his father is dead.

At the cemetery, the trees are coming into leaf, everything brushed with a sheen of green, the deep smells of the newly mowed grass and the freshly dug earth blending into one long, low note. From the grave, over the words of the prayers the Orthodox rabbi is chanting, Reichman can hear the rumble of the river, swollen now with rain water and snowmelt. The river, always in one place, always on its way somewhere else.

Predictably, Roz hasn't come for the funeral; it took Reichman two days just to get her on the phone, and her ambivalence is such that in the end, it wasn't worth it for her to drop everything and get a flight from London just for this. But even as Reichman's analyzing her neglect, he's forgiving her, too, forgiving her for leaving him to take care of this alone.

Reichman tosses in the first shovelful of dirt, hears it clatter onto the wood. Reichman's boyhood Hebrew doesn't *come back,* it wasn't away someplace; it was waiting for him all along, nestled somewhere in the deeper reaches of his brain. *"Yisgadal, v'yitkadash shemeh rabbah,"* Reichman says, the small group of Jews who have come to this burial chiming in with *"b'ra chu,"* their voices lifting up into the bright April air in a chorus.

⌒

Since she found the bandanna with her birth certificate and photo, Blue's more distracted at the diner, mixing up orders, forgetting to bring the customers their coffee or their bills. Her tips are slipping down, and she's glad now—she wasn't before—that the waitresses don't pool their tips as they've told her some restaurants demand they do, because she doesn't want to show them, doesn't want to admit how much she's messing up.

"What the hell is with her now?" Bethany says in a hot whisper to Tiff, as they pass in the kitchen, arms filled with platters of food, or with piles of empty glasses and plates.

In between her appointments with Dr. Reichman, now it's all she can think of: her birth certificate, the name, Brenda LaPlatte, and she practices saying the name under her breath, practices sometimes writing it. Who is Brenda LaPlatte? Where did she live, and what did she do?

Easter Sunday, and the diner's decorated with cut-out cardboard eggs in pastel colors. She pulls plates of lamb with mint jelly in pinched paper cups toward her through the kitchen window, carries the plates to the tables of customers dressed in their Easter best, the women with bright corsages of miniature carnations or gardenias pinned to the lapels of their pale yellow or pink suits, the men smelling still of aftershave and soap.

Once Dr. Reichman verifies her birth certificate, after that, what will he find? The name of her grammar school, an address of a home? Already she's pulling back from the life, such as it is, that she's been making here in Intervale. *Her life,* she has to remind herself, but now, now that she's got a name, now that Dr. Reichman's trying to track down who she is, this life of hers feels more distant, and whatever-came-before feels as if it's closer in.

She walks down to the river a few more times, and every time she looks carefully down at the ground as she goes, but there's nothing more out here, nothing to be found except the trash spit up from the river. Out there, the water's a roiling rumble, swollen by the melted ice and spring rains. There'd be no crossing it, if one wanted to.

⌒

In the pool, Reichman cuts through the water slowly, feeling a sob gasp up in his throat every time he turns his head to breathe. He watches the tiles beneath him slide by, and remembers his snorkeling trip with Amy in the gin-clear Caribbean, how it was like flying over a lawn of waving grasses where fish brighter than flowers grazed in the puffy coral and silky sand.

He stops at the far end of the lane, takes off his goggles, wipes his eyes. He looks up at the clock: just after five. Somehow he's nearly gotten through shiva, the first seven days of the world turned inside out, a group of Havarah members corralled by Newman into meeting each night at Reichman's house, so that he could say Kaddish at home those first seven nights. Except for Pesach, when he forced himself to join them at the Unitarians' building, forced himself to attend the service portion of the celebration. Tonight's the last night in the seven first days of his mourning, and he's planning tonight to feed these members of the Havarah, these strangers who've been so damn nice to him that he can't help but reciprocate.

And then, as he curls into a flip turn, remembering again why all this is, *his father is dead,* his chest begins to quiver with the crying, and he thinks, he isn't annoyed, or mad: he's just sad, and he floats back down into the water, counting his laps in his head.

⌒

Annie's coloring in the sunroom when Reichman approaches. She's forgotten her ten o'clock appointment with him, so absorbed is she in the picture she's making, painstakingly coloring in every moment of the page. *Coloring blue for my sadness, red for my rage.*

He sits on the sofa beside her chair. "Hi Annie," he says, and as she looks up at him, he feels something drop away, some pretense he's been putting on with her. His sadness blows through him so fully he can't try to hide it, and he wants to say, "My father died," but of course doesn't, instead reigns himself in. He looks at her drawing: tiny red and blue scratch marks intersecting, like a Van Gogh. "What are you drawing?" he asks.

"It's rage and sadness," she says, speaking so clearly for the moment around her cleft lip that he's taken aback.

"What does the drawing tell you about them?" he asks.

"Oh, the rage spills out onto the page. You know, I've been mad my whole life," she says, and looks up at him. "And the sadness, that goes with it, too, along for the ride with nothing to hide."

"What do you mean, with nothing to hide?" In a crazy way, this statement of hers makes sense to him, but only on an intuitive level; he needs to discern how lucid she is, and he fears he's spent so much time talking with her that he can no longer tell if she's making sense.

"Well, the sadness I think is because of the anger. I mean, if you're angry, you lose something, right? And then you're sad. And the sadness has nothing to hide, because it isn't guilty, it isn't the feeling to blame, it doesn't have the stain of the name."

Reichman nods, scratches his fingers into his beard. "The sadness is pure," he says, and she nods at this, again looking up. "Yeah, that's right. The sadness will river me, I mean, will deliver me like a river back into my home," she says, drawing short, sharp marks on the page with her blue crayon.

At his desk, Reichman writes up his notes on Annie, then dictates into his microphone his reasoning behind authorizing her release in one week: she's fairly coherent, she has an understanding of her emotions, and she's on an even keel with her medications. He recommends twice-weekly visits to see him, and states clearly that she must continue with her meds, but even as he's signing off, he knows she won't, knows that he's releasing her back into her world of voices and visions.

He looks up at the clock then: his only chance to say Kaddish now that the *shiva* period is over is by going to the Orthodox synagogue for the evening service at seven, and now it's nearly four. *The sadness will river me, I mean, will deliver me like a river back into my home,* he hears Annie say in his head. Just time to clear his desk, grab a sandwich at the cafeteria. He moves quickly. Thirty days, he promises himself. For thirty evenings in a row, he'll go, and hope that the prayer really does lift his father's soul heavenward, wherever that is.

~

I told the doctor about the feelings spilling onto the page, but not the details. Does the story ever matter? Does the story ever make sense?

My sheaf of pictures lies neatly on my dresser, weighted down by Kitty and my other things. The pile of papers grows until it nearly blows, even though it takes me a whole day to make just one. There's the red and blue of sadness and rage, and there's the white on white of the bright light waiting for me at the tunnel's end. There's the cluster of silky lavender pigeons, and the bad black marks.

I told the doctor about the feelings, about the pictures I can make if I go slow and take my time. He's letting me go soon, he said so himself.

And then I'll be back on the road, out on my way, hitching a ride into the day.

Reichman stops in his office between his swim and the minyan, just in case, just to see. There's the usual sheaf of messages on his desk, and he looks through them eagerly, the cancellations and the pleas for appointments, the hospital reports, the copy of his signed authorization granting Annie Blaise's use of grounds. And then, there it is: a message from Hal Gordo in Boston, calling to confirm the birth certificate, calling to say they've found some of the records of Brenda's early life. The message gives a number at the Department of Social Services for Reichman to call if he wants to know more. He knows this means the baby—Blue—went into some kind of state care. It can't mean anything good.

It isn't much, but it's something, he thinks. At least now he knows that this birth certificate is real, and he can imagine a girl, scared, fifteen years old, in 1960. Blue's mother. Did she leave her baby at the hospital, did she run away, abandoning the baby as she herself was most likely abandoned in her own particular way? Or did she take the baby, Brenda, Blue, and raise her as best she could?

He looks at the clock: it's almost six-thirty, and he packs up his things, carefully folds the paper with the information on it, weights it down with his glass ball globe, and heads out to the synagogue.

She must have been born to this, born into this loneliness. When will Dr. Reichman ever have some news for her? Maybe there is no one out there to find: maybe she never belonged to anyone. Maybe, she thinks, no one is looking for her. No one but that crazy woman following her around, acting as if she knows her, acting like she's got some claim.

What does it mean to love someone? At the QwikMart, Blue stands before the rack of magazines, with their bright spring colors, their lemon yellow and lime green, and reads the titles of the stories: *Sex Secrets You Must Know, How Men Think,* and *Is It Love?* She pulls a magazine out from its slot on the shelf, flips through the pages until she finds it. There's a photo of a pretty young woman holding out both hands, palms up, and in one palm is a big red heart, in the other a key. She looks puzzled, brow wrinkled up, looking as confused as Blue feels.

But standing in the market reading the article, Blue finds it tells her nothing. She shoves the magazine back in the rack, mad, its cover now marked with her fingerprints. At the checkout, the boy says, "How're you doing?" and she just says "Fine," as she puts her milk and bread on the counter.

She sees the row of cigarette boxes that lie stacked behind his head. A cigarette, that's what she wants, that's what she needs. "I'd like a pack of cigarettes," she says, and the kid at the counter, being a nice Intervale boy, doesn't say sarcastically, "Well, we've got about hundred kinds," but just says, "What brand?" and she scans the brands for one that might fit. "Camel," she says, liking the picture of the animal on the neat white packet, which looks to her clean.

He passes the pack across to her, and she pays for her things, then tosses the cigarettes into the bag.

What's love? she thinks, and thinks then she should have asked that boy; he's probably in love with a girl. He probably knows better than anyone what love isn't and is, what love can mean.

Up the concrete pathway to her building, and the remains of winter linger here, the wash of silt and sand from melted snow, a mitten lying on the pavement, waiting to be claimed.

From her window, settling her things on the counter, Blue sees the pickup truck again, pulling up, idling in the spring evening, window rolled down. From the front window of her apartment, Blue can see into the cab, but she can see only the hands of the driver at the wheel, not the driver's face. The hands move, lighting a cigarette, and as night approaches and the street goes dark, Blue can see just a cigarette's lit tip.

She remembers then the beach, the bonfire on the sand, how she could see the wick of her mother's cigarette glowing orange above the flames, as if her mother had taken a tiny circle of the fire, a spot, and held it in her hands. She remembers watching the fire from inside the house, from behind the windowed wall, watching her mother dancing on the beach by the fire, watching her mother stumble and fall.

Now, Blue watches this stranger's cigarette pass from the lighted dash into the secret dark recesses of the cab, glow bright, then pass forward again.

She's half-hidden behind the curtain, and she's left the lights off, so she's sure she can't be seen as she watches her watcher as if in a dream.

⌒

Rita isn't surprised when at the roadhouse the jukebox switches off and the lights suddenly go out, and the singing begins, *"happy birthday to you,"* and here comes Stelly carrying a cake, shielding the candles from the breeze she makes by crossing the room to where Rita stands, pool cue in hand, just about to make her shot.

She waits for a long moment before blowing the candles out, even though she knows what she wants; she doesn't have to think about this. Still, a birthday wish is a powerful thing, and she doesn't want to waste it, not this time, not this special year. She focuses, with everyone standing around her, watching, and she wishes, as she often has on birthdays: *let me find my twin.* But this time, this year, she knows it will happen, knows it has to come true.

And then she blows, and the thirty-one candles flicker, then quit, and then a few, scattered, re-ignite, and she blows again before realizing they're trick candles, and like the flame a little laughter's beginning to start up among the people standing in a semicircle around her, until she straightens, laughs too, then makes a face at Stelly, clenches her face and her fist in a mock threat.

"Hey, Stelly," she calls across the table, "I'm only thirty now. You don't have to push it."

"It's one for good luck. Not that you need it," Stelly calls back, and everyone laughs.

"Speech, speech," Jake shouts from the back, and Rita's scared for a moment, but then she says, "Well, I guess I just want to say that I have a good feeling about this coming year, and that you guys are the best," she says, then lifts her bottle of beer, and everyone drinks.

"Okay, okay, let's get that off the felt," Claude says, coming over officiously, picking up the cake, settling it on a nearby table, handing Rita a knife from the kitchen. The lights come back on to their usual dim level, and the music resumes, the jukebox groaning back to life.

After she cuts and serves up the slices of cake, Rita hands Bart his plate and he says, "Oh no, I shouldn't," as he's taking the fork into his hand.

She stands to one side with him, licks the first forkful of sugared frosting from the tines, and Bart says, "What did you wish for?"

"You know it's bad luck to say."

"Come on, Rita, I'm your best friend."

"No," she says, forking up a dollop of blue and white icing. "I'll just say it involved finding something."

"Hhmmm. I can only imagine. True Love," Bart says knowingly.

"Not quite. You may be surprised."

"Oh?" Bart raises his eyebrows at her. "You have something in the works you haven't told me about?"

"Kind of. I don't know yet. And until I know, I'm not saying anything more," Rita says, and then, hearing a new song skip onto the jukebox, she puts her paper plate down on the table, already moving her shoulders and hips to the music. "Won't you dance with me? It's my birthday," she says to Bart, but he shakes his head. "You know I can't dance. Go find Al or Jake," he says, and she does, dancing through the crowd, taking Jake's elbow as she passes, leading him onto the dance floor, singing along and clapping her hands.

~

Reichman's just arrived at his office at the hospital, having checked in with the nurses and made his inpatient rounds, when the ringing phone makes him hurry his key in the lock, and he picks up the receiver just in time.

It's a woman's voice, a friend of Ira Aronson in the social services department in Boston calling him back. "We've found the records you were looking for," she says.

"Go ahead," Reichman says, forcing his voice into its professional depth, even though he knows in this moment he's too involved, cares too much about Blue.

"We've got a Brenda LaPlatte at St. Elizabeth's Hospital on January 27, 1960. But there's more to it, not on the birth certificate but in her file, noting that she was put into foster care. She was a foundling, abandoned."

The confirmation of this wells up in Reichman like a wave: *of course.* Blue would have had something enormously tragic in her distant past for her to become so thoroughly awash in amnesia.

"But if she was abandoned, how is the mother's name on the birth certificate?"

He writes quickly as the woman tells him more. The mother, fifteen years old, had left the baby on the steps of St. Elizabeth's Hospital. "That's really the way it often happened, in the fifties, sixties," she says. "The girls who were in that kind of situation just did what they'd always seen done in movies." The baby's grandmother had called later and reported that the mother was Colleen LaPlatte, and that she left town.

"Did anyone track her down? Did she ever come back?" Reichman says into the phone, no longer thinking of Blue, just thinking of the pain that must have been lodged in that young girl's heart for her to leave her baby and never look back.

Arrested for abandoning the baby, three years at Framingham Women's Prison, and then, nothing. A few cursory calls were made, to friends of the girl, but the grandmother of the baby seemed to have little interest in the whole matter, and so the baby was put into foster care.

Reichman writes down the names of the foster families that were recorded. The woman in Boston tells him she's sorry, she can't tell him much more. Six months in a group home when the child was eight, then a whole year's history missing like a book missing a page. A chapter, Reichman thinks. No wonder she slipped into a fugue: the real question is, when wasn't she in a fugue, if ever? The last record is that she ran away when she was fourteen, and since then, they've got nothing.

Finally, he writes down her own name, thanks her for her help. "If you come up with anything else . . ." he begins, and she says she'll call back again if she does, but he knows this is probably it, probably all that he'll get. She's got other matters to contend with now, living children she's responsible for, children waiting for someone, anyone, to rescue them.

Reichman looks down at his notes. He's written so fast that his handwriting has come out in an inky scrawl, a scrawl like his father's handwriting, which all his life he's tried so hard not to copy. He's still standing up, and goes now to the window, winds it open, and looks down at the lilacs starting to bloom on the hospital lawn. Someone planted them years ago; they must be at least fifty years old, as old as he is. Someone who cared about having color and a sweet scent sharpening into the spring air.

Isn't every adoptee in a sense in a fugue? Stumbling along without a bloodline, without the marvelous map of a parent's aging to follow, without a sister mirroring a hand gesture, with no brother's musical talent to mime? The adoptee moves through her years without ever seeing a face that holds the beautiful, terrifying image of her own within it, subtle, hidden, alive. There must always be that question, tucked away, nascent: *where did I come from?*

When should he tell Blue about this news? And how? He leans against the window frame, suddenly worried, no, more than that: *deeply afraid,* that this means the end. He's occupied himself so well with this one patient that he knows he's projected onto her all his loneliness; finding her past, helping her to remember has become his excuse. And now, now that he's finding out who she is, now what will he do?

⌒

Annie Blaze sits on the bench between two towering lilacs at the side of the hospital as if she's waiting for someone. She remembers the smell of the lilacs from someplace in her childhood, that scent like burning sugar. A house, one of the nicer ones, a place where they took her in for a winter and a spring. She remembers pressing her face into the big puff-ball lilacs, then breathing in, as if the sweet scent could erase everything else.

Sitting there, she looks as if she's waiting for someone, but in all her months in the hospital no one has come, and no one is coming for her now, and from the hospital window Alison Crue looks down, thinking, *she's lost.* She goes down in the elevator, stops in the hospital store, then sits beside Annie on the bench, heaving out a sigh, turning her face to the sky. The spring day is perfect, the sky picture-book blue, white clouds puffing by, more the setting for a story of a little girl planting a garden than a story of a bunch of crazy people locked up together.

"Sure is pretty out," she says to Annie, and Annie doesn't turn, but mutters, "Yeah. I guess it's good timing the doctor gave me grounds, huh?"

"Yeah, I guess so. You know what that means," Alison Crue says.

"Any day now I shall be released," Annie says. She says this while pushing her fists up in the air, but says it without enthusiasm, and the discrepancy between her voice, nasally, affectless, and her behavior makes Alison wonder if maybe Dr. Reichman's releasing her too soon.

"Here, would you like a fireball?" she says, holding open her hand, and in her palm rest two twin red balls, each snug in its cellophane envelope.

"Really? You mean it? Thanks," Annie says, and slips the fireball into her mouth, where it burns brighter and brighter, like something powerful and new. She leans her head back against the bench, enjoying the warmth of the sun on her face, and she looks then almost like she could be anyone, her matted hair neatly clipped short and growing in clean, wearing clothes she found in the hospital rummage box. Except for her lip with a cleft that runs nearly all the way to her nose. In this moment, she doesn't look like a woman who teeters between this world and that.

Soon enough she'll get out, soon enough she'll go back.

What happens to the riverbank in spring? Does the river swell up with rain and melting snow? Is it a rumble and a roil, or is it smooth as light, pale as a silver braid? Is the rabbit still there, and the home that I made?

In his hospital office, his sandwich still wrapped in a wax paper envelope, Reichman thinks maybe it's best that he hasn't told Blue about her history, about the foster homes, at least not yet. She has to be ready, and in the meantime, the more information he can get his hands on, the better. He wants to present her with as much as he can, not just hand her more fragments and shreds.

But he's stymied in his search. The physician listed on the birth certificate is retired to Florida, and the grandmother, Blue's—Brenda's, he corrects himself—grandmother is dead, and by now, in that section of Boston, skinny apartment houses and falling down duplexes, most likely any childhood neighbors have moved away.

He picks up the notes again, leafs through the addresses and names until he finds the last foster home listed, the one from which she ran away for the last time, when she was fourteen, nineteen years ago. It's a long shot, but he calls information, asks for Phelan, and there's a number listed, at the same address, and hand shaking, he dials, and waits for the ring.

"Hello," a man's voice yells into the phone.

"Good afternoon," Reichman says, hearing at once how stilted he sounds. "I'm calling with kind of an odd situation—"

"You selling something? We don't buy on the phone," the man cuts in.

"No, no, not at all. The thing is, I'm working on behalf of someone who I believe may have lived with you at one time, a Brenda LaPlatte, a foster child."

"Yeah?"

"Well, first of all, is this the right Phelan? Did you have a foster child named Brenda LaPlatte, about twenty years ago, around 1975?"

There's a pause on the phone, and Reichman thinks for a moment the man has hung up. But then, "Yeah, I think we did. I think so. I don't know. We had a bunch of them kids. We tried to give them a home, you know. Nothing wrong with that, is there?"

"No, no sir. But you do remember her? She ran away from your home, the paperwork says."

"Oh yeah, that one. The runaway. That's one I'm not likely to forget. She was terrible trouble, right from the start. A real smart aleck. I said to my wife we shouldn't keep her, but she insisted. But who are you, why do you care?"

"Well, I'm her physician, and she's here, in Maine, and she's got amnesia, and we're trying to find any living relatives of hers."

"Yeah? Amnesia, huh?"

"And, well, it seemed you were the last family on record she lived with, and we thought maybe—"

"Look, I don't want any trouble. We already had the whole damn investigation when she ran off, and they found out we were fine, we didn't do anything to make her run off like that. Forget it," and the phone clicks off in Reichman's ear, and he's left with the echo trembling there, the echo of the silence that must have been Blue's childhood.

⌒

Since the first years of his residency, Reichman hasn't had to give his patients too much news, hasn't handed out diagnoses, watching the patient's face for that tremble of shock, or the laughter that spills out on hearing: *negative.*

But now, Blue. He's got to tell her the news, and he's got all the papers together, and when he goes to the door, says, "Blue? Come on in," he's ready, prepared.

"I found some information," he begins, thinking it's the first time he's been the one to start a session.

Blue looks scared, he thinks. "You did? Do you know who I am?"

"Well, yes and no. There's still a lot of digging to do, and I'm afraid there isn't much information about your most recent past."

But that's what I want, Blue thinks. *I want to know who I am, now. Who I was just before.*

"I've found some records that indicate that you were put into foster care very early on, and that you lived with a few different families. I only found one of the foster families still listed," Reichman says. It's only a partial lie. He did look up a few of the others, but most were homes in which she lived only three months, or sometimes, six.

"What did they say? Did they remember me?"

"Yes, they did. It was the last home you were in, the one you ran away from when you were fourteen," he says.

"Well, what did they say? What did they say about me?"

"They really didn't remember much, Blue. The man I spoke with said he remembered that you were very smart, and you ran away." He isn't lying; he's only stretching the truth, he tells himself, knowing this too is a lie. But which would be worse?

"Oh." Blue's disappointment fills the air of the room like smoke. "So there's no one after that? They don't know where I went, or what happened to me next?"

"No, I'm afraid not. I'm sorry. But I'll keep looking. Now that we have your name, there have to be some other records out there, maybe something more recent." Is it wrong of him to lead her on like this? What if he's giving her hope where there is none?

Blue's gone silent, her gaze catching on the line of rooftops outside his office window. She's thinking of how she could make a jump from roof to roof, out there.

"Blue? What are you feeling?"

She turns back to him. "You mean I was abandoned?"

Reichman draws in a deep breath, lets it out like a sigh. "I wouldn't say abandoned, Blue. Maybe your mother knew she couldn't care for you properly and so gave you away. She was only fifteen."

"I don't like this. I don't think this is true," she says then, quietly. *No, no, no,* inside her head like a bell.

Reichman isn't surprised she's reacting this way, rejecting the history now they've found it, especially because it's so damned bad. No wonder she went into a fugue; no wonder she's been so resistant to reclaiming her memory, no wonder she hasn't wanted to go back.

⌒

Reichman catches himself staring out his window in his office at the hospital. He's been watching a robin fly from the pine tree out, then back again, and as he watches, he realizes its got a nest in there. Such a common summer bird here, in Maine, ubiquitous, but lately, his window open to the warming air, he's been listening to its song, appreciating the simple, perfect melody, as if the robin's song can bring him from his grief into the waking, necessary world.

Now, he turns to the stack of papers he's collected on amnesia during the winter. Wasn't there one titled something about persistent fugue, one that mentioned the search for the amnesiac's origins?

Yes, here it is. Fugue patients often turn up at their places of origin, the paper points out, like a criminal returning to the scene of a crime, and often these places *are* crime scenes, the place where the patient witnessed an atrocity, the place where the inability to live in the world was nailed down: the place of their youth. Reichman thinks of the old man he read about, a death camp survivor, who took an apartment near Auschwitz after the war and every day now walks to the camp, now a museum, asking visitors if they want to hear his story, telling his story again and again. "This is the spot where I last saw my mother," he says. "These are the barracks where we were kept." Every day, even on Shabbes. Is he in a fugue?

Return. What is it we spend our lives returning to? Return makes him think *t'shuvah,* the return, the introspection and penance of turning back to Torah and God, turning back into Judaism. What you gain and what you give up that's at the heart of Yom Kippur, at the heart of saying Kaddish. At the heart of being a Jew?

And Blue? Could Blue have returned to her origins? Could she have originated right here, in Intervale? *Wait,* he thinks, with the cold realization starting to burn in his chest: he hasn't checked medical records right here at the Intervale Hospital.

He moves quickly, then, his blood quickening, calls down to Medical Records. "Hey Stacy," he says, and she says, "Hi Dr. R., what's up? Did you make any progress on that Annie Blaise you were looking for?"

"What a memory you have," he says, knowing as he's saying it he's hoping the compliment will buy him some favors. "No, we're still waiting for something from law enforcement. You'd think now they're getting those new computers in they'd be able to look up someone's fingerprints without waiting months."

"Yeah, well, down here we try to do better than that. What can I do for you?"

"I have another name I'm looking for. How about last name LaPlatte, first name Colleen. Middle name McGlew. Sorry, I only have the year of birth, 1946."

"Hold on," she says, and he can hear her computer keys clicking under her nails. "I've got—oh yeah, here she is. Dead."

"Dead?" Reichman tries to assimilate these two poles of information at once: *Yes, she lived here, and now she's dead.*

He pitches for a moment into the finality of this. "You're sure? When did she die?"

"I'll send you a copy of the record, but it looks like a little over a year ago, no, a year and six months. Liver failure. Died right here at Intervale Hospital."

"Okay. Relatives?" It's going too fast, Reichman thinks. Wait. This means he was right, and Blue did return to her origins. Her mother *was* here, and died just a year before Blue arrived. *T'shuvah*, to her mother, her birth mother, the one who abandoned her how many years ago? Thirty-four.

"Yeah, one. A daughter, Rita LaPlatte."

——

The conveyer belt clanks to life, and Rita pauses a moment before getting to her feet, feeling so tired she could just stay sitting, and for a moment she even imagines how it would feel to do this, to just sink back into the molded plastic seat, watch as the papers fall from the rolling metal belt and onto the floor.

But she's too well trained, and it's only a few seconds before she's on her feet, and then, with the first papers that she stacks and ties, she sees the headline: AMNESIAC HAS ROOTS IN INTERVALE. If she could, Rita would pull the switch, stop the press, because she knows what this means, and yet she can't, she has to wait, and she stacks the papers, holding her excitement tight in her chest, feeling as if she's about to burst. But she's still cautious as ever, and makes sure that no one will see her slip one paper under her arm as she jumps into the cab of her truck.

Once she's out of the *Gazette* parking lot, Rita pulls off to the side, reads the article through. They believe her mother was from Intervale, but they're waiting to publish her name, they're trying to find her next of kin. The article says only that Blue was adopted, put into foster care. It doesn't make any mention of twins.

Just the way she always figured the story went. Her own mother, her real mother, giving birth to twins. This must be how it feels to win the lottery, Rita thinks. On the roadside she reads the article through one more time, then puts it aside, pulls onto Route 3, turns WKID on high, and plans her next move.

After her route's done, Rita heads home. It must be her *twin*. How could this be happening? It's like a dream come true, and she kneels in front of her altar, lights a white candle for thanking the universe for making it happen. She remembers all the good signs she's been seeing lately, finding the woman out on the bridge, getting the lottery tickets with the wolf on them. Maybe her luck really has started to turn, and now she'll be able to get what she wanted all along. Get what she deserves.

In her bedroom, Rita stands in front of her closet door staring in. What will she wear? She wants to look good, wants to look like she should. She clatters the clothes past on their hangers. A dressy T-shirt, the white one with the shimmering silver beads stapled into the cloth? Or something more down-to-earth? Her stone-washed jeans.

Who is she kidding? Blue knows her for exactly what she is, already. How will she even get her to talk? Does Blue remember seeing her when she followed her this winter? Why did she go into the diner like that, asking Blue if she had a twin? God, how can she cover that up? What would Blue want with her anyway, *loser loser loser*, she says to herself in the cave of her head.

She pulls on her jeans, her black sweater with the sequins stitched in around the neckline. Why hasn't she at least tried to do something else, do something more? If she'd started something before now, she wouldn't be in this fix, she'd be able to say that she's taking courses somewhere, that she's just working at the *Gazette* to pay the rent, to support herself while she's in school. What about the course Bart signed up for this spring at the Intervale Community Center?

She checks the glowing bedroom clock: she knows Blue's schedule, and she's still got a little time, so she picks up the phone, calls Bart at home.

"Hey," she says, without any preliminaries. "Is it too late to get in on that course you're taking?"

"I thought you said Music for Listeners sounded like the most boring thing a person could do, if I recall correctly."

"Well, yeah, I know, I was being harsh. I've just been thinking about it, and I've got to do something, you know, I've got to get out of this rut that I'm in."

⌣

It's to the river Blue takes her new information, takes *what Dr. Reichman told her:* she's a woman from Boston, a woman without a family, without a home. A baby shuttled into foster care. Of course, she thinks, I knew it. And she did, didn't she? Those nights all winter long, lying on her back on her living room floor, the pulse beating in her wrist and neck: *alone, alone, alone.*

Out here, by the river, she feels more alone now than she did before. Dr. Reichman won't use the word *abandoned,* but this word persists in her, as she watches Random nosing in the grass, coming up with just an empty paper bag this time.

Abandoned, she thinks, breathing in the river wind, as she sits on the big rock, feeling the sun warm on her face. *Abandoned,* and now, she thinks, *found?*

She breathes the smells in, too: damp earth, old and new leaves. So what if that was her origin? At least now she's got a start. She looks up: an orange and black motion high in the tops of the new green leaves. She looks again: a *redstart,* she knows, and remembers then walking out in the woods, a woods not unlike this, walking with someone, a woman with a flash of blonde hair, both of them tilting their heads back to look up into the trees. *Tenderness.*

"Random," she calls, and hears a rustle in the leaves, then here he is, panting back up to her. "Don't go too far," she cautions, even though she can see this isn't necessary: it's as if she's all he's ever known.

But now she's supposed to make a new life, again? What about her life right before the fugue?

She must have had friends, and someone more than that, too to remember, the paper flowers blooming in the glass, the voice saying *make for me a snow angel.* This is what she's longing for, this is what she wants to find; not this life of going in each week to talk to her psychiatrist, of being watched by the girls at the diner as if she's an animal who at any moment might turn, and bite. She wants to find the person who loved her. The person she loved, too.

"Random," she calls out again, suddenly afraid he'll run off for good, suddenly so afraid that she'll lose him that she starts to feel a panic rise up. "Random!" she shouts, and then there's a thrashing in the undergrowth, a noise of dogtail slashing leaves and tree branches, a little cry, and here he comes, a silky bundle of limp fur hanging from his mouth, its eyes wide in animal terror. It's alive, but Blue can see the blood mixing with saliva along the pup's mouth, and in one motion she bends to the ground, her hand finds a stick, and she raises it, even as Random's looking up at her so hopeful and proud.

At the sight of the stick (*does he remember the stake in the cement square? does he remember how she came to claim him?*) he drops the rabbit, crouches low, whines out a whimper that Blue hasn't heard since that first day she found him.

Still, she's still mad. So angry, and unsure, really, why. She grabs his collar, and he continues to crouch low to the ground and cry. "You idiot," she spits, shaking his neck.

And then she lets go, crouches on the path herself, covers her face with her hands. Random raises his head, tentatively, whimpers again, but his loyalty's outrunning his fear, and he inches over to her, lays his nose on her knee. "I'm sorry," Blue says, putting her hand out to rub his soft head. "Let's go," she says, "come on," and they keep walking up the path, and then they start running, and together the two of them run alongside the river, up toward the bridges, as if by her running she'll outstrip whatever it is that's catching up to her fast.

~

High up on the railroad bridge, Rita thinks this is dangerous, to be walking across the rickety planks over the rippling waters, stepping beam to beam, so easy to slip, so easy to trip. Half way across she stops, looks out over the water, her legs a little shaky, her breath coming fast.

From her perch, she can see the other bridge, the Route 3 bridge. *The bridge where I found her*, she thinks. And then, as if by magic, Rita sees someone walking across the bridge opposite. She watches as the figure pauses right at the center of the bridge, and she thinks with a jolt, what if I saw myself over there? What if I looked up and it was me looking back at myself?

But it isn't her, of course. The bridge is so far away it's all Rita can do to make out that it's a person on the opposite side, and deflated, suddenly no longer afraid, she crosses to the other side and scrambles down the embankment to the shore.

And then she sees her. First, really, she sees the dog, racing into the underbrush as if on a mission, as if on a search. And then, here she is, Blue, her sister, her twin, what she's been wanting, what she's been missing.

Rita tries to strike a casual pose, jams her hands in her jacket pockets, glad that she dressed carefully. "You see?" she imagines saying to Bart, if she could ever tell him any of this, if she could ever confess.

She waits, slows her pace. The dog ignores her, and Blue isn't paying attention; she's looking out toward the water as she's walking, and soon they're so close that Rita says, in a normal voice, not too loud, striving for a tone of neutrality, of equanimity, "Hi."

Blue starts. "Oh," she says, and her eyes fill with fear. How did this woman know where to find her? Is she following her every move?

"Hi," Rita says again. She's stopped in her tracks. "Listen, I just wanted to tell you, I mean, I didn't follow you down here or anything, but I want you to know something. I think maybe it can help you."

"Yeah?" Blue says, cutting her eyes left, then right. "What?" She's ready to run, ready to bolt.

"Well, you know when I asked if you had a twin? At the diner that time? Well, the thing is, I think I'm her. I mean, I don't have a lot of evidence," Rita says, hearing in her head Bart saying, *What do you mean, a lot? Like, you don't have one shred!* But Rita goes on: "But I really think you may have a twin. I think that I'm her," and here she pauses, waits for this to sink in. Waits for Blue to drop her guard, come closer in.

But Blue just stands there, looking around a little nervously, shifting her eyes left to right and back again, looking down at her feet as they sink a little into the spring-softened sand.

"I mean, I don't want to freak you out. Listen, I live above the stationer's, on Main. You know where that is, right?" Blue nods, yes.

"Well, if you ever want to come by, if you want to know more, come find me, okay? That's all," and Rita stops, waiting still for Blue to say something, not walking on, not turning away.

"Look," Blue says, "Just leave me alone." Then she calls out, "Random!" and walks past Rita, toward the railroad bridge, away, leaning down to tousle the dog's head and ears, leaving Rita standing on the riverbank.

Blue doesn't turn, not once, to look back at Rita, to smile or wave or call back that she was just kidding. Rita knows; she watches Blue's silent retreating back the whole time, standing perched on one big stone, hands jammed into the pockets of her jeans, watching until woman and dog disappear under the railroad bridge, where the river curves south and then pulls out beyond the town. She realizes then, *dummy,* she didn't even tell Blue her name.

⌒

Looking through his father's things, Reichman's struck by how little there is; there were only a few boxes his father wanted to keep, from all the spoils of the house in Brookline. Reichman's incorporated some of the furniture into his house, his mother's candlesticks, the rose wing chair and some of the black and white family photos, but most of it's been sold or given away to charity. When Roz comes to visit from England this summer, they'll sort through what remains.

But in the guest room his father has tucked away his personal things, so few and so neatly arranged that Reichman thinks his father must have known he was about to die, and realizes then that of course he knew: he was

eighty-four, his memory couldn't trap even the simplest beads of daily negotiations, and he was moving up to Maine to live with his son. *What, I should
think this could mean maybe a vacation to Italy?* Reichman can hear his father
joke, and he smiles, laughs a little.

He looks in the closet, runs his fingers down the arm of his father's
good suit, a suit he only wore once after he moved to Intervale, for his meeting with the Orthodox rabbi. From the dresser, he picks up his father's
watch; the second hand is still sweeping the face. He looks out the window,
then, looks at the view his father looked at for the last weeks of his life. The
ferns have now unfolded from their winter curls, and Reichman can see a few
blooms on the apple tree. Was this the wrong thing to do? Was it selling the
house and moving up here that killed his father?

Reichman knows better; his father was dying, was on his way out, his
mind focused on the world to come, whatever that is. Outside, the early
morning is bright, and clear, the air rinsed by the night's brief rain. By the
bed, here's his father's battered old siddur, and Reichman picks it up, turns
to the first pages, his fingers remembering to turn the pages, right to left,
hooking into the pages like a trout catching onto a hook.

He can read the Hebrew words of the morning prayers, even though
he isn't sure what they mean, can't quite capture from his memory if *da'at's*
intelligence or worship. *"Kadosh, kadosh kadosh,"* Reichman reads out loud,
feels that trembling again in his voice that means he's about to cry. He puts
the siddur down, then sees his father's tallis, folded and lying on the
straight-backed chair.

He picks up the tallis as if it's a living animal, as if he should be careful,
as if it might bite. Why wasn't his father buried in it? he wonders, then
remembers how the Orthodox rabbi said something about his father's "unusual
request." Reichman's own tallis disappeared from his possession sometime
during college, when the last thing he wanted was a reminder of his history,
a reminder of his past. A loss he had thought his father never forgave.

Now, his hands and arms remember how to sweep the tallis onto his
shoulders, even if his mind forgets the prayer. Wrapped up in the cottony
cloth, Reichman lies down on the bed, cradles himself. Embraced by the
tallis, he doesn't choke back his crying, doesn't make himself stop.

Blue walks through the town, from one end to the other, then circumnavigates the whole place: from her row house on River Road, she turns left, heads into town, past the QwikMart, all the way until the wide road becomes Main Street. She passes Hansen's Variety, and Crystal 'N Sands, and Bodeo's. She passes the stationer's, and the big glass door that leads upstairs to the apartment where, she knows, Rita lives. Number 27 Main. Then up the hill, to the hospital grounds where she sits on a bench looking out over the town, watching.

She sits a long time there in the sun, and closes her eyes. She's come so far: she remembers then the plane lifting off the ground in its terrible roar, remembers looking down to see the blue ocean below.

She looks up, sees two gulls sail overhead, then dip down toward the river.

What doesn't she remember? She may never know, never be sure. The gulls pass back overhead; or are these a different pair? And Blue feels the late afternoon sun dissipating, feels the chill in the air begin, and starts down the hill to her appointment with Dr. Reichman, hoping he'll give her the answer, hoping he'll know what to say.

But as she approaches his building, her legs go so heavy, like sandbags, she thinks she can't go in. Can't possibly. *No.*

The big round clock face planted at the corner of Elm and Main says it's precisely four. Maybe she could walk around the block, and then be at least a little late, and delay, delay, and then she suddenly remembers that she did want to get some aspirin, and the drug store is right there, so she quickly steps across the street and into the door with the big Rx.

Five past four, the big clock reads on her return. She bolts back across, and before she can convince herself not to, she opens the door to Dr. Reichman's office. His door is open, and she comes in, breathless.

"Sorry I'm late," she says as she's sitting, taking her jacket off, putting the little waxy white bag down carefully beside her on the sofa. She offers no other excuse than this.

"That's okay," Dr. Reichman says calmly. He's been expecting this, this resistance to finding her identity. Then, "I found out something else, and I wanted to ask you about it before doing anything," he says.

"What?" Blue says, her eyes darkening in the way they do when she's girding for disappointment.

"It seems there's a possible relative of yours here in Intervale. Not your mother, but a relative of your mother's." He lets the pause stand open between them, careful not to go into it first.

"A relative? How do you know?"

Reichman explains the research at the hospital, the pattern of fugue patients returning to their origins, watching Blue carefully as he speaks. He doesn't tell her that it seems her mother is recently dead. "So you could think about whether or not you'd like to meet. I could set it up; I would be there, too," he says, wondering if he's going to far with this. Is he letting his own desire to solve everything push her too far? Will it push her away?

"I don't know," Blue says, turning then to look out the window at the bright day. "Can I think about it, or do I have to answer today?" and Reichman backs off, retreats to what he knows will work best: "How do you feel right now?"

"Sad," she says. "Lonely." She tells him then how that woman has been following her, even came into the diner a few times, and now has stopped Blue in her tracks to say that she's her twin.

Twin? Reichman wants to bolt forward: could it be possible this woman is right? Could this be the Rita LaPlatte listed as the next-of-kin? But this discovery, this revelation, isn't his to make. "You have to understand something, Blue," Reichman starts. "People project their desires onto each other all the time. It may mean more about her than it does about you."

"But the whole thing just isn't right," Blue says, determined to convince Dr. Reichman, but instead, she feels the tears start to leak from her eyes, the quivering in her voice begin.

"What do you mean?" he asks, making his voice quiet.

"How could I have been abandoned like that? What kind of person would just leave a little baby on the street? And those genes are my genes? That's part of me? If that woman who's following me around is related to me, I'd rather go back to being alone."

The tears come now, and the sobbing, and Reichman tells her what he tells all his patients who fear they're somehow stained by their parents' bad behavior, that it isn't her, it isn't who she is, that there is no determination in genes alone, just in what we make with them.

⌒

Blue takes a kitchen chair—now she's got two—out to the porch that faces the woods and the river. To call it a porch is a bit of a stretch; it's more like a rickety wooden bare flight of steps, ending up here, with a landing just big enough for a chair, an ashtray, a woman, a dog.

She opens her new pack of Camels, unwinding the little cellophane wrapper, tapping the pack against her knee, hard. She lights the cigarette, cupping her hand around the match, and when she first inhales, the bitterness makes her feel a little sick, but smoking like this gives her a link to the past, to her other life, to the person she thinks of now in the third person. *Brenda.* The woman with her face and name and history and past. She reminds herself: *"me."* She exhales long and silently, like making a big ghostly sigh.

It's early evening, and the spring smells in the air, loamy and sweet, the spring blood running inside the hard trees, making the leaves push out of their little budsacs, makes her feel excited, makes her feel like she wants something. *Desire,* she thinks. Something she hasn't felt much since she came to.

Blue rolls the ash from the cigarette's tip. Takes another long drag.

What's to remember? Why remember *this,* or *this,* or *this?* If Blue had all her memories laid out before her now like rows of pretty tiles, blue and brick and water-green, which ones would she choose? Which would she be willing to lose? She'd run her fingertips across the surfaces, choose this one, painted white with a picture of a stylized bird in blue, or this, a solid tourmaline. A tile with a red bull's eye, or another one striped black and white. What difference would it make, *this* or *this* or *this?*

After all, she'd still end up the same, here, in this riverside apartment in this broken-down row house, waiting. What difference if her childhood took place against a backdrop of scattered papers and trash windblown across varied skimpy yards? So what if she was abandoned, shuttled from one home to the next, with only the few belongings she could carry to call her own?

Blue goes inside, comes back out with a pad of paper and a pen. She's going to write a letter, and for a moment thinks that if she just sits down and starts to write, she'll be able to trick her mind into coming up with an address and a name of someone she should send it to. She starts out: *You.*

I was looking for you in the track of all those dark years. I wanted you to come for me, she writes. *I wanted you to persistently find me, again and again.*

She lights another cigarette, and the curve of the match smoke rising up triggers a feeling in her, a memory of a feeling.

I wanted you to come after me, press yourself against me in the night. Bunny, I'd call you then, whisper it against your neck, when I knew you couldn't hear. But you never heard it; I was too cautious, and who wouldn't be? Look at me, orphaned early and orphaned again. How could I trust anyone? How could I trust even you?

I don't want this searching anymore. I don't want to make up a past, or find out that all I've got is a woman, half-crazy anyway, who lives above a stationer's shop and follows me through the winter town. I don't want someone who makes believe she's got the same twisting strands of DNA binding her to me. What I want is someone who knows me, knows the me of me's, someone who has a reason to love me, someone with a reason to care.

What I want, beloved, what I want again is you.

Blue crushes her cigarette out with her fingertip. She's writing to someone, and it sure isn't Rita LaPlatte, isn't anyone here, in Intervale. But who is it, then? Down below, she can see Random nosing in the grass, and she's jealous of him, of his sensory delights, the way for him it's always simply *now, now, now.*

It can't be true, born to a mother who dumped her in the street, torn and re-planted in so many foster homes that now Dr. Reichman can't find even one that's willing to claim her. *This can't be right, this can't be me,* she thinks, and lights another cigarette.

———

Rita trudges up the sidewalk, her feet slowed. It's just dawn, and she's so tired she can barely move, and thinks that next time, she won't stay out so late, won't drink quite so much. Certainly won't stay over in some guy's filthy trailer. *There's always next time,* she sighs to herself, mounting the stairs, holding onto the railing for support.

At the top of the stairs, she stops, feels that she's being watched, and as she climbs the last three steps, she sees the watcher, lying at the foot of her own apartment door, a dog, the brown and white dog she's seen with Blue, a mixed up mutt with lots of spaniel, a little retriever, and at first, Rita's scared, she feels that quiver in her heart, that rumble of warning, remembers the dog Ed had that year, the year that she was eight, a big Doberman, lean and sleek and mean. But this dog looks up, beats its tail against the carpet that lines the hall, expectantly, as if he's been waiting for her, as if he knows who she is.

Beside the door, Rita finds a bag of dog food, two bowls, and a leash neatly coiled in on itself. That's it. She looks, but there isn't any note, no message left for her by Blue. By Brenda, her sister. This is Brenda's dog, isn't it? The dog beats his tail against the carpet again, lowers his head, gives out a little whimpering cry. Rita bends then, gingerly touches his head, then pets his neck, until she feels a collar buried there under the fur. She scrambles around, and finds first a rabies tag, with the name of the vet, and then, still shiny, newly minted, a heart-shaped nametag: Random. Blue's gone, just like that, and Rita's abandoned again, just when she had found her twin, just when she'd finally got her chance. But is Blue leaving her a secret message here, telling her something she wanted to hear, that she was her twin, after all, and by leaving her the dog is she telling her they were linked to each other through their mutual beginning under the watchful eyes of the wolf?

It must be, Rita thinks. She opens the door, gets the dog and his things inside. He must be hungry, she thinks, and pours some of the food into one of the bowls, pours water into the other.

Then, while he eats, she goes to her altar, to make a little offering. She lights a white candle, a candle for thanksgiving, closes her eyes. Blue's gone: she's lost her twin, again; she had her brief quick chance, which she blew. *Rue.* And her shellacked shell cracks just a bit, and for a moment, sitting there before the flickering candle flame, she cries.

⌣

At the train station, she half expects someone, Dr. Reichman, or Rita, or even one of the girls from the diner, to appear just as the train pulls up, to come running across the platform, to stop her. But here's the train, here's the one-way ticket in her hand.

Blue can feel her heart beating in her chest. *Ticking like a whistle or a stitch.*

Here's the conductor, helping her up the steps. Is this her seat, then, this one? No, here, alone by the window. Here's the scenery, the clustered houses of Intervale, yards blooming now with iris and peonies, then the line of row houses, her own among them, her former house, that is. *Where I once lived.* Here they go over the bridge then, passing over the river, and as Blue looks out the window, presses her face to the glass, she sees the bridge opposite, *where I was found, where I was born,* she thinks again now, and she doesn't look back, doesn't look down.

⌒

Reichman doesn't always know what's happening when a patient misses an appointment; how could he? He isn't God, after all, just a lowly human being with a knack for getting people to talk, emote, and sometimes, if the winds are right, to change.

While waiting for a patient he'll sit at his desk as the hour clicks up and then the minutes tick past, three, five, eight, ten, fifteen, and later, he'll pick up his messages and hear the patient, plaintive or defiant, drumming up some excuse that really means: *I couldn't stand to see what I was seeing.*

But today, Reichman knows, even as the minute hand sweeps up near the hour, even before it ticks one minute past, that Blue won't be coming in today. He just feels it: he knows. She's gone, and won't be back. At his desk, he looks out the window; the hillside across the street is washed a pale, bright green, and outside, the sun is shining in that indomitable spring way that insists: *all's right with the world, you have nothing to fear.*

He glances at a few journal articles, but he can't even pretend to concentrate. He picks up the glass ball, shakes it until the snowstorm appears, swirls over the chalet, over the "AUSTRIA" sign, the pines, the tiny bird perched on the roof. He wants to hurl the ball across the room, watch it smash against the bookshelf, snow scattering everywhere, and he imagines that were he to do this, the tiny bluebird would fly up from the wreckage like an angel in a cartoon, fly up to flit around the room, singing.

⌒

The sky is still dark the next morning when Rita pulls the pickup off to the side of the bridge. Once they're outside, she's glad she wore her sweatshirt underneath her down vest, because although morning's leaking in along the horizon, down here by the river it's still cold, in the wind that lifts off the water even late in spring.

Out here, the riverbank's unfolding to spring's firm hand, the bramble bushes sprouting in pale green, violets flecking in among the rocks and stones, and there's a smell of something fresh, and new and promising and clean borne on the wind coming up from the river.

Rita hasn't been down here much since she was a kid, when she and her best friend Marni would come down here to skip flat stones across the water. And now, the spring smell from the river, fresh and muddy at once, jolts her back to the time when she was a teenager, and she stormed down here in a rage, after hearing her mother on the phone, just before her grandmother died, saying again something about the twins. *Twins.* She's sure she heard that. And yet, at the time, her mother gave her an Indian burn on her wrist, saying, *"Will you just shut your food hole about the twins? You don't have a twin, okay? You've only got me."* And Rita ran from the house, snatching her mother's last pack of cigarettes on her way, then sat down here by the water, smoking and kicking at the stones for one whole long night and half another day.

She looks around now, thinking, well, now any chance of finding her twin is gone. She bends, snaps the dog free from his leash, but he doesn't scamper away, just looks at her quizzically. "Go on," she says, "run away, run away," but he just noses off to the side, and she follows him then, under the railroad bridge, along the green shoreline, the dog sniffing around the tree trunks, the rocks, pushing his snout deep into the leaf litter.

Soon, Rita calls to the dog, "Random, come on," and she starts to run, back toward the bridges, back to the truck, along the bracken edge of the water, and the dog chases her, jumps to her chest, takes the lead, and she chases him, and like that they go, panting, breaking loose.

Near the bridges, they rest, the dog returning to his investigation of the leaves, Rita sitting for a moment on a river-handled log. Rita thinks, why hasn't she ever come down here before, why hasn't she come here since she was a kid? She finds a patch of leafmeal that's dried and warmed by the morning sun and lies on her back, looking up, up at the straight bones of the trees, the only motion a little bird spiraling up the trunk of an elm.

On their way back to the truck, they walk more slowly, but soon feel themselves being watched, and the moment Rita sees the rabbit hop away into the underbrush she calls, "Random, stop," but he's gone, off like a shot, all instinct and sudden muscle, and Rita follows, panting, then leaning over to catch her breath, to spit onto the ground. Isn't there in her a shivery memory of this, of running out by the water with dogs, with the wolves, of bending double and seeing red?

No, she knows now, and calls again, "Random," and here he returns, shaking his head side to side, with nothing to show for all his hustle and haste. Together they walk back to the truck, Rita pats the seat and Random leaps up, and together they drive back home again.

~

At the Intervale Diner, Bethany and Tiff clack their gum and click their nails against the countertop. "Well," Tiff says, "it's a quarter past eight. Where is she? Who does she think she is?"

After Blue doesn't show up the second day in a row, no message, no call, Eleanor takes it upon herself to drive over to River Road, check things out. She gets the address from Mac, who shrugs off her worry, saying plenty of girls have up and quit on him, plenty of girls just aren't reliable.

Upstairs at the row house, the door to Apartment Number 3 is clearly marked, with a number, and, above the buzzer, a name in Blue's clear, stiff hand: "B. Doe." And in the lock, a set of keys. Eleanor presses the buzzer gingerly, and when she hears it ring, she can tell it's echoing throughout the empty apartment. She turns the key, opens the door, steps inside. In the kitchen, the red-edged table stands surrounded by its four red plastic-seated chairs, and in the living room and bedroom the few pieces of furniture look to Eleanor like sad animals, abandoned there. A big green armchair, stuffing coming out of the seams, and in the bedroom, the bed, its stained mattress bare. The noise of the river comes in the open windows. Eleanor walks through the room, each one immaculately swept and mopped, perfectly clean, the smell of ammonia still cloying the air. She hears her shoes soft across the bare wood floors. There's nothing here; nothing at all has been left behind.

AMNESIAC DISAPPEARS
By Ruth Addison

The woman who surprised Intervale last fall by her appearance on the Route 3 bridge has disappeared.

According to police, the woman, who had taken the name Blue Doe, failed to attend her job at the Intervale Diner on Tuesday. According to Mac MacQuire, owner and operator of the diner,

when Ms. Doe failed to report, he asked one of the employees
to stop by her apartment on River Road to see if she was sick.

("Hah. He didn't give a shit about her," Eleanor will say to Tiffany as they
read the account in the *Gazette*. "If I hadn't of gone down there, we'd still
be wondering where she was.")

The apartment was empty except for a few pieces of
furniture, and thoroughly cleaned.

The landlord of the building, Stiles Wellington, owner of
Stiles Wellington Realty, said that his tenant had been living
there on a month-to-month basis. He declined to comment
on accusations that he had made an exception to his policy of
requiring a security deposit equal to three months' rent, and
said only that his tenant had been paid up on her rent.

Police are not treating Ms. Doe's disappearance as a crime
because no foul play is suspected. It is not being treated as
a missing persons case because no one has reported
Ms. Doe missing.

"It looks like she just moved on," Police Chief Martin
Kelsy said.

～

Released, Annie scrambles down the embankment from the Route 3 bridge,
nearly tripping over the rocks covered now with the new shoots of ferns and
undergrowth. Here, the winter's snows and freeze have done little to heal the
brush still blackened and singed by her fires, but still, the new spring growth
is starting, pale bright green rising from the burn. Here, the water's rushing
past, clearing from its muddy brown, and the river seems even wider than
when she was here before, wider than when she first arrived.

Under the railroad bridge, she beats the bushes with her hands, looking: *where is it?* Where's her nest she squirreled away before the fires began?
Here's her cardboard tent all collapsed, soaked through, dissolved into pieces
lying scattered on the stones. *So much for that old home, home of the bones in
the blood-black night.* But here, tucked under some bushes, protected by the

shelter of the bridge, here's the knapsack she found, its neck cinched up tight, ready to choke.

She sits under the bridge, leans back against the stalk, and in the spring sun dappling through the metal filigree, she opens up the knapsack to see what treasures she left for herself, to see what it is that's inside.

First, the clothes: she'd forgotten the clothes! Good warm turtleneck and even underwear. Good, she'll be able to use them where she's going, wherever it is that she goes.

At the bottom of the knapsack she finds the blue Maxwell House can that has doubled as tin drum and safe deposit box, and she pries off the plastic lid. Inside, there's her collection of things, a seashell, its edge bitten and cracked, a pencil she's held onto all this time, a rabbit's ear, jagged-edged, but the fur still soft. The fork that washed up on shore: that's a handy thing to have.

Something's missing: where's her paper? Her birth certificate with her original name, the name of shame that bore the original taint of original sin: *Brenda LaPlatte,* the name like a crack on the head, the paper that made it along with the locket from family to family, home to home. And then she remembers, remembers tying it up and sailing it down the river in the reed basket she made, with the photo she found and the lucky rabbit's foot, *right before the fires that drove me straight inside the wires.*

But here, buried in the knapsack, the wallet she found in the pack just before the fires, with its many bills still tucked inside. And here, in a tiny pocket in the wallet, a locket, just like her own, like the tiny heart-shaped locket she keeps stored in Max. Or did she send that away too, with the other things? She plays the weight of the locket between her hands, running it on its chain up and back.

And here, in the secret leather envelope the passport, with its photo of a dark-haired, blue-eyed woman looking out at her, looking startled. *Lucille Rachel Abramson,* the passport says, and it must have been meant for her to find, it must mean someone sent this to her, because it's got Annie's own birthdate: January 27, 1960. It's got a big round stamp: *Mexico. It looks enough like me,* Annie thinks, *just like me but without my twisted rabbit lip.*

Lucky Lucy, she thinks, and tucks the passport back into the secret pocket, back into the knapsack. Between the shirts and the pants, here's a sheet of thin blue paper, folded. The letter, the second page of the letter!

She opens it up, settles back against the bridge to read. "Now that I've found out what happened after my family—they're still my family, aren't they?—moved to Mexico, now that my search is nearing its end, I'll be able to come back to you soon. It took some charm and not a little cash but today I got the name of the town my birth mother moved to, Intervale, Maine, and I found out something else, too: I've got a sister there. And not just one sister—I can't believe it, but I've got a twin. Somewhere. There's more to it, but I'll save the rest for when I see you.

"I'll wait and mail this letter to you when I get to Intervale, because I want it to have the postmark for you to look at, so you can see where I am. Do you know that I love you, know that you'll be with me, even here, lying onto our backs as we fall into the snow side by side, making snow angels together? You with your silly fears that I would come here and never return. You must know I'm nearly on my way back to you, so that you must wait for me to come find you again." It's signed in the same stiff, clear hand: "Luce."

Annie rustles through the pockets of the knapsack, and there's something else in here, too, something she'd missed before, a little notebook, and she sinks down onto her haunches, opens it up, and reads the notes neatly penned down onto the page, scattered words, *Boston, abandoned, distressed,* and then some addresses, some names. *Baby abandoned at curbside of hospital; Framingham prison,* and finally: *Intervale, Maine.*

And written there, in the notes, Annie's own same mother's name, the name of the mother who left her at St. Elizabeth's, the mother on her own birth certificate, the mother who she dreamed of, but who never, ever came back. *Colleen McGlew LaPlatte.* And her own birthdate, again: *January 27, 1960.* Then another name, first written bold, and then in lacy script: *Lucy LaPlatte.* And the word, underlined twice: *twin.*

And then, more notes, like black insects on the page: *one baby: cleft lip, abandoned, hospital—one baby: adopted, two months: me.*

She finishes flipping through the book, thinks she has what she needs, new knapsack, a new ID, some cash to spend to help her on her way, and rises then from the beach, shrugs the pack onto her back, finds a strong tall stick for walking and for warding off the voices that already are beginning their whispering inside her head, whispering *sing a song of nonsense, you were left to die, four and twenty baby bones baked in a pie, and when the pie was opened the birds were made of string, now aren't you an ugly dish to set before the king?* and she leaves her encampment, climbs back up the embankment, up to the bridge that spans the wide river rising and falling with the sweet wind of early summer.

~

At the Intervale Diner, Reichman waits; he's early for his dinner with Ira Aronson, a function of how eager he is for the information Aronson has found. Or a function of how ready he is to connect with someone, to have a lunch date that could lead into friendship. How the yawning space left by his father's death, and the smaller space left by Blue's sudden departure just days before so badly still need to be filled.

He's a little sickened by the smells of bacon, of French fries splattering in grease, but when the waitress comes, he orders coffee and starts perusing the menu, and then here's Aronson, energetic, breezy, taking the seat across from him.

Aronson doesn't bother with preliminaries. "I think I've got it pieced together," he says, just as the waitress reappears. "Corned beef," he says, and Reichman says, "Me, too," feeling like he did when he was a kid and only wanted to copy Roz.

"It seems there was a young girl, fifteen, Colleen LaPlatte, who gave birth to twin girls in Boston on January 27, 1960," Aronson says. "One twin she took with her, but the other she left on the steps of St. Elizabeth's Hospital. She was later charged with abandoning her baby, and the twin she took with her was put up for adoption."

Reichman takes a draw from his coffee. His hand is shaking, and his heart's beating hard. "The adopted one, what happened to her?" he asks, thinking even as he does that he knows.

"Adopted by a Jewish family, as a matter of fact. Abramson, of New York City, who later moved to Mexico. Artists," Aronson says, shaking his head in bewilderment and, perhaps, envy. "They named the baby Lucy."

Blue, Reichman thinks. Her memory of the taxis pulling up in the snow, the steam heat hissing on, the tall ailanthus tree outside the window. The blue tiles, warm in the sun beneath her bare feet.

"And the other baby, the twin who was left at St. Elizabeth's?" he asks, more to erase the thought that's scribbling across his brain: now that he's found out, now that he knows, it's too late.

"Apparently the mother left that twin because she had a deformity—"

"A cleft lip," Reichman says, even though now his heart's beating so hard he can feel the racing in his chest.

"And palate," Aronson adds.

The plates arrive, Tiffany sliding them onto the table, saying "Two corned beefs," and twitching away.

Reichman leans back for a moment; for a moment, he's stunned.

"This twin, the one left behind. She was raised in foster homes in Boston? Brenda LaPlatte?"

"Yeah," Aronson says, picking up his sandwich. "How did you know? I thought you said you'd had trouble getting the information, but it sounds like you'd make a pretty good PI yourself."

Reichman picks up his sandwich, too. "I guess I had the information, but I was interpreting it all wrong. Isn't that too often the case? Everything you have is right in your hands, but you don't recognize it." He remembers the blue bandanna lying open in his palms, with the photo of Blue, and Annie's original birth certificate. Not Annie, he tells himself, Brenda LaPlatte.

The two men eat together in silence for a few moments.

"But what about the mother, the woman who was arrested? Colleen LaPlatte?" Reichman asks. "What's the sentence for abandoning a baby?"

"Here's the thing," Aronson says, excited now, trying to talk fast around his sandwich, slapping his palm onto the table. "She lived here, in Intervale. Three years in prison, then she moved here."

"That seems pretty severe," Reichman says.

"That's the way it was. Maybe they also charged her with endangerment. Chances are she had some young law school intern representing her pro bono, right? Anyway, I'm not sure why she ended up here, but that made all the rest of the research easy. Had one daughter, named her Rita, who attended local schools. Still lives here in town, as a matter of fact."

"And the mother, Colleen LaPlatte, died almost two years ago, here at the hospital," Reichman finishes, and Aronson nods. "You got it," he says.

Reichman pays the bill, saying, "Really, I owe you much more than this," and the two men leave the diner, walk out into the parking lot, the evening summer sun glinting off the windshields of the cars, off the big plate glass windows. "Listen," Aronson says, "Renee and I are having a party, Memorial Day. Why don't you come by?"

"Sure," Reichman says. He means it, too, feeling almost weightless with an emotion he can't quite name: relief? Or grief?

Reichman drives toward home, but when he passes the bridge, he pulls off to the side, stops the car, walks back to the midpoint. *Where Blue was found,* he thinks, looking down.

The river's bloated with rain, muddy and stirred up with spring. Even from this height he can see the brush and tangled up bushes are still scorched on their undersides. But they're starting to push forth their brave new little leaves, everything coming in green.

Annie Blaise, he thinks. Cleft lip, cleft palate, the psychosis twisting up in her as she was shuttled from home to home to home. Changing her name, not just once, he's sure, looking for who it was she might be. And Blue, raised in a family, but with enough instability so that her search for her birth mother and the injury to her head were enough to kick her into her fugue.

And Rita. Just as he thinks of Rita LaPlatte, Blue's younger sister, he looks down at the riverbank, and sees a woman down below, a brown and white spaniel—the dog Blue had found, he's sure—running beside her, nosing in the burnt riverbank bushes.

He almost calls down to her, but no. What would be the point? To tell her she had two older sisters, twins, both of whom have gone again, each unreachable in her own unique way? Each of them, Annie and Blue— Brenda and Lucy—he's sure he'll never see again, he'd never be able to find if he tried. Plus, he has no reason, he has no right.

He watches as Rita and the pup—Random, he thinks—disappear around the curve under the railroad bridge, then he crosses the bridge to his car, gets in, but instead of heading home, he turns the car around and goes back into town, where he'll have a swim, and then stop by the synagogue to say Kaddish again.

Below the bridge, the water thunders along the grassy banks, thick with all that it's collected on its run, running past the burnt pricker bushes and muddied reeds, under the railroad bridge further down, as high up over Intervale the ghosts of the mothers and fathers shuttle and spin, and the sky washes rose and deep, azure blue.

San Francisco, 1996
New York, 2003

Blue was designed and typeset on a Macintosh computer system using QuarkXPress software. The body text is set in 10.5/14.5 Adobe Garamond and display type is set in DIN Scriften and Avant Garde. This book was designed and typeset by Cheryl Carrington and manufactured by Thomson-Shore, Inc.